LIAR!

Books by Fern Michaels

On the Line
Fear Thy Neighbor
Santa Cruise
No Way Out
The Brightest Star
Fearless
Spirit of the Season
Deep Harbor
Fate & Fortune
Sweet Vengeance
Holly and Ivy
Fancy Dancer
No Safe Secret
Wishes for Christmas
About Face
Perfect Match
A Family Affair
Forget Me Not
The Blossom Sisters
Balancing Act
Tuesday's Child
Betrayal
Southern Comfort
To Taste the Wine
Sins of the Flesh
Sins of Omission
Return to Sender
Mr. and Miss Anonymous
Up Close and Personal
Fool Me Once
Picture Perfect
The Future Scrolls
Kentucky Sunrise
Kentucky Heat

Kentucky Rich
Plain Jane
Charming Lily
What You Wish For
The Guest List
Listen to Your Heart
Celebration
Yesterday
Finders Keepers
Annie's Rainbow
Sara's Song
Vegas Sunrise
Vegas Heat
Vegas Rich
Whitefire
Wish List
Dear Emily
Christmas at Timberwoods

The Lost and Found Novels:

Secrets
Hidden

The Sisterhood Novels:

19 Yellow Moon Road
Bitter Pill
Truth and Justice
Cut and Run
Safe and Sound
Need to Know
Crash and Burn
Point Blank
In Plain Sight

Eyes Only
Kiss and Tell
Blindsided
Gotcha!
Home Free
Déjà Vu
Cross Roads
Game Over
Deadly Deals
Vanishing Act
Razor Sharp
Under the Radar
Final Justice
Collateral Damage
Fast Track
Hokus Pokus
Hide and Seek
Free Fall
Lethal Justice
Sweet Revenge
The Jury
Vendetta
Payback
Weekend Warriors

The Men of the Sisterhood
Novels:

Hot Shot
Truth or Dare
High Stakes
Fast and Loose
Double Down

The Godmothers Series:

Far and Away
Classified
Breaking News
Deadline
Late Edition
Exclusive
The Scoop

E-Book Exclusives:

Desperate Measures
Seasons of Her Life
To Have and To Hold
Serendipity
Captive Innocence
Captive Embraces
Captive Passions
Captive Secrets
Captive Splendors
Cinders to Satin
For All Their Lives
Texas Heat
Texas Rich
Texas Fury
Texas Sunrise

Anthologies:

Home Sweet Home
A Snowy Little Christmas
Coming Home for
Christmas
A Season to Celebrate

Books by Fern Michaels (*Cont.*)

Mistletoe Magic

Winter Wishes

The Most Wonderful Time

When the Snow Falls

Secret Santa

A Winter Wonderland

I'll Be Home for Christmas

Making Spirits Bright

Holiday Magic

Snow Angels

Silver Bells

Comfort and Joy

Sugar and Spice

Let it Snow

A Gift of Joy

Five Golden Rings

Deck the Halls

Jingle All the Way

FERN MICHAELS

LIAR!

KENSINGTON
PUBLISHING CORP.

www.kensingtonbooks.com

KENSINGTON BOOKS are published by

Kensington Publishing Corp.
119 West 40th Street
New York, NY 10018

All Kensington titles, imprints and distributed lines are available at special quantity discounts for bulk purchases for sales promotion, premiums, fund-raising, educational or institutional use.

Special book excerpts or customized printings can also be created to fit specific needs. For details, write or phone the office of the Kensington Special Sales Manager: Kensington Publishing Corp., 119 West 40th Street, New York, NY, 10018. Attn. Special Sales Department. Phone: 1-800-221-2647.

The K with book logo Reg US Pat. & TM Off.

Library of Congress Control Number: 2023930888

ISBN-13: 978-1-4967-4129-5
First Kensington Hardcover Edition: June 2023

10 9 8 7 6 5 4 3 2 1

Printed in the United States of America

PART ONE

Chapter One

How It Started

1983

Chad Pierce Sr. hit the lottery the day he met Camille. Figuratively speaking, that is. He had been on the sailing team in college, and once a year he and his pals would meet up somewhere for their annual bacchanalian reunion. That particular year it was Newport, Rhode Island, during the America's Cup match. Even into his late twenties, Chad still enjoyed carousing and drinking until the wee hours of the morning. That is, until he spotted the lithe, stunning woman leaning on the railing of the yacht club veranda. Her gaze was on the sunrise as wisps of her bangs gently caressed her face. Her white silk scarf floated with the breeze. Chad was gobsmacked. She reminded him of Michelle Pfeiffer in that stupid, sophomoric movie The Hollywood Knights. It wasn't because of the character she had played. It was because she shared that same striking, understated beauty.

Chad slowly moved off the lounge chair that had served as his bed. He was lucky no one had spotted him sleeping, rather recovering, from a night he could barely remember. He looked down at his rumpled clothes, sniffed at his armpits and jerked his head away in disgust. But that woman. He had to meet her. He looked around for a porter or someone who might know the lady's identity and who might be discreet enough not to run him off the property. He spotted a steward setting up tables for brunch. He riffled through his wrinkled Bermuda shorts, hoping he still had some cash in his pocket. Fortune smiled on him, and he pulled out a twenty-dollar bill. He waited until the steward was within loud whispering range and he could see the man's name tag.

"Psst. Selwyn."

The man was startled but quickly noticed Chad pressing his finger to his lips, indicating he should say nothing. Chad motioned for the steward to come closer. Once out of the woman's line of sight and earshot, Chad pulled Selwyn to the side. "Sorry, old man, but could you tell me who that lovely young lady is?" Chad made sure to reveal Andrew Jackson's face on the proffered bill. He then apologized for his appearance. "A night out with the boys. You understand."

Selwyn had seen his share of misbehaved, spoiled and often drunk young men. Newport was rife with them. Especially in the summer, during yachting season. Selwyn also knew to remain invisible, never directly interacting with the clientele unless they needed something. Rarely did any of them offer him money for information. He hesitated, but remembered that the young man had been hanging about the night before with several other men dressed in similar regalia. He gently pulled the bill from Chad's fingers.

"That would be Camille Atherton Tindale. A very nice young lady." Over the years, Selwyn's Caribbean accent had softened but the singsong cadence remained refreshing and comforting. When addressed, he always made things sound easy, with a nod and an "absolutely" or "no problem" followed by "right away." He continued. "She often comes here early in the morning. She likes to feed the ducks." He grinned at the disheveled young man, eyeing Chad up and down. "If you want to have the pleasure of her company, I might suggest a shower, a shave and a fresh set of clothes."

"Right." Chad was appreciative of the man's kindly straightforwardness. "Can you tell me where she lives?" Chad had immediately recognized the Tindale name. A very wealthy family.

"Oh, no. That would not be correct, but what I can do is tell you that she and some of her friends are planning a little party this evenin'. Some kind of celebration. Six o'clock, if I am correct in my recollection." He pointed to his head.

Chad grabbed the man by both shoulders. He wanted to give him a big kiss. "Thanks, old chap!" Chad patted him on the shoulder and skedaddled to go clean up his act and figure out a way to meet the very beautiful, very rich Camille. It would take a bit of finesse, but that was one thing Chad was extremely good at. Charm, poise and skill. When he smiled, his green eyes sparkled and the dimple in his left cheek made him even more appealing. He could make you believe you were the only person in the room and you had his full, undivided attention. Yes, his demeanor could charm the pants off anyone . . . and it had. Many times. But this time . . . this time it was different. There was something special about that woman, her wealth notwithstanding.

Chad had grown up in an upper-middle class family on Long Island. They were well-to-do enough to enjoy a summer house in the Hamptons, which was where he had learned to sail. He attended a state college, graduated and began working at a local bank. But his family's finances were nowhere near Camille's. Not even close. Because he had grown up privileged enough, it was easy for him to navigate his way around the elite, and he made it a point to surround himself with rich friends. While he couldn't afford a $975 pair of Brunello Cucinelli boat shoes, he could pull off the $295 two-tone Sebagos. The salmon shorts and Polo shirts were easier to match as long as he was wearing his Burberry belt. A signet ring and Seiko sports watch finished off the package. Luckily, he had packed enough for the long weekend and had another set of clothes waiting for him at his friend's house, where they were staying. Next, he had to convince his buddies to stop at the Conanicut Yacht Club for cocktails. It didn't take much to talk his friends into another night of debauchery. He simply wouldn't mention his real intentions for fear they might derail his plan.

That evening Chad and his three friends arrived at the yacht club at around five thirty. They gathered around the large patio bar, Chad positioning himself so he could keep an eye on the arriving patrons. His heart sank when he saw Camille enter with another man. This was going to be more difficult than he'd imagined. But then Camille gave the man a peck on the cheek and he proceeded to another table, where a lovely young woman greeted him with a more substantial kiss. Chad thought he was going to break out in a sweat.

"What's up, mate?" Chad's friend Steve elbowed him.

"Uh, nothing. I thought I recognized someone."

Steve chuckled. "Yeah, last night was a doozy. Took me all day to sober up."

Chad gave a snicker. "You got that right."

"Speaking of last night, where did you end up?" Steve asked, recalling not seeing his pal guzzling copious amounts of coffee that morning with the others.

Chad indicated one of the lounge chairs on the side of the veranda.

Steve howled. "Man, you are too much. What happened to that babe you were hitting on?"

Chad stared into his glass of Scotch and chuckled. "I have

no idea." He looked up to see Camille greeting three female friends. From what Chad could gather from all the hugging, it appeared they hadn't seen one another for a while. He tried not to stare at the group of women. They all seemed to be around the same age except for one, who may have been slightly older, but not by much. He noticed Selwyn carrying a champagne bucket over to their table. Clearly it was some kind of celebration. Selwyn looked in Chad's direction and gave him a very subtle nod. When the cork popped, the women gave a dainty cheer and applauded as Selwyn poured each of them a glass.

Chad was careful not to stare, but it wasn't easy. Camille was wearing a silk Georgian floral dress, her hair pulled back with a matching ribbon. Chad was keenly aware that his timing had to be impeccable. But he also didn't want to lose his nerve. It was now or never. He extricated himself from his buddies, snapped a gardenia from one of the planters and casually walked toward the table where the women were sitting.

"I beg your pardon, ladies." That smile of his stopped them in their tracks. He gave a slight bow with one hand behind his back. "My name is Chad Pierce. I realize this is quite unconventional, but I couldn't help noticing how stunning you are." His eyes locked with Camille's. He pulled his arm around and presented the flower to her. "Please excuse my impertinence, but if you could do me the honor of joining me for dinner one evening, you would make me the happiest man on the planet." He quickly cleared his throat. "That is, if you are so inclined and not attached to anyone else, although I would find that extremely hard to believe."

Camille smiled up at him and extended her hand. "Camille Tindale. I am pleased to meet you. And yes, this is a bit unconventional." The other women were chuckling. "But how do I know you aren't a serial killer?" Camille's friend Elle snorted, trying to keep the champagne from flying out of her nose.

Chad was deadpan. "I can give you a copy of my dossier, or would you prefer a chaperone?"

"I think we should invite Mr. Pierce to join us." Elle looked at the other women. "That way we can all assess the situation." She, too, was deadpan.

"Oh, I wouldn't think of barging in on your dinner," Chad said politely.

"Ah, but you already have," Camille said slyly. She looked at her companions. They shrugged in agreement.

Chad flashed that smile again. "I am with a few of my sailing mates." He nodded over to where his buddies stood with their mouths agape.

Elle was the next one to speak. "Then I think we should make this a party. What do you say, girls?"

"Sure!" Maureen raised her glass.

"Sounds like fun!" Liza chimed in.

"Why not?" Camille replied.

"Really, ladies. I sincerely do not want to impose on your dinner."

Elle was the first to answer. "Not at all."

Chad looked around. "I'll talk to Selwyn and have him move us to another table. Excuse me for a moment. I'll rally the troops."

He motioned to Selwyn and explained the party was expanding, and could he please find a space that would accommodate them? Eight in all. Chad was also astute enough to slip him another twenty.

"No problem, sir. Will do it in a jiffy."

Chad then went over to his buddies, who were still in a state of shock. "Gentlemen, we have been invited to join those lovely ladies for dinner."

"Wait. What?" Drew asked.

"You heard me." Chad then lowered his voice. "These are very influential women, and they seem to be in the mood for fun."

"Only you, Chadster." Larry used his nickname for his friend. "Well, I'm in the mood for some fun, too."

"I'll pick up the check and we can divvy it up later," Chad added.

"Oh. Trying to impress the lovely blonde?" Larry asked.

"Indeed." Chad winked, paid the bar tab, and they moved to the table Selwyn had arranged. Introductions went around the table, along with more champagne and laughs.

The evening went swimmingly. Elle explained how the women had met in Europe while Camille was on an art tour. Elle had led the tour group. Before they left Paris, the women promised to get together over the summer. That made for interesting conversation as the men were also having a reunion of sorts.

The talk continued long after dessert was served, one of the subjects being who might win the big race. Of course, everyone was rooting for the defender, the *Liberty* from the New York Yacht Club, but the Royal Perth Yacht Club's *Australia II* was making a good show of it. They had tied the race at three wins each.

Chad slipped his credit card to Selwyn, hoping he wouldn't be over his limit. Something like that could ruin everything, so he excused himself and followed the steward into the main hall. "If there is a problem, I don't want anyone to know," Chad said sheepishly.

Selwyn ran the card through the device and printed out the receipt, saying, "We won't know until tomorrow, when the bank opens."

Chad wrote down the phone number of the home where he was staying. "If there is an issue, please call me and I'll make it right."

Selwyn smiled. "No worries. I am sure you will."

The group agreed to meet up again the next day to watch the seventh race together. The *Australia II* ended up taking the Cup with a margin of forty-one seconds. It was the first time in 132 years the Cup went to the challenger. In spite of the loss, the mood was festive and jovial, and Camille was enchanted with her audacious new friend. After the race they strolled arm in arm back to the yacht club, leaving the other partygoers behind.

"I have to go back to New York tomorrow," Chad said as he took her hand. "It has been my greatest pleasure spending time with you." He kissed the back of her hand.

"Mine as well." Camille hesitated for a moment. "I'll be in New York next month. My family owns an apartment on Sutton Place. Perhaps we can have dinner then?"

Chad tried to keep his cool. "Yes. That would be wonderful." He kissed the back of her hand once more. "How shall we be in touch?"

Camille reached into her purse and pulled out a fine linen card with her name and phone number embossed upon it in gold lettering. "I plan to arrive on the first of October. You can call then and leave word." She smiled, turned and floated back toward her friends, who were also bidding each other adieu.

Two weeks later, Chad phoned Camille and they made plans to meet at La Grenouille, a historic and award-winning restaurant on East 52nd Street with excellent food and a romantic atmosphere. It was a gem for special occasions. And Chad believed this was certainly special. He also chose it so he could suggest walking Camille home afterward, as it was only a few blocks from her parents' apartment. For Chad, the stars were aligned.

Camille was in her mid-twenties when she first met Chad. She was coming off a very bad breakup, which was one of the reasons she had fled to Paris. She had to get away and immerse herself in a distraction. The timing of the art tour was perfect and the tour guide, Elle, was as passionate about art as one could be. Elle was five years older than Camille and working on her PhD in art history. They hit it off from the get-go. Elle was married to Richard Stillwell, a real estate attorney in Buncombe County, North Carolina. Elle was the kind of person you could confide in, and boy, did Camille need a sympathetic ear and a shoulder to lean on.

Camille explained how her ex had humiliated her after their two-year engagement. Just three months before Camille's wedding, her father discovered her fiancé was cheating on her with one of her father's personal assistants. In addition to being a scoundrel, Camille's fiancé had the nerve to cheat with someone from within her family's business. Camille was mortified. The wedding invitations had already been sent out. The bridal registries were complete. The Ritz-Carlton had been booked for the reception, and the honeymoon in Greece was paid for.

Camille went on to explain to Elle how her father broke the news to her and suggested she go to Paris, where she could put some physical and emotional distance between herself and her friends. Her father also put distance between the rogue ex-fiancé and his job, firing him in front of the staff and then having the security guards escort him out of the building.

Harrison Tindale Jr. took great pleasure notifying everyone in his circle of friends and associates that under no circumstances should they hire his former future son-in-law No one was going to hurt Daddy's little girl. The rumor was the ex-betrothed hightailed it to another state. The situation was never spoken about again. Not at home. Not at the office. Not ever.

Now, many months later, Camille realized it was the best thing that could have happened to her. She had made a very good friend in Elle, and she was smitten with a captivating, alluring, handsome man. All thanks to Elle. Had Elle not suggested the impromptu dinner party at the yacht club, Camille would not be walking on air right now.

The romance was a whirlwind. But to be certain Camille wasn't getting involved with another ne'er-do-well, Harrison Tindale hired a private detective to find out exactly who Chad Pierce was. As it turned out, Chad came from a decent family. He was educated and ambitious. He worked at a bank and got a promotion after his first year. He had no criminal record and everyone who was interviewed thought highly of him. With all the right boxes checked, Harrison was relieved his daughter had found an acceptable suitor. And Chad seemed to make her happy. Harrison couldn't remember how long it had been since Camille smiled so much. Even when she was engaged to the cad, she never seemed as happy as a bride-to-be should be. Maybe back then her instincts told her something wasn't quite right, but now there was someone new in her life. Someone who brought her joy and laughter.

With the size of his bank and Chad's financial experience, Harrison knew he could create a job for his soon-to-be son-in-law. And because of Chad's experience, the word "nepotism" would not be tossed around much. Or so Harrison hoped. Harrison's desire was to keep the family business within the family and not sell out to some greedy bunch of impresarios. His family had made their money the hard way—they'd earned it. They had survived the Depression and created jobs, and he wanted that legacy to continue. The only thing left was the prenuptial agreement, which Chad gladly signed. There was no way Chad was going to screw up this relationship.

Chad had never been in love before he met Camille. He never even thought he was capable of it. His father was a

stoic, his mother a bit of a drunk, although they never referred to people in their circle of friends as drunkards. Probably because most of the women cracked open the sauce at
noon and no one was going to throw stones. This was a
whole new life for Chad, and he was going to be a good husband and partner. If only he could get over his feelings of in-
feriority. Maybe in time, when he could prove his worth to
Camille and her family.

Chad and Camille were married at St. Bartholomew's Church
within a year of first meeting. The reception was held at the
Waldorf-Astoria Hotel. They didn't want to have it at the
Ritz-Carlton; that would have been too weird, given Camille's thwarted original wedding plans. Although the guest
list of 500 people remained the same. A second reception was
held at the Tindale estate in Newport. That guest list was a
modest 300, including Selwyn and his wife. Before Camille's
mother could protest at the idea of inviting a member of the
yacht club waitstaff, Camille reminded her family that Selwyn was partially responsible for introducing her to Chad.
Camille's mother never said another word, and the night of
the event no one even recognized Selwyn as a steward, with
him in his tailored tuxedo and his stunning wife wearing a
sexy Norma Kamali dress. Over the years, Camille would
grow fonder and fonder of Selwyn. But never more so than at
her wedding reception.

As a wedding present, Camille's parents gave her and Chad
a three-story town house on Sniffen Court, a very small historic district in the Murray Hill neighborhood of Manhattan.
A year later, Camille had their one and only child, Chad James
Richard Pierce Jr., whom everyone referred to as J.R. for Ju-
nior.
Camille continued her philanthropic work from her home

office and tended to J.R. Unlike her friends, Camille refused to have a nanny raise her child. They did have two house-keepers, but that was their sole responsibility: keeping up with the household chores and maintaining the kitchen and other supplies. Chad worked long hours and started a financial advisory branch of the bank. When the time came, J.R. was enrolled in Manhattan's Trinity School. With J.R. in school and Chad moving up the corporate ladder, continuing to prove his worth to the company, Camille resumed some of her volunteer duties at the Metropolitan Museum of Art. Life was good, steady and rewarding—until J.R. began his freshman year in high school.

Despite having private tutors, J.R.'s grades plummeted, forcing his parents to transfer him to a different private school. This time it was Horace Mann, which had a more diverse environment. That lasted a year. From there, he was sent to Hackley, a private boarding school in Tarrytown. His father thought removing him from his comfortable surroundings and his equally spoiled friends might inspire his son to straighten up. J.R. only had two more years to go before college—provided he could get into a college. Sadly, after a few months of skipping classes and being caught smoking numerous times in the stairwell, J.R. was expelled and sent home.

Camille was heartsick over her son's inability to focus on his schoolwork. Even after months of therapy for J.R., there didn't seem to be any diagnosis except for laziness and apathy. It appeared J.R. was trapped on the wheel of entitlement, something his parents regretted. J.R. lived a charmed life. The eighteen-year-old was pampered by both his mother and father. He drove a $50,000 car and carried a platinum American Express card, the bills for which went directly to his father's office. J.R. had failed miserably at his several boarding schools, and now his father was desperate for him to get into a high-profile college. J.R.'s parents therefore decided a complete change of scenery and a stricter environment might shake him into a sense of responsibility. Frustrated and exasperated, they enrolled him in Briarcliff Academy in Massachusetts for his senior year. The school specialized in college preparation and had a no-nonsense reputation. It was known for its very strict regime, equal to the best military schools in the Northeast.

The first semester proved successful and J.R. passed with respectable grades, making him a candidate for perhaps a small private college, where his father could make a sizable donation for J.R.'s entry—but without a lot of scrutiny. Chad Pierce Sr. could not afford a scandal like those idiot Hollywood people. Slowly, J.R.'s grades improved, and Camille and Chad Sr. were once again optimistic about their son's future. Chad Sr. had long ago given up on the idea of an Ivy League school for his son. At this point, any college would do. He had to have *something* to brag about to his Wall Street friends, who were always playing the one-upmanship game. Even comparing watches involved a volley of "mine's better."

Chapter Two

The Family Nightmare

Sniffen Court, NYC
2003

One late April evening, forty-eight-year-old Chad Sr. was in his study on the main floor of their town house. He cracked open a new bottle of the Macallan Rare Cask, which sold for close to $400 per bottle. He glanced at the Macallan 1926 with a price tag of $75,000, but he'd rather wait until he had an audience to flaunt it to. He knew it was silly. He really had no reason to doubt himself. He had proven his worth at his father-in-law's business, and his marriage to Camille was solid. He wondered if his anxiety was because of his mother. She was rarely sober and had done mean things to him when he was away at college, like the time she gave his stand-up bass away. He would escape the shouting matches his parents had when he was growing up, getting lost in his music. When he asked her why she had gotten rid of his instrument, she said the noise bothered her. He had been almost heartbroken. How could she do that to him? Without asking? Without any concern for him?

Now he scoffed at the memory. *No wonder he was insecure.* This was textbook psychology. But everything had
changed when he injected himself into Camille's life twenty
years earlier.

The one thing Chad Sr. was truly proud of, and adored,
was his beautiful wife, Camille. She came from money. Lots
of it. Not at the level of the Vanderbilts, Rothschilds or Get-
tys, but the Athertons weren't far behind. Camille was refined in her demeanor, her clothes, her shoes, even her
handbags. Her radiant skin and perfectly manicured hair and
nails were a sure sign of self-care and self-respect. Camille
was genteel. Elegant without being a snob, as were most of
her friends. It would often grate on her when she was out to
lunch with them and one of her companions would snap her
fingers at the waitstaff. *Why couldn't they be gracious?* she
would think to herself. *We should be appreciative, not arro-
gant. We live very entitled lives.* But she would just sit back in
her chair and sip her martini, or her Bellini, or whatever the
latest cocktail craze was.

Camille sometimes cringed at her husband's bravado, but
then again, that was part of his appeal. His swagger hid his
need for approval. Her biggest hope for her son was that he
would grow up with a little more humility than his father.
Granted, Chad Sr. was a charmer, but he was also a status
seeker. At least he was when they were first married. He
wanted to be sure everyone got to know his name. To his
credit, his ambition did the bank a lot of good. But he still
often appeared to have something to prove. Either to himself
or someone else. Camille's therapist suggested her husband
was insecure. She reminded Camille that she came from an
exceptionally successful and wealthy family. "It's hard to com-
pete," the therapist noted.

"But we aren't in competition." Camille sighed.

"Maybe *you* aren't, but clearly he has something to prove."

Camille sometimes wondered if that would ever happen. Would her husband ever fully achieve a sense of accomplishment?

Now Chad read the *Financial Times* as he sipped his single-malt scotch in his study. Camille was in her office, adjacent to their bedroom on the third floor. She was working on plans for her next fundraiser. Chad was startled when his private phone rang. He checked his watch. It was after ten p.m. No one called at that hour unless it was a dire emergency. He sat upright and answered with, "Chad Pierce."

There was a lot of static on the other end of the line. "Hello? Who is this?" Chad asked.

A gravelly, electronically enhanced voice answered. "Listen very carefully. We have your son. If you want to see him alive, you will follow our instructions. Do not call the police. We will be in touch." Then the line went dead. Chad stared at the phone. Was this some kind of a joke? He hit *69 to see where the call came from. He got a recorded message in response: "The number you have reached is not in service." He furrowed his brow and wrote down what the caller had said. A few minutes later, Camille came down the stairs.

"Who was that on the phone?" she asked casually. Chad didn't answer right away. She looked at her husband. "Chad? Is everything all right?" Now there was a bit of worry to her tone.

"Honey, I'm not sure." He tapped his pen on the pad. "Sit. Please." He got up from his chair and took a crystal rocks glass from the sideboard and poured Camille a drink.

"Chad? What is going on?" Her eyes followed his every move.

He handed her the glass and waited for her to take a sip. "The person on the phone said they have our son."

"They what?" Camille immediately moved to the edge of her seat.

He read the words he had written down back to her. She looked at him in disbelief. "I don't understand. *Who* has our son?"

"I don't know." Chad shook his head. "I tried *69, but the number is not in service." He opened his leather address book and began to dial the phone.

"They said not to call the police?" Camille asked in a hushed tone.

"I'm calling the school."

After a few rings, a stern voice at Briarcliff answered. "Briarcliff. How can I help you?"

"Good evening. Apologies for calling so late. This is Chad Pierce Sr."

The man's voice on the other end of the line softened a bit. He didn't want to anger one of the school's biggest benefactors. "Yes, Mr. Pierce. How can I help you?" he repeated.

"I realize this is an odd question, but have you seen my son on campus today?"

The man paused for a moment before answering. "No, sir. I don't recall seeing him, but I was in my classroom all day."

"Is there someone who can check to see if he's in his room?" Chad fought to keep his voice even.

"Certainly. Hold one moment and I'll ring the floor resident adviser." Several minutes passed. It seemed like an eternity until the person got back on the phone. "Mr. Pierce? I don't mean to alarm you, but Chad is not in his room. His roommate said he hasn't seen him in two days. He thought he might have gone home for a long weekend."

Chad steadied himself against his desk. Camille took a long pull of her drink. By the look on Chad's face, she knew something terrible was happening.

"Could he and his friends have gone off on some class trip? Some excursion?" Chad was grasping for a reasonable explanation.

"No, sir. There are no activities off campus this week. That's why his roommate thought he might be heading home." He paused. "Is there someone else I can call for you?"

"Can you check the infirmary? Maybe he got hurt playing sports?" Now Chad was really straining for a good excuse for his son's absence. He could hear the person on the other end of the phone riffling through papers.

"I'm sorry, Mr. Pierce, but no one has been logged in or out of the infirmary for the past few days."

"I see." Which he really didn't, but what else was there to say? "I would appreciate it if you could check with some of his other classmates. Perhaps they can shed some light."

"Absolutely. I'll do that."

"Thanks much. I appreciate it." He hung up the phone. Tears were now streaming down Camille's face.

The two jumped when the phone rang again. When Chad answered, he was greeted by the same strange, staticky voice as before. "I hope you didn't call the cops."

"No. Of course not." Chad took a deep breath and continued. "Tell me what you want and I will make it happen."

"Tomorrow."

"Tomorrow what?" Chad struggled to hold his angst in check.

"Instructions." Then the line went dead.

Chad tried *69 again and got the same recorded message.

"What is happening?" Camille was also trying to avoid becoming hysterical.

Chad took her in his arms and held her close. "Sweetheart, I don't know, but we will figure this out."

"But how?" she whimpered.

"I don't know, but we will." He then held her at arm's length. "They said they will call tomorrow with instructions."

Camille slumped into a chair. "Tomorrow? We have to

wait until tomorrow? How do we even know he's still alive?"
She began to sob at the thought of something horrifying happening to her son. Chad stroked her hair.

"I am sure they want money. And they will have to give us proof."

"But what if they can't?" Camille was now officially hysterical.

Chad lifted her chin and wiped her face with his handkerchief. "We can only pray, hope and wait."

Chad supported Camille as she went up the stairs to their bedroom suite. He fluffed her pillows and gently helped her climb between the silk sheets and sat at the edge of the bed. He handed her the glass of Scotch. Her hands were trembling. Camille was always poised and bubbly regardless of the circumstances, but on this night, she was frail and deflated. Chad hated to see his wife this way. He vowed he would do whatever it took to bring his son home.

"In this day and age, we are easy targets." Chad tried to rationalize what was happening to his family. "They will ask for money, but we will demand proof of life before they see a penny."

Camille looked comatose. "Proof of life?" She could barely get the words out of her mouth.

"I know this is hard to wrap our heads around, but we have to remain strong and steadfast. They want money, and they know they can't get it without meeting our demands."

"What are you talking about?" Camille looked confused.

"Our demand of proof that our son is alive and will be returned to us." Chad waited a beat. "They can't have what they want without giving us what *we* want."

"But what if . . . what if . . ." Camille broke down again.

"Honey, I truly believe that if they have any expectation of getting money, they will understand they have to produce our son alive and well."

Camille settled back on the bed and closed her eyes. Their two Yorkies, Lucy and Ricky, looked confused. The dogs could sense something in the air. Chad spoke to them quietly. "Mommy is all right." He hoped Camille would be able to drift off to sleep, although that was a lot to expect under the circumstances. He kissed her gently on the forehead and gave the dogs a pat on their heads. "I'm going downstairs. Try to rest."

Camille Atherton Tindale was born into wealth, but her family hadn't had money two generations earlier. Her grandfather, Harrison Tindale Sr. weathered the Great Depression by saving cash earned from a grocery store he owned on the Lower East Side of Manhattan. Everyone was touting the stock market, but he was skeptical. And it was a good thing, too—he was one of the few of his peers who didn't lose everything on that fateful day in 1929.

He worked diligently, sometimes eighteen to twenty hours at a stretch, building his grocery store into the largest in the neighborhood, offering items not otherwise easily found by the influx of immigrants. But when the stock market crashed and people were left with no jobs or money, he rationed whatever he had in inventory. Then it occurred to him that people without jobs would need money, and he began lending funds at a very low rate of interest to people he trusted. He, much like his neighbors, had come from Europe to start anew. They had the courage to leave their homeland for a better life in the land of opportunity.

In order to have a future, Harrison Sr. had to preserve the present. To do so, he created what were now referred to as mini banks. He believed in reinvesting in his community no matter how long it took to be repaid, provided he could support his own family. It took over ten years for the country and the economy to crawl back to solvency. During that time, Harrison created the Metropolitan Savings and Loan, where he amassed a large sum from the interest and payments he received. In 1934 he applied for certification as an FDIC-insured institution, giving him more credibility and more customers.

But Harrison Sr. never forgot the Depression and was frugal with his money. One wouldn't call him cheap, but he did not squander his wealth. When he retired, his son, Harrison Jr., took the reins and parlayed the bank into one of the largest in the state. With the family's growing wealth, Harrison Jr. was more comfortable spending money and began investing in real estate. He purchased a large penthouse apartment with a wraparound terrace on Sutton Place, and a modest house in Westport, Connecticut, where he and his wife and daughter spent the weekends. That was where Camille learned to ride horses. Through most of her childhood, Camille preferred the bucolic tranquility of the countryside, choosing to leave the noise and chaos of the city behind. She loved animals, but her father prevented her from having dogs in the apartment or the house. When she and Chad married, that was her one demand: dogs. At least two.

Camille attended private schools and was an exceptional student. She took piano lessons, French lessons, art appreciation, and horseback riding in Central Park when they weren't at their country home in Connecticut. Camille had everything she wanted or needed, but it was impressed upon her that she must be discerning as to how she spent money. Frivolous activities were not encouraged. From the age of thirteen, Camille was expected to do a minimum of six hours of charity work per week, either at the local hospital or at their church. Despite her inherited wealth, Camille learned how to give back to the society that had provided a very good and comfortable lifestyle for her and her family.

Camille's academic record and community involvement

made her an excellent candidate for college. She was accepted at Dartmouth, considered one of the top three colleges for art history, bringing her closer to her desire to become a curator for an art gallery. When Camille left for Dartmouth, her father sold the Connecticut house for a very large profit and invested in an estate in Newport, Rhode Island, where the family spent their summers. Camille didn't care much for the water but enjoyed watching the boats from the yacht club, where her father kept his eighty-five-foot yacht. It certainly wasn't the largest at the yacht club, but it was big enough for them to travel to Cape Cod or Martha's Vineyard should they be so inclined. For the most part he kept it docked in Newport. It was really his only indulgence, besides his daughter. Even so, he was careful not to spoil her rotten.

Of all her peers—from grade school to the present—Camille was the most open-minded and well-rounded. Perhaps that was why she had little patience for most of the women in her social circle now. They lacked humility. But Camille? She was the most respected and best-liked among their contemporaries.

After college, Camille began her master's degree at New York University while working as a docent at the Metropolitan Museum of Art, organizing tours for schools and clubs. Her exuberance and passion for art and her delightful personality made a perfect combination. Both NYU and the museum were a short half-hour bus ride and, depending on the weather, she would walk from Sutton Place to the museum. She didn't feel the need to spend money on taxis during the day. After dark was different, however. She never wanted to be stranded on a sidewalk at night. When she wasn't working or studying, she spent time with the curators, learning as much as she could until she was eligible for a full-time job. She got her master's in less than two years, and her employment at the Met was inevitable.

Even those who might be jealous of her found it hard to dislike her. With the exception of her mortifying breakup, now a seldom-recalled memory, Camille Atherton Tindale led a charmed life.

But that night she lay in bed cuddled with her two Yorkies, Lucy and Ricky, terrified that her only child was in grave danger. It was the worst nightmare she could imagine.

Chad returned to his study, where he could pace and think, and poured two fingers' worth of Scotch into his glass. He looked over at the $75,000 Macallan 1926 and realized how insignificant it was. How trivial.

His mind raced as he wondered what the price tag for his son would be. He could certainly come up with large sums of cash, but not overnight. He debated whether or not he should call the police. Not yet. He had nothing to tell them, and the caller had been quite specific about that. He thought about phoning his father-in-law but decided against that too. The man was in his mid-seventies with a heart condition. Besides, what could he possibly tell him? He decided to wait until he had all the information from the kidnappers. *Kidnappers.* The word sent a chill up his spine. Why *his* son? True, the family had wealth, but most of it was still in the hands of Harrison. Not that Harrison wouldn't step up to save his one and only grandson. Chad paced the floor. He checked his watch again. It was almost midnight. He decided to call his longtime buddy and best man, Larry Willis.

Larry had been there the night Chad first interjected himself into Camille's life. Larry had started a private investigation and security firm and worked for some of the biggest celebrities in New York. He was accustomed to handling many sensitive situations. Chances were he was still awake, trolling the internet for unscrupulous characters. He picked up on the first ring.

"What in the heck are you doing awake at this hour?" Larry grunted into the phone.

"Larry, I think I have a problem. A big one." Chad let out a big whoosh of air.

"Oh, no. Don't tell me you went and left Camille."

"Don't be ridiculous," Chad said with emphasis.

"I didn't think so. Hell, I'd have to shoot you myself." Larry dialed back the humor. "So, what's up?"

Chad described the two phone calls as Larry listened intently.

Larry's background working alongside the FBI gave him lots of contacts in almost every area of criminal investigation. "Do not call the police. They'll want to invade your home with electronic equipment."

"What's wrong with that?" Chad asked, a bit befuddled.

"If the kidnappers have any brains, someone will be watching your house. You don't want anyone to notice any unusual activity."

Larry had a good point. Sniffen Court was an alley constructed in 1893 as a line of carriage houses to mitigate the noise and smell of the neighborhood's horses. It remained a stable area until the 1920s, when automobiles gained in popularity. Eventually, the ten stables were sold and converted into brownstone town houses now fetching prices into several million dollars, all neatly protected by a wrought-iron gate at the sidewalk on East 36th Street between Lexington and Third Avenues. A passerby could easily spot activity in front of any of the brownstones.

"I suppose you're right." Chad tried not to sound defeated. "What do you recommend?"

"Well, you can have one visitor. That shouldn't set off any red flags, especially if he's dressed in a pair of jeans and wearing a Poland Spring jacket," Larry continued. "I'll park the truck on East Thirty-Sixth and carry a gallon into the court-yard. George will remain in the truck and keep an eye on the street."

George was Larry's partner. Chad knew he could be trusted to help without asking too many questions. "Where are you going to . . . never mind." Chad realized this was not an unusual activity in Larry's line of work. He was a chameleon of sorts. Blend in with the environment. Make yourself invisible.

"Did they say when they would call back?" Larry asked.

"No. But I would imagine before I go to work. I doubt they would think I'd keep a chunk of money here. I mean, I keep some here, but I have no idea how much they are looking for."

Larry grunted. "True. How much they know about your family's worth might determine the price. On the other hand, maybe they'll make it a relatively small sum. Something easy for you to put together quickly in cash, so they can pick it up and split. How about I come by around seven thirty in the morning?"

"I have a meeting downtown at nine."

"It's important you keep to a normal schedule. You don't want to draw any attention to yourself."

"But what if the person calls and I'm not here?"

"The person or persons probably know your schedule and will most likely call the same number."

"Right. Thanks, Larry. By the way, what do you want for breakfast?"

"Does Camille still make those killer pancakes?" Larry remembered how Camille insisted on making breakfast for Chad and J.R. every morning. It was their time together, before they had to go out to face the world. "That is, unless she's not up to it. But keeping busy is the best way to keep from falling apart."

"Right again, Larry. You're on a roll. I think she'd be up for it. If not, I'll do my best."

"Heaven forbid. I've seen you in the kitchen. That in itself is a crime. See you in the morning."

"Larry?" Chad stopped.

"Yeah?"

"Thanks, pal."

"Anything for you." Larry ended the call.

Chad felt some relief knowing he had outside support. Larry was an easygoing but take-charge kind of guy. A good combination in his line of work.

When Chad returned to the bedroom, Camille was half awake. "Larry is coming by tomorrow morning around seven thirty. I promised you would make pancakes."

Camille shook some of the sleep from her head. "What are you talking about?"

Chad explained Larry's plan to Camille. "I guess I'll have to make enough for George, too." She gave him a tired smile.

Chad knew the news that Larry was helping would lift Camille's mood. Even just a bit. Larry had worked on a number of cases for the family and the bank over the years, and he was always successful in finding the culprits.

Chad undressed and joined Camille in bed. He wrapped his arms around her and whispered, "Everything is going to be all right. I promise." Chad knew he was making a pledge for which he had no guarantee.

They were both awake at six a.m. the next morning. Camille pulled on a jogging suit even though she knew she wasn't going anywhere. But it was comfortable, and that was exactly what she needed. She pulled back her hair with a headband and scrutinized her face. She sighed as she dabbed a bit of blush on her cheeks and applied lipstick. She knew trying to hide the bags under her eyes was futile. She stepped back and gave herself one more look. She was presentable enough. Chad kissed her on the top of her head and then went through his morning routine. He said he'd meet her in the kitchen.

Camille phoned Mildred, the housekeeper, to tell her not to come in that morning. The fewer people about the better. She also phoned the school, reassured the alarmed headmaster that everything was fine and that J.R. would be staying at home for a few days. Camille was in a daze. She knew the kitchen like the back of her hand, but she suddenly couldn't remember where she kept the pancake mix. Her eyes welled up with tears. She brushed them away. "That's not going to help," she told herself out loud. Sure, she could easily fall apart, but that would only put more pressure on Chad. She lifted her chin and stomped toward the pantry. If necessary, she could call Mildred back and ask her where things were, but she had to be strong. Act normal. It wasn't at all like Camille not to have it together. Sure, she went to a therapist occasionally, but so did everyone else living on the East Side of Manhattan. In no way did that sully one's reputation. At least not in Camille's situation. As far as anyone was concerned, Camille was one of the most capable people in her circle. She rummaged around and found everything she needed to start breakfast. *Normal. Act normal*, she kept repeating to herself.

By the time Chad made it to the kitchen, Camille had everything ready to start the pancakes as soon as Larry arrived. "You mean I have to wait until he gets here?" Chad teased her.

Camille handed Chad a bowl of berries. "Start with these."

He looked down at the fruit and grunted. "Oh, whoopee."

Camille chuckled. It was the first light moment since the phone call the night before. She looked at her husband. In spite of the salt-and-pepper hair, he still had the good looks of Richard Gere. She hoped she was aging as well.

Chad gave her a quizzical look. "What?"

Camille smiled. "You are as handsome as ever."

"And you are as beautiful as the day I first saw you." He came up behind her and put his arms around her waist. "When this is over, we are going to take a holiday."

She leaned into him. "When this is over, it *will* be a holiday."

The buzzer rang, indicating someone was at the gate.

"Must be Larry." Chad went to the wall phone. "Yes?"

Larry's voice came over the line. "Delivery."

Chad buzzed him into the courtyard and went to the front door. Lucy and Ricky followed closely. When Chad opened the door, he pretended Larry was simply delivering water for the cooler. They gave each other only a nod until Chad closed the door behind his friend. Larry set down the five-gallon jug. "I forgot how heavy water is." He slapped his friend on the shoulder. "How are you holding up?"

Chad grimaced and shrugged. "I'm numb."

"Camille?" Larry asked cautiously.

"She's a trouper . . . working on those pancakes for you." Chad motioned for Larry to follow him to the rear of the house.

The two men entered the kitchen. "Come over here, beautiful." Larry motioned for Camille to give him a hug.

Camille set down her spatula on the counter and moved toward their friend. As soon as she put her arms around Larry, she began to sob. Then hiccupped.

Larry nodded to Chad, and soon the three of them were in a group hug. They let Camille cry. She needed to let it all out. It took several minutes before she could regain her composure and disengaged herself from the two men. "Sorry." She wiped her face with the kitchen towel hanging from the belt of her apron, not realizing she had smeared pancake batter on her face. The two men couldn't help but laugh. "What?" Camille looked shocked. "What is so damn funny?"

"Your face." Chad turned her toward the reflective surface of the vent over the stove. He wiped her cheek with one finger and gave it a lick. "Yummy. But I think it would be better in the skillet."

Camille slapped him with the towel, getting batter on his tie. Keeping up an attempt at some levity, Chad licked his tie. "Oh, for heaven's sake." Camille wasn't sure which was more disturbing, flinging batter or Chad eating the raw mix off his clothes. "Take that off." She shook her head and returned to the task at hand.

Larry took a seat at the table and asked Chad to go over last night's conversations again. Chad untied the knot in his tie and read from his notepad, then looked up. "That's all I've got. Which is nothing."

"Have you spoken to any of J.R.'s classmates this morning?"

"No. I was hoping his roommate would call. According to the headmaster, J.R. missed the last two days of classes and no one has seen him. Everyone thought he was heading here for a long weekend."

Larry nodded as he pulled a small utility bag from his jacket and showed Chad its contents. It was an assortment of gadgets and gizmos. He explained he was going to connect the phone in Chad's study to a tracking device. "We should probably get that taken care of right away."

"Good idea," Chad agreed.

Camille turned down the griddle, checked her face again for any traces of batter and followed the men into the study.

"Under the best circumstances, this device can trace the calls to the originator, or close proximity, and it's capable of recording conversations. But first things first." Larry's stomach growled in protest.

With great interest, Chad watched the instruments Larry produced, as he was familiar with the ever-changing sphere of technology. Chad still questioned whether Y2K had been a scheme developed so start-up tech companies could make money on people's fear. He wondered how such brilliant people could build such complex systems but not think about something so obvious as the digits of a year. It made no sense, and three years later nothing of any consequence had come of it. Chad grunted.

"What?" Larry looked up.

"Just thinking about how far we've come with technology and how it seems to change every day. It's hard to keep up. We have had to invest and reinvest in everything. It's staggering." Chad peered as closely as he could without getting in Larry's face. "That is quite impressive."

"It's smaller and more high-tech than what the feds use," Larry explained. "They have a bigger budget, but I know what to invest in without all the politics and red tape."

Chad continued to scrutinize the equipment. The piece that attached to the phone was the size of a nickel, and the tracking device was the size of an Apple iPod.

"I'm going to show you how to install this in your office. Just be sure no one sees you do it. You don't know who may be watching." Larry held the items in each hand. "Once it's hooked up, you can put the tracking device in your drawer."

Something occurred to Chad and his expression changed. "Wait. Aren't law enforcement officers the only people allowed to trace a call? And only after they get a subpoena?"

Larry gave him a smirk. "Are you serious?"

"Well, yes. I don't want to be breaking the law," Chad said with conviction.

"We're breaking the law because someone else is breaking the law, my friend," Larry said smugly. "I'll take the heat if it comes to that."

"Isn't it a federal offense?" Chad was clearly focused on the questionable legality of what they were doing.

"Yes, and so is kidnapping." Larry stood up from the desk and stared Chad in the face.

Chad blinked several times. Larry had an excellent point. How stupid of him to even question it. Then he asked, "What about my BlackBerry?"

"The calls can be tracked by cell towers," Larry said. "I doubt they will call you on it because if they have half a brain, they would know that. Which is probably why they called your landline here in the study." Larry furrowed his brow. "How do you suppose they got that number?"

"From J.R., I guess," Camille chimed in as she watched from the doorway. "Is there anything else we can do?"

"Not at the moment. It's a waiting game and it stinks," Larry said.

"All right, you criminals. There is a whole lot of batter that needs to be cooked," Camille said half-seriously. At that very moment, she didn't care what they had to do to get their son back.

The men followed Camille back into the kitchen, where she turned up the heat on the griddle, gave the batter a little more liquid and continued to mix and then pour. Camille was flipping the first batch of pancakes when Larry became animated and stuck his nose in the air, inhaling the aroma of pancakes on the grill. "Ah, heaven."

Camille rested a pile of flapjacks on the table. For the first time in a while, they all held hands and prayed. Camille had a lot of hope in her voice and neither Larry nor Chad was about to burst her balloon. The men gave each other a silent look.

Larry was the first to speak after the prayer had ended. "Wow! Camille, you outdid yourself! These look delicious!" He stabbed his fork into a pile of pancakes covered in Camille's special lingonberry syrup. This was her secret sauce, something her grandmother had taught her to make. The taste was a cross between a cranberry and a raspberry. Sweet and tart all at the same time.

Camille began a second batch of pancakes as Chad and Larry devoured the first. She returned to the table with two separate plates. "This one is for me." She plopped down a sizable portion in front of her seat.

Larry gave her a big grin. "You still look like Michelle Pfeiffer, even in your gym clothes."

Camille smiled back. "Thanks, Larry. I know you're only saying that because you want more pancakes."

"That much is true. About the pancakes, I mean, and you too! But I always envied my pal over there." He jerked his thumb toward Chad. "He did catch the prettiest girl."

Camille leaned on her elbows and grimaced. "I would like to be known for my remarkable intellect as well."

"I gotta say, you were really smart to marry this guy. As much of a pain in the ass as he was. You know he always persuaded us to do things the right way."

Camille moved her gaze toward her husband. "Really? How?" she asked with a bit of sarcasm and skepticism. "I thought he was the instigator of the group."

"Nah. He just wanted that kind of reputation." Larry dug his fork into another pile of deliciousness.

"Do tell." Camille's interest was piqued. This was another insight into Chad's insecurity.

"Well. Remember the night he boldly interrupted your dinner with your friends?"

"Yes. How could I forget?" Camille answered.

"True. He made sure all of us paid our share of the bill for the entire table."

Chad grimaced and gave Larry a wide-eyed look, as if to say, *Please don't blow my cover.*

"That seems fair," Camille said as she raised her coffee cup to her lips. She gave her husband a wink. She knew Chad had picked up the check that night, but she also assumed his friends had chipped in. That would have been the right thing to do.

"And he gave Selwyn a very nice tip," Larry added.

"That seems fair as well," Camille said.

"See? That's what I mean. Mr. Do-the-Right-Thing. I used to call him 'Mr. Goody Two-Shoes.' "

This comment brought a chortle from Camille as she tried to keep the coffee from coming out of her nose. "Now, that is something I would never accuse you of, darling." She patted Chad's arm with one hand while she dabbed her nose with her napkin. It was true that when she'd first met Chad, he had been smooth. A bon vivant. She appreciated his desire for fine taste and charming conversation. And he was funny. But most of all he was kind.

"You have to admit, on that particular evening he was the instigator, was he not?" Camille said, referring to the dinner crashers.

"Oh, for sure. We had no idea what he was up to!" Larry agreed.

Their conversation was abruptly interrupted by the sound of the phone ringing in Chad's study. They each bounded out of their chairs and dashed toward the study. Larry noticed the lights on the device were working. "Keep him on as long as you can."

Chad answered with more confidence than the night before. He hit the Speaker button so everyone could hear what was being said. "Hello. This is Chad Pierce."

A raspy, electronically altered voice replied, "One million. Small bills. Day after tomorrow."

Chad tried to get a word in before the caller ended the one-way conversation. "How do I know he's okay?"

The raspy voice said, "Tell Daddy you're okay."

Chad could hear his son in the background. "Dad!"

Then the phone went dead. Chad's hands were sweating. He was relieved and distressed at the same time. "He's alive." Chad let out a big sigh and hugged Camille.

Larry made a face. "The call was too short to get any traction. Next time speak slowly. Repeat everything he says back to him. We only need a minute."

Chad stared at the phone. "I suppose they are going to give me instructions tomorrow if they want the money the next day."

"Sounds about right," Larry agreed.

Chad stepped away from Camille's grip on his arm. "Looks like we have work to do." Chad's instincts kicked in and he was back to being stoic. He had to be. He had to think clearly.

"Should we call my father?" Camille asked.

"I hope that won't be necessary. If I get to the office within the next two hours, I can put the wheels in motion. Most banks don't keep a lot of cash on hand, so it may take longer than they're giving us." He wiped his brow with his handkerchief. "Larry, can you stay with Camille for a bit?" He pulled a fresh hanky from his desk drawer.

"Sure. Let me check in with George to see if anyone suspicious has been hanging around." Larry went back into the kitchen and called George on his walkie-talkie. According to George, no one was loitering or lurking in the area. Everyone looked as if they had someplace to go, including the dog walkers with several pooches on leashes.

Camille and Chad returned to the kitchen and went over what they needed to do next. Chad would install the tracing device on his office phone and arrange for cash transfers from several of his accounts. He would stress the utmost confidentiality to the branch manager and anyone else who had to be involved in the transactions. He figured it wouldn't involve many, but one slip of the tongue could turn the entire transaction into a disaster. Chad kissed Camille, gave Larry a bro hug and headed downtown to the Financial District.

Camille poured herself and Larry another cup of coffee and nodded for him to sit. "I can't expect you to do the dishes without an ample supply of caffeine."

Larry patted her hand. "At least we know he's okay."

Camille took a gulp of her coffee. "Yes, he sounded okay. I mean, all we heard was him saying 'Dad!' but his voice was recognizable and he didn't sound like he had been tortured." A chill went up her spine.

"This will all be over in two days." Larry was trying to reassure her.

"I hope so." Camille gave him a weak smile.

"Okay. So let's get these dishes done before George has a conniption."

"You start on the plates and I'll make a fresh batch for you to take to George."

"Deal." Larry rolled up his sleeves and began rinsing the plates and putting them in the dishwasher.

Camille placed the hotcakes in a foil container and put them in an insulated bag with a fork and napkins. "I trust these will make it to the truck?" She held the handle of the bag as Larry tried to tug it from her hand.

"Yes, ma'am."

Camille gave him a hug and walked him to the door. "Thanks, Larry. I don't know what we would do without you."

"Likewise. You two are the best people I know."

Chad walked to Lexington Avenue and hailed a cab. It took over twenty minutes to get downtown to the bank. The FDR Drive was one long parking lot. The cab driver ditched the Drive and hustled through local streets until they got to

Maiden Lane. Chad glanced down the street to where the bank once stood. The company's original office was only a few blocks from the site of the World Trade Center. The neighborhood was still in a shambles, with many stores and offices boarded up. Chad counted his blessings every day. He and his father-in-law had discussed moving the offices to Midtown a few years before. Even though they shared a car every morning, the twenty-minute ride could often become a forty-minute stall in traffic, bringing both men's blood pressure to a boil. Harrison had some heart issues but insisted he would continue working, so they had negotiated for a building on Madison Avenue, a short walk from Harrison's Sutton Place apartment and Chad's Sniffen Court town house. The ten-minute walk each morning was good exercise and decreased the stress of their commute downtown.

Chad admired Harrison's resolve, but that generation had witnessed many horrific things. Now he would be faced with the shock of his only grandson being abducted. Survival, persistence and determination was mandatory for the entire family. With any luck, the transaction would be swift, and he could report good news to his father-in-law, or perhaps never have to mention it at all.

Chad entered the marble lobby of Popular Bank. He greeted the security officer and signed in. Ever since September 11, 2001, almost every major building in New York City had guards, security, and metal detectors. The Financial District was no exception. In fact, the New York Stock Exchange building was still surrounded by concrete barriers. Unless you had credentials, you couldn't get within fifty feet of the building. It was still eerie, even all these months later.

Chad got into the elevator and pushed the button for the twenty-third floor. The receptionist greeted him with a big smile and a "Good morning, Mr. Pierce. Mr. Elizondo is waiting for you in the conference room."

"Thanks, Louise." He gave her his most charming smile. He tried to appear natural. It wasn't easy, knowing his son was being held captive somewhere. He had to get through this meeting and do it as quickly as possible without seeming rattled. He entered the large conference room where five of his colleagues sat at a large mahogany table. "Good morning, gentlemen."

Rico Elizondo rose from his chair and greeted Chad with a handshake. The others nodded and smiled. This discussion was about installing ATM machines in as many venues as possible. It was a fast-growing part of their industry and there was a big push by manufacturers to raise the price of the machines. It was important for banks, particularly the smaller ones, to band together so they, too, could have a footprint in convenience stores. Chad knew a decision would require additional meetings, so his strategy was to present an outline and then schedule another meeting for the following week. With any luck, he wouldn't have this terrible crisis interfering with his thoughts by then.

Fortunately, he had come prepared and had copies of his proposal ready for the executives sitting at the table. He briefed them on what he believed would be a good strategy, quickly reviewed the prospectus and asked if there were any questions or other considerations. The men seemed stunned at how well-prepared Chad was, but then again, wasn't he always? Or maybe it was his brisk delivery. He silently questioned himself. Was he being too abrupt? Could they tell something horrendous was lurking in the shadows? Elizondo got up from his chair. "Great work, Chad. We have a lot to consider. I'll appraise every one of your recommendations and we can explore the results of our findings. Next week?" Elizondo looked around the massive table. The other men nodded in agreement. "Fine. Then it is settled. We will meet again next week. Same time?"

Chad almost lost his train of thought. "Yes. Yes, that will be fine."

Elizondo walked Chad to the elevators. They shook hands. Chad was relieved his palms weren't sweating.

When he reached the lobby, he hustled to grab a cab to Midtown. He had a lot of scrambling to do. Putting together a million dollars in small bills wasn't an easy task, even for a millionaire. There would be a lot of paperwork to fill out. One couldn't withdraw large sums of money without setting off regulatory alarms. Since 1970, any withdrawal over $10,000 required the participating bank to report it to the government. The rule had been initiated by the FDIC to curtail money laundering. In addition, most banks didn't have a lot of cash on hand. Chad would have to put in an order to the bank manager. With any luck, the money would be available the next day, but certainly not before.

Chad made as many discreet phone calls as possible to banks where he felt safe to discuss large amounts of withdrawal. He said he needed a down payment for a condo in the Caribbean and an Aston Martin for his wife's birthday. He made a note to tell Camille about this, in case anyone asked if she was enjoying her new car. In his circle of colleagues, neither of these scenarios was a stretch. By noon he was able to get confirmations on a total of $250,000 to be available by the end of the day. He still had $750,000 more to go. He wondered if maybe he should ask his father-in-law. He decided against it until he was out of other options. Several phone calls later, the sum was close to a half million. The rest would take more time. He was startled when his private office line rang. Then he thought it might be Camille. "Camille?" he asked after he picked up.

A gravelly voice responded. "No, Pops. How's it coming on the money?"

Chad stared at the phone. Only a handful of people had

this number as well as his home office. He remembered what Larry had said earlier and repeated the caller's question. "How is it coming?" He paused, squeezing out more time. "A little slowly. It's not easy—" His sentence was cut off. "One more day." Then the phone went dead.

Chad wondered what that meant. Were they giving him an additional day, or did he only have one more day? Chad immediately called Larry on his cell and explained what had happened. Chad rubbed his eyes with the bottom of the palm of his hand. "Larry, they said 'one more day.' I don't know if that means an additional day or tomorrow. I've only been able to come up with half of what they want."

"They'll have to call you again to give you instructions. Just keep doing what you have to do. I'll check in with you later."

Back at the town house, Camille was trying to keep herself distracted by working on the layout for a new catalog. It was going to be one of the most comprehensive exhibits of European sculpture in the history of the museum. She thought she heard the phone in Chad's study ringing and ran down the stairs to answer it. "Hello?" she asked breathlessly. Her skin went cold when she heard the voice.

"Tell your husband further instructions for delivery day will come tomorrow."

"Hello? Hello?" Camille was shaking. She immediately called Chad at his office and relayed the brief call.

"That's a relief." Chad sighed.

"A relief?" Camille tried not to shriek. "What do you mean, a relief?"

"That person just called me here. When I tried to explain that getting a million dollars isn't as easy as one would think, he said, 'one more day,' and I didn't know what he meant and then he hung up. Maybe he realized their demands were too challenging." He took a breath. "Obviously, they want the money. There's nothing in it for them if they harm J.R."

Camille took a few deep breaths. She was becoming more accustomed to this harrowing situation and sounded calmer than she had before. "I think you may be right. I have a gut feeling about it."

"Tell me." Chad knew Camille always had her feminine intuition, or "radar," as he put it, on high alert.

"It seems to me these people are desperate and are willing to make a small concession to get what they want. I don't think it's any kind of vendetta or trying to make a political statement. As you said, there is nothing in it for them unless they turn him over to us." Camille stopped. "Although that doesn't mean they won't harm him in the process."

"I agree. They want money and they want it fast, but I don't think they're stupid."

"I hope you're right. I hope we're both right," Camille agreed.

Chad softened his voice. "How are you holding up?"

"Okay. I'm okay, considering." Camille sounded convincing.

"Good. I'll check back with you in a couple of hours and let you know how much I've been able to accomplish." Chad's BlackBerry rang again. "Gotta go. It's Larry. Maybe he has something. Love you."

Chad hung up his office phone as he picked up the cell. "Anything?"

"Not exactly, but we were able to get some background sounds identified."

"Really?" Chad seemed surprised.

"A tractor."

"A tractor?" Chad was stupefied.

"Or some kind of farm equipment. I suspect the call came from a pay phone on a highway near a farm."

"You were able to get all that from a few seconds?" Chad was even more amazed.

"We took the sound recordings from all the calls so far and pieced them together. The calls from last night didn't give us anything, but this morning and then the recent call to the house gave us about thirty seconds of ambient sound. We ran it through a processor and narrowed it down to a tractor."

"Larry, you are incredible." Chad was heartened.

"Well, we couldn't zone in on the location, but at least we know it's not in the city." Larry grunted. "Only a few hundred thousand miles of farmland. But I doubt they ventured too far away from New York."

"Camille and I were saying that they are probably desperate for money, and that it's probably not any kind of vendetta. Or anything akin to the Patty Hearst kidnapping by the Symbionese Liberation Army. An attack against capitalism, if I remember correctly."

"Yeah. That was some kind of crazy thing," Larry agreed. "But we can't underestimate these people either." He paused. "How are you coming on the funds?"

"I should be halfway there by the end of the business day. At least I gave the banks a heads-up for tomorrow so they'll have the cash and I won't be on a begging mission."

"Good," Larry replied. "Hang in there, my friend. I'll check in with you later."

Chad gathered all the documents he needed and headed to the first bank on his list. He arranged for several of the branches to put together whatever funds they had available. He then went to another financial institution where he had several money market accounts. He began to worry about carrying so much cash around, so he hired a private car for the few hours it would take to drive uptown, downtown and crosstown. At least he wouldn't be standing on a corner trying to flag down a cab. He made one stop at the town house to drop off the first batch of cash and put it in the safe. He then went to the next branch to pick up another several thousand. He made at least a dozen trips in about four hours, knowing he would have to repeat the process the next day. His only hope was that everything would come together without tragedy striking.

As the car pulled in front of the wrought-iron gates of Sniffen Court, Chad spotted the Poland Spring truck parked on the side of the street. He glanced toward the driver, and sure enough, it was George, Larry's partner. Chad signed the voucher for the car service and gave the driver a sizable tip. "Pick me up tomorrow? Here at eight thirty?"

"Yessir," the limo driver responded. Chad figured the fewer people who knew about his activities the better, and having the same driver would eliminate getting another person involved in his relay race for cash.

Chad approached the parked truck. George rolled down the window. "Just keeping an eye on things." George smiled and extended his hand.

"I really appreciate what you and Larry are doing for us."

"Are you kidding?" George replied. "Anything for you guys." Then he smiled. "Pancakes tomorrow?"

Chad patted George on the shoulder. "I'll see what I can do."

"I'll be here until ten tonight if you need anything," George called out the window.

"Thanks!" Chad hustled toward the front door of his brownstone. He wanted to lock the cash in the safe as quickly as possible.

Camille met him at the door, and he swooshed past her. "Everything all right?" she asked.

"Yes. Sorry, darlin'." He stopped, backed up and gave her a kiss. "I just want to get this into the safe." He walked to the bookcase, where the safe was hidden behind a fake shelf of books. He stared at the loot. "Despite all my years in banking, a half million dollars is still impressive. And it weighs fifty-five pounds. I don't know how I am going to handle one hundred and ten pounds of money."

As soon as he was finished emptying out his duffel bag, he closed the safe and pulled Camille into his arms. "What a day."

She grabbed his hand. "Come." She walked him out to their small patio, where a bottle of Louis Latour Puligny-Montrachet was chilling in a wine bucket. A platter of jumbo shrimp, lobster and crab claws sat on the table.

"What's the occasion?" Chad was pleased but also confused.

"I figured we may be broke after tomorrow, so we might as well enjoy ourselves tonight." Camille always knew what to do, regardless of the situation.

"Do you know how much I love you?" Chad pulled her close and held her for a good long minute.

She tried not to get teary-eyed, but it was a comfort knowing they had each other, no matter what.

He held her at arm's length. "Hey. It's going to be okay." She leaned back into him. "Look at what you've done." He gestured to the food and wine. "Even under all this stress, you figured out a way to make the day end in a civilized and loving manner."

"Aw shucks." She wiped a tear away and handed him the corkscrew. "Get busy. I almost started without you."

Chad obediently opened the wine and poured two glasses. He pulled out a chair from the café table and motioned for her to sit as he took the chair next to her. He raised his glass. "Here's to us. And J.R."

They clinked glasses and sat silently for a while as they sipped their Chardonnay. Camille had just begun to serve the seafood when the phone in Chad's study rang. Both jumped up and dashed toward the sound of his private line.

Chad took a deep breath before answering. "Chad Pierce."

Again, a distorted voice replied. "Howz it goin', Daddy Warbucks?"

Chad hesitated and repeated the sentence. "How is it going?" He paused. "I told you earlier, it's not as easy as you might think. There's paperwork." Another pause. "The government tracks every transaction over ten thousand dollars."

"Well, then, do it, old man. No more waiting. You got until tomorrow to get it together. Instructions soon." Then the line went dead.

Immediately, Chad's BlackBerry rang. "Larry? Did you get anything?"

"We're working on it now. I want to do another ambient sound check. Give me about an hour."

"Thanks." Chad clicked off his cell phone. "He needs another hour. Let's go finish the wine before the chill is gone." He grabbed Camille's hand and walked her out to the patio this time.

Camille looked at Chad. In the twenty years since she'd met him, he'd never looked haggard. But today he did. She could see the pressure was wearing on him. They tried to keep the conversation light. Chad commented on how bad the traffic was getting in the city and Camille discussed the layout of the museum catalog. The sky was turning dark. They had been sitting there for over two hours when the phone in his study rang again. They bolted to answer it.

Once again, the raspy voice gave instructions. "Wednesday. There is a shack in a field on the west side of Route 34 in Colts Neck between Laird and Concord. Bring the cash to the shack. Do not have anyone follow you or you won't see your fair boy again."

Chad repeated the instructions. "Wednesday. Shack. Route 34. Laird and Concord. But how will I know he's okay?"

"After you deliver the money, wait one hour at Delicious Orchards. Then go north to Newman Springs Road. There's a Sunoco station there. Your son will be on the side of the road."

"What?" Chad's mind raced to the worst. The decibels in his voice increased. "The side of the road?"

"Don't worry, Pops." Then Chad heard a crackling sound, followed by his son's voice in the background again.

"Dad! Please! Help!" Then the phone went dead.

Larry called immediately. "Somewhere along Route 537 near the Due Process Stable."

Chad snickered. "How ironic. In 1995 the original owner, Robert Brennan, was fined seventy-five million dollars for defrauding investors. Then, in 2000, he was arrested for bankruptcy fraud, obstructing justice and money laundering."

"Yeah," Larry replied. "Didn't he get nine years?"

"He did, but he was released early for good behavior. And then he came back to work as the general manager, but that didn't last long."

"Chad? I hate to ask you this, but are there any investors you may have pissed off?" Larry couldn't imagine Chad doing anything illegal or improper, but he had to ask anyway.

"Me?" Chad wasn't surprised at the question. It was a natural thing to ask. "No, Larry. I have a good life. A good gig. Why would I blow it?"

"You think it's just a coincidence that your son is somewhere near a place where the owner bilked investors of millions? Maybe some kind of revenge?"

"Revenge? For what?" Chad paused. "Unless it's just someone familiar with banking, but I doubt it. I cannot possibly think of someone who would do this to us." His voice calmed. "Besides, that part of Jersey is filled with farms and horses."

"True. And it's an easy shot from the City. I can take a ride down there tomorrow morning to see if there is any activity. Should we set up cameras?"

"No. I don't want anything to go wrong. If they think they're being watched, they may do something to J.R."

"So you're willing to give up a million dollars and walk away?"

"I don't have a choice, Larry. He's my son."

"I get it. Just needed to ask. You can always alert the authorities after he's safe. Not that your call will do anything except have the feds keep an eye out for someone spending lots of cash."

"Thanks. We'll talk tomorrow. George said he'd be here in the morning."

Larry laughed. "That guy will do anything for a free meal."

Chad hung up the phone and poured a brandy for himself and Camille. "Everything is in play."

Camille sighed.

"But . . ." Chad paused, then gave her a grin. "You have to make breakfast for George."

Camille chuckled nervously. They were both relieved and tense at the same time. Things were moving.

Chad carried their snifters back to the kitchen and helped clear the dishes. "You have been such a champ during this," Chad said to his wife.

"And so have you." Camille gave him a tired smile.

"Let's finish up here and watch some inane movie. There's nothing else we can do for now."

"Maybe I should freshen up his room," Camille said pensively.

"Let Mildred do that tomorrow. It's been a very long day."

"Should I tell Mildred to come tomorrow or not?"

"How did you leave it with her?"

"I just told her not to come in today. I should call her."

"Will you be okay with her coming here? I mean, everything is still up in the air."

"I don't want her to think anything has gone awry. Besides, I can keep myself occupied while she's here in the morning."

"What if they call?" Chad asked.

"I won't answer the phone. Then they'll have to call your office. Besides, I really don't want to talk to those people. I might start screaming at them."

"Good thinking." Chad nodded. "So, a movie?"

Camille looked down at her two dogs. "What do you say? Another brandy and *There's Something About Mary?*"

Lucy gave a yap of approval and Ricky wagged his tail.

"I was going to vote for *Fargo* but looks like you guys already have it planned." Chad refilled their glasses as Camille and the dogs sprang up the stairs.

Chad pulled out the DVD from their massive collection, inserted it into the DVD player and queued up the film. Camille returned from the bathroom in a pair of light cotton pajamas, her hair in a short ponytail. He smiled at her. She looked refreshed for the first time since the night before.

Camille, Lucy and Ricky settled into their king-size bed. Every night it was a race to who would get near the pillows first—Camille, Lucy or Ricky. Then the game of "move over" would start when Chad came to bed.

Chad kissed her on the forehead. "This will all be over soon."

The following day, Camille made her famous pancakes and Chad handed them to George on his way to meet the car service. "All clear?" Chad asked him.

"Same people, same dogs," George said. "Thanks. I may have to come back tomorrow." He grinned. "Larry and I are leaving for Jersey in about an hour. Anything you need from me before we head out?"

"I can't think of anything, George. And I can't thank you enough."

"All right, then. We'll be in touch later." George patted him on the back, and Chad got into the black town car that was waiting for him.

The car made the rounds to the various financial institutions where Chad had made arrangements for the cash. It was over two hours later when they finally circled back to the town house. Chad realized Mildred would probably be there, so he phoned Camille. "Hey, honey. Is Mildred there?"

"Yes. Why?"

"I have the rest of the cash and I want to put it in the safe, but I don't think all of it will fit, and I don't want Mildred snooping around."

Camille realized Mildred was within earshot. "I'm putting a grocery list together with her now, so I'll be sure to order some of your favorite. Raspberry?" She glanced at Mildred and gave her a wink.

"Brilliant," Chad replied. "I'll be there within the next thirty minutes."

"Perfect. See you for dinner. Love you." Camille could not have acted more normal if things actually *were* normal. She turned to Mildred. "Put some of that raspberry preserve on the list, and a couple of rib eyes, too. Chad's been working like a fiend and could use some good, red meat."

"Yes, ma'am." Mildred scribbled on the notepad. "Do you want me to go to D'Agostino now?"

"Yes, before they get too busy."

"Do you want me to wait for them to put everything together?"

"Why don't you pick out the steak and vegetables and let them do the rest? They can deliver all of it this afternoon," Camille continued. "And when you get back, could you put a fresh set of linens on J.R.'s bed and give it a good once-over? We're expecting him for the weekend."

"Oh, how nice! It's been a while. How is he doing in school?" Mildred asked innocently.

"He's doing very well. It was the best thing we did, sending him up to Massachusetts." Camille was lying, but she was convincing.

"Glad to hear it. I know things were a little up in the air for a while." Mildred didn't want to overstep, but it was no secret J.R. had failed or been kicked out of several schools. "I'll get on this right away." She perused the list. "We probably could use more pancake mix and lingonberry syrup."

Camille chuckled. "Chad had a friend over for breakfast yesterday. They must have eaten two dozen each."

"Oh, you should have told me you were having company. I would have come to help."

"Larry insisted I make him his favorite pancakes, so that's why I didn't think it was necessary for you to come in."

Mildred didn't seem surprised or suspicious. She grabbed her purse. "I'll be back in a jiffy."

"Take your time. Especially picking out those steaks," Camille urged, wanting her to avoid rushing.

About a half hour later, Chad grunted through the door carrying two duffel bags, each weighing over twenty-five pounds. "Where can we put these so Mildred won't find them?"

"In my office. I'll pretend I'm working on the catalog. She won't bother me in there."

Chad hurried with the two bags tucked under each arm. "Whew, this is some kind of workout."

Camille opened the large bifold doors of her art supply closet. "Under here." She pointed to a spot on the floor. Chad was sweating. "You'd better change your shirt before you go back to work."

"Good idea." He quickly loosened his tie and unbuttoned his shirt. Camille handed him a damp washcloth that he took into their bathroom. "What if Mildred comes back before I'm gone?"

Camille leaned against the doorjamb. "You do live here, you know. You really don't have to explain anything to her."

Chad scoffed. "I'll just tell her I spilled coffee on my shirt and had to change."

Camille was shaking her head. "You'd think we were Bonnie and Clyde."

"Well, we didn't rob any banks," Chad added as he pulled on another button-down shirt.

"No, we just cleaned them out," Camille said wryly.

"Now look who's being the funny one." Chad smiled. He kissed her on the cheek. "Everything is going to be all right. Larry is checking out the drop location so I'll have an idea of how close I can get with the car. It's a lot of weight." He paused. "I wonder if they even know how much a million dollars in twenties weighs? TV and movies are never accurate."

"That will be their problem to solve." Camille patted Chad on the ass. "Now get going in case they call your office again. I told you I won't answer the phone here."

"Righto." Chad hustled down the stairs, out the door and past the gate. He slowed his pace. The hardest logistical part was over. Just thinking about it made him sweat. Twenty banks in twenty-four hours. And 110 pounds of cash. Chad walked the twelve blocks to his office. He needed to slow his pace again, get a grip, act normal. He was anticipating two more phone calls. One would be from Larry giving Chad a heads-up as to what he could expect at the drop site. The other would be from the kidnappers, confirming the time.

He checked his watch. It was almost two. He felt his BlackBerry vibrating in his pocket. It was Larry.

"Confirming a shack in the middle of a field, Route 34 between Laird and Concord. But it's not a working farm. The place looks like it hasn't seen a tractor in at least a decade or more. So they musta been calling from someplace close by, but not here."

"How far is it from the road?" Chad asked, thinking about the load he was going to carry.

"Several hundred yards. Maybe two football fields' worth." Chad groaned. "Is there a place for me to park?"

"Not on the property. There's an old split-rail fence. Looks like you're going to have to leave the car on the side of the road. The shack is literally in the middle of nowhere. I'd say it's surrounded by maybe a hundred acres."

Chad's back was aching at the thought of the physical exertion. He was in excellent shape for a man of forty-eight, but lugging 110 pounds over a quarter mile could knock the wind out of him. He would have to do it in two trips.

"Thanks, Larry. I'm going to need a massage after this."

"You ain't kidding," Larry said. "Let's hope everything goes as planned. Do you want me to wait in the parking lot at Due Process?"

"That would be great. Just in case . . . just in case . . ." He stopped speaking when he was at the crosswalk with a half-dozen other people waiting for the light to change. "I'm heading to my office." He figured Larry would know he wasn't in the most advantageous place to talk.

Larry continued the one-sided conversation. "What time did they say?" he asked.

"They didn't. I'm guessing they'll call again to confirm."

"You'd think so."

"I'm not sure if I'm dealing with geniuses or idiots," Chad said as he lowered his voice.

"Probably a mixed bag of both," Larry replied. "Call me when they give you the time frame."

"Will do." Chad clicked off the phone and placed it back in his pocket. He went through the revolving doors, said hello to the security guard and took the elevator to the twentieth floor. He smiled and greeted everyone he passed on his way to his corner office. Normally, he left the door open, but today he needed some privacy. It had been one hell of a forty-eight hours and there were still another twenty-four to go. He went through both his email and desk inboxes to make sure he hadn't overlooked anything during this harrowing experience. He certainly couldn't afford to lose any more money or anger any of his clients. He riffled through the papers. Nothing urgent. He checked his email and stopped in his tracks. There was a photo of his son holding a piece of paper. It read: "Noon or Dead. Your choice."

Chad immediately phoned Larry and explained what had just come in. Larry explained the person could have used a coffee shop Wi-Fi hot spot to send it, and it could take a day or so to trace the internet service provider.

"How did he look in the photo?" Larry asked calmly.

"Unshaven. Rumpled." Chad kept staring at the photo.

"Anything in the background?" Larry asked.

"No. Just wood." Chad was rattled. He hadn't been expecting this kind of communication. Even though the entire situation was perilous, the word "Dead" hit him like a punch to the gut. "But the photo looked menacing."

"It was meant to." Larry's tone remained even. "They want to be sure you're on track and you're not going to ignore their threats."

"If you say so, Larry." Chad was weary.

"Just follow the instructions."

"How will they know I delivered the money?"

"They said to wait an hour. They'll check the drop-off point. I'm sure they'll be on the lookout for anyone. If they're satisfied, they'll bring him to the gas station."

Chad's hands were shaking. He had been in crisis mode and hadn't had a whole lot of time to think about what was happening. He kept putting one foot in front of the other to get things done, and to make sure Camille wouldn't unravel. Having your child abducted was more than any parent could endure. He picked up the phone to check on Camille, even though it had been less than an hour. At least he had something new to tell her—the time of the drop. With any luck and the heavens shining on them, the family would be reunited within twenty-four hours. Once he reached her, Chad also told Camille the kidnappers had sent a photo, and J.R. looked okay under the circumstances. Camille took the news well. Most likely because Chad did not mention the word "Dead."

Chad decided to call it quits early; he couldn't focus on anything anyway. He told his staff he was leaving, and if something important came up to call his home office. No one thought anything of it. On his way home he stopped at a shop and purchased four nylon duffel bags. They would be lighter than the ones he'd used earlier, and this way he wouldn't be giving up his good leather luggage. He was confident the kidnappers would not be concerned that the money was not in Louis Vuitton bags.

When Chad arrived home, he went into the kitchen, pulled out a chair and loosened his tie. "One more day and all of this should be over."

Camille was on the patio, setting the café table. The steaks were on the kitchen counter, salted and getting the chill out of them. She walked in, wiping her hands on a towel that matched her apron. In spite of everything, she still looked radiant. He pulled her close to him and rested his head against her waist. "I swear, you look good in everything." He tugged at the smock. "And you have become the chef du jour."

"I let Mildred go home after the groceries were delivered. The fewer people around here the better." She moved away from her husband and checked the big hunks of beef. "I had her refresh J.R.'s room. I told her he was coming home for the weekend." She handed Chad a bottle of Châteauneuf-du-Pape and a corkscrew. "We'll give it time to breathe."

"Speaking of the weekend . . . We should talk about what we'll do with J.R. after he comes home."

Camille looked puzzled. "What do you mean?"

"Do we really want him to go back to boarding school after all this?"

"No, of course not." Camille hadn't given it any thought until now, but her answer was automatic.

"He's going to have to finish. This is his last year and he's come very far. It would be a shame for him to lose all the credits and his grades. We both know what a struggle this has been."

Camille took the seat across from him. "Why don't we see how he is feeling? Thinking. He's been through a horrible, traumatic event. Let's give him some breathing room."

"I suppose you're right. I guess I am anxious for life to resume a level of normalcy."

Camille frowned. "I don't know if anything will ever be normal again. This is something that will take all of us time to recover from."

Chad knew Camille was right. "Good point. We'll take it one day at a time." He changed the subject to dinner. "Those steaks look delicious."

"Mildred gave the butcher explicit instructions and supervised every step of the way."

Chad chuckled. "I bet she did." He stood up. "I'm going to change. Give me a couple of minutes and I'll fire up the grill." He pecked her on the cheek.

Then the phone rang in his study. It was as if someone had been watching every move he made. When he was home, when he was in the office. It was uncanny. And creepy.

"Chad Pierce," he said once he had run to the phone and picked up.

"Everything ready?" the raspy voice asked.

"Everything is ready. Tomorrow. Noon. Route 34. Laird and Concord. Small bills." He stopped short of telling the caller the bags were heavy. *Let them find out for themselves.*

"Nighty night." The call ended.

Camille scurried into the study with a panicked look on her face. Chad held up his hand. "No worries, love. They were just confirming."

Camille let out a huge breath of air and steadied herself, holding on to the edge of Chad's desk.

"It's going to be all right." He pulled her against him again and stroked her hair. "Come on. Let's try to relax and enjoy our dinner. I'll be down in a minute." Chad headed for their bedroom and Camille went back to the kitchen. She didn't wait for Chad to return but poured herself a glass of wine and went out to the patio. She took a few minutes to gaze at the landscaping. It was a small area with stone walls separating their property from the neighbors, giving them a sense of privacy. The English ivy that climbed the walls had been there long before they moved in twenty years earlier. She wondered how old it was. Decades for sure. There were some blue hydrangeas and boxwoods, and a small area where Camille kept her herbs. Camille loved to cook. She had spent a good amount of time in France and learned from some of the best. One thing that had stuck with her was the use of fine herbs. Every year she would grow tarragon, chives, parsley and chervil outdoors. In the winter she kept a small greenhouse window box that also included basil and oregano for when she wanted an Italian flare. She was snipping a few bits of parsley and tarragon to make a dressing for the salad when Chad returned wearing a pair of flannel slacks and a crew-neck sweater.

Chad sidled up behind her, wrapping his arms around her and nuzzling her neck. "I love you so very much, Camille. I am happy you are my partner in life."

Camille's face became a waterfall, the tears dripping down her cheeks. She tried to pull herself together. Again.

Chad rocked her back and forth, as if they were slow dancing. He wiped her tears. They took a few silent moments in each other's arms.

Camille was the first to make a move. "Please?" She held up her half-empty glass.

Chad looked at her for a moment before he asked, "Would you say your glass is half empty or half full?"

She cocked her head. "That would depend on what is *in* the glass."

"Excellent point." He poured a bit more wine into her glass and filled his. "Here's to us. Our family."

They clinked glasses, both letting out heavy sighs.

Chad turned on the grill, then pulled out a chair for Camille. He took both her hands into his. "This is how it's going to go down tomorrow."

She looked at him intently. She knew her husband would have all the bases covered. Even those he didn't know about. Chad always prepared for every possible scenario, although admittedly, this was his first ransom drop.

"After dinner I'll transfer the money into the duffel bags I bought on the way home. They're lightweight, and I'm going to need all the help I can get." He took a sip from his glass. "Larry is going to drop off a car first thing in the morning. He'll take my car to Due Process. I'll drive his Range Rover to the drop point. I'll park on the side of the road and try to make the drop in two trips. I figure I can carry twenty-five pounds under each arm." He playfully curled his biceps.

Camille couldn't help but smile.

"Then I drive to Delicious Orchards and hang out in the parking lot for one hour. After which I go to the Sunoco station a few miles north." He paused. "Once I pick up J.R., we'll meet up with Larry at Due Process. I will call you the minute I have him in the car."

Camille gave a short huff. "Okay. This is going to be fine." She didn't know who she was trying to convince.

Chad put the steaks on the grill while Camille went to get the salad. It was a quiet, calm, peaceful dinner. Even the usual sounds of traffic in the background seemed muffled and distant. A little over an hour later, they cleared the dishes and took the rest of their wine into Chad's study. He opened the safe and began transferring the funds into two of the nylon bags. "Is Mildred coming in the morning?"

"No. I told her we were both going to be out and the house is tidy enough. She'll be back day after."

"Good. I didn't want her to be around when I shuffled the duffels." He made a goofy grin at his silly rhyme as they proceeded up the stairs. They went into Camille's office and transferred the money from the closet into the remaining bags. "I'll bring these downstairs so they're ready when Larry gets here."

After finishing the task, Chad poured two glasses of cognac and brought them to the bedroom. He handed Camille a snifter. "I thought this might help us get some sleep."

"Good idea in theory." She smiled and took a whiff of the Rémy Martin VSOP. "Did you put some orange bitters in this?"

"You have a good nose." He smiled as he gave hers a little tap with his finger. "Yes, a cognac cocktail."

She took a sip. "Nicely done." She patted the space next to her, which barely had enough room now that Lucy and Ricky had claimed their space. Chad wiggled into the sumptuous linens and rested his head against the padded headboard before wearily closing his eyes.

Chapter Three

The Rescue and Beyond

2003–Present

Neither Camille nor Chad got much sleep the night before, nor did the dogs. With Camille and Chad tossing and turning, the dogs were being bounced all over the bed. Finally, Lucy took to the chaise longue in the corner and Ricky found refuge at the foot of the bed. It was around five a.m. when Chad decided sleep was futile and got up. He showered and dressed while Camille insisted she could get some shut-eye by beating her pillows into submission. After thirty minutes of wrestling with the linens, she, too, got up and showered, the dogs following her into the master bathroom suite.

Chad was shaving when she stepped out of the stall and wrapped a towel around her hair. She looked at the clock on the vanity. It was only six o'clock. "So, what shall we do until Larry arrives?"

Chad gave her a wink and a grin. "Pancakes. What else?"

"What time is he getting here?"

"Around eight. I want to leave by nine. Under normal circumstances, it should take me about an hour and a half, but it's always a crapshoot during rush hour, even if the traffic is going in the opposite direction."

"I wish you would take me with you." Camille sighed.

"Honey, we discussed this. It's best if you stay here, just in case."

"In case of what?" Camille grew tense.

"In case they call. I don't know. Please, let's not have this discussion again. Let's just think positively and do everything according to the plan."

"You're right." Camille began to blow-dry her hair. She shouted over the noise, "Will George be on the lookout again?"

"Absolutely. That's a lot of money to move around."

"Will Larry be following you?"

"No, but he will be close by. We don't want to take any chance that someone will think we've veered from their explicit instructions."

Camille pulled on a new jogging suit and gave her face a once-over with a bit of tinted moisturizer, blush and pale lipstick before tying her hair back in a short ponytail.

Chad put on a pair of jeans, a long-sleeved Polo shirt, socks and loafers. He couldn't have appeared more casual but it was a far cry from what he was experiencing inside. He looked at his collection of watches and opted for the simple, stainless-steel OMEGA. No sense in looking ostentatious. Besides, he might have to sell a few of his better watches once this was all over. A million dollars was a lot of money, even for his family. Most of it was tied up in bonds, stocks and real estate. His net worth was maybe five million, not counting Camille's money, which he never did. The money he'd accumulated over the past twenty years was hard-earned and made on his own. Granted, his father-in-law had given him a job, which he worked at diligently, and their town house had been a wedding present. But Chad paid the taxes and upkeep. The only thing he didn't pay for was J.R.'s education. Harrison insisted on handling it and had long ago set up a trust for J.R. that included private school and college.

Camille was in the kitchen, putting the ingredients for breakfast together. It was a good thing Mildred had noticed they were almost out of pancake mix and added it to the list the day before. At exactly eight the buzzer at the front gate rang, and Chad let Larry into the courtyard. They decided to wait until they finished breakfast before loading the car. No sense in putting a pile of cash outside the gated court even if George was on duty. There was much too much to lose at this point in the game.

The conversation was somber, but not morose. They kept to the facts and went over the plan. Everyone was confident they had it mapped out correctly. Camille thought she was going to jump out of her skin, but she kept it together. As did the two men. No one wanted to show any sign of fear or angst—even though they were all feeling both inside.

Camille was the first to get up and start to clear the table. "I'm not rushing you boys, but I want this day to go by as quickly as possible."

Larry smiled. "As do we all."

Camille fixed a container for George and handed it to Larry while Chad gathered the duffel bags and set them in the front entry.

"I'll bring the first bag out and give this to George." Larry grabbed one of the bags. "Man, these are heavy."

"I know." Chad grimaced. "Guess we're not the agile athletes we used to be, eh?"

"You were the athlete. I was the nerd." Larry slung the strap over his shoulder. "Be right back." Once outside, Larry popped the back door of the Range Rover sitting just past the wrought-iron gate. George was parked directly behind it. He nodded to Larry.

Chad followed with two bags. "Show-off," Larry kidded his friend.

"There's one more." Chad looked over his shoulder at Camille, who stood in the doorway. He handed the bags to Larry and went back to the house for the last bag of loot. He held Camille close. "I'll be back in a few hours with our son." They clung to each other for about a minute before Larry cleared his throat, indicating they needed to hit the road. He gave Camille a wave and a thumbs-up.

Even though they were almost certain no one was watching or following them, they had agreed that Larry should take a different route to Colts Neck than Chad, then proceed to Due Process Stable Golf Course. He had friends who were members, so it wasn't unusual for Larry to be around the premises.

Chad started the Range Rover and decided to take Lexington Avenue instead of the FDR Drive. Traffic was the usual state of chaos, with taxis, buses and pedestrians all racing to get to where they needed to go. Chad kept his cool, as difficult as it was. But he felt strangely confident things would turn out all right. Maybe he was in denial of what could go wrong, but he reminded himself of a book by John-Roger and Peter McWilliams called *You Can't Afford the Luxury of a Negative Thought*. Negative thinking could be debilitating, and he had to be in his best form in this moment.

The route through the city, the Lincoln Tunnel, then on to the NJ Turnpike had its usual stops and starts, but once Chad got on the Garden State Parkway, it was a breeze to exit 116 in Holmdel. From there, the country roads had few vehicles. He slowed when he saw the Sunoco station, then continued for another two miles and spotted Concord on the left. There was a grove of trees and then a very large field that seemed to stretch for acres. He slowed again, squinting to spot the shack. He almost passed it because it was quite a distance from the road, just as Larry had described. He checked his watch. It was ten forty-five. He didn't want to wait in that particular spot, so he drove a little farther down the road to see how far Delicious Orchards would be. It wasn't far. Maybe a little over a mile. He realized the kidnappers were sending him in opposite directions. First it was south, then wait, and then north.

Chad had over an hour to contemplate who these people might be. Clever, for sure. Then it occurred to him—would this be the last he heard from them? Would they come back for more money? No. It wasn't blackmail. Just a kidnapping. He snickered at the thought. *Just a kidnapping.* He resisted the temptation of going inside the orchard's shop to get a cup of coffee. There was no way he was leaving a million dollars alone in the vehicle. He was getting antsy. It was the longest hour of his life. Finally, around eleven forty, he decided to head back to the drop point. He figured it would take him almost fifteen minutes to make two trips back and forth to the car. He hoped a police officer wouldn't stop and check why a Range Rover was stopped on the side of the road. One more thing to make him anxious. *Great.*

He drove north and made a U-turn just past Concord, then doubled back to the spot closest to the shack. He pulled as far off to the side as he could onto a patch of gravel and weeds. He looked both ways before he got out of the vehicle. There was still very little traffic in either direction. He went to the rear passenger seat and pulled out two of the bags. He thought he could carry two at a time, but after about an acre's worth of walking he broke out in a sweat. He looked around. Not a person or cow in sight. He decided to leave the two bags in the field and go retrieve the other two. It would be easier to do it in stages, and that way he would be able to see if anyone was on the move. It would also alleviate the worry of leaving half the money unguarded in the car. He jogged back to the vehicle and pulled out the rest of the stash. Yes, this was a much better plan.

He continued to the shack with the first two bags. The place was deserted. It was a ramshackle structure about eight-by-ten feet, with a very old door barely hanging on its hinges. He wondered about the soundness of this location. But it wasn't his idea; he was just following directions. He placed the first two bags on the floor, which was covered in inches of dust. It didn't appear anyone had been here for a long time. There was no sign of his son or anything that belonged to anyone. No scraps of clothing, food wrappers, empty bottles or cans. It was completely deserted save for the dirt.

He quickly hustled to the area where he'd left the other two bundles, heaved them up and waddled back to the shed. His legs were going numb, as were his arms and shoulders. He dropped the rest of the load, shut the door and began to walk back to his car. No wonder they had picked this spot. If anyone was watching, they would spy the police in a heartbeat. How they would retrieve the money was another story. Not being a terribly religious man, Chad stopped for a moment and prayed that in the next hour and ten minutes his son would be safely returned to him.

Chad drove back to Delicious Orchards, as instructed. This time he went inside and bought a coffee and a piece of crumb cake. Not that he had an appetite, but he figured it would use up some of the time. He couldn't decide if the previous hour had been the longest in his life but decided it was at the top of his list. He browsed the store, trying to knock away the minutes. A cherry pie caught his eye. That would make a nice dessert for the homecoming dinner. Chad was feeling more positive. He went outside and ate the cake and drank the coffee at a picnic table. It was a lovely spot. He understood why Camille loved the countryside. Then he felt a pang of guilt. They had been married for over twenty years and they still did not have a country home. He then reminded himself that Harrison's place in Newport was always available to them. But it was a bit of a haul. Over three hours on a very busy, unsightly highway. The drive was never pleasant, as opposed to the one-hour drive to Westport, where Camille had spent her high school summers. Maybe that was what they needed in their life. A place of peace and quiet. That was a conversation for another day. He checked his watch again. Fifteen more minutes. He thought about calling Larry but decided against it. *Follow the instructions. Do not deviate. No one intervening.*

He walked slowly back to the vehicle, started the engine and waited a few more minutes. He wanted to be exactly on time. It was one on the dot as he pulled into the gas station. He looked around. No J.R. He almost started to panic when he saw a disheveled, dirty kid a few hundred yards away staggering down the road. The kid almost looked as if he was drunk. Maybe drugged. Chad jumped out of the car and ran toward him. "J.R.!" He grabbed the waiflike creature and hugged him.

J.R. finally spoke. "Dad." He collapsed into his father's arms.

A gas station attendant witnessed the encounter and ran toward them. "Is everything okay?"

"You got some water?" Chad helped J.R. to the passenger side of the car. He opened the door, and J.R. climbed in and sat sideways with his legs dangling over the edge of the seat. The attendant dashed back with a bottle of cold water, opened it and handed it to J.R., who proceeded to pour some of it over his head, then guzzle the rest.

Chad got to eye level with his son. "Are you all right?"

J.R. squinted up and replied with a whisper. "Yeah, Dad. I'm okay."

There was a moment of awkward silence between the two of them and the gas station attendant. The attendant had no idea what was going on, and Chad didn't want to let on that his son was just returned from a heart-wrenching kidnapping. Chad turned to the man in the overalls. "Thanks very much." He reached into his pocket to pay for the water and give the man a tip, but the attendant refused. Chad helped J.R. get situated and then buckled his seat belt for him. He pulled out his BlackBerry and dialed Camille.

"He's safe," Chad said as the tears welled up in his eyes.

"Oh, thank God." Camille began to cry. But it was a good cry. "Let me speak to him, please?"

Chad handed the phone to his son.

"Mom?"

"Sweetie. Are you all right?" Camille was excited and relieved. Her voice sounded like it was an octave higher than usual.

"Yeah, Mom. I'm okay."

"I am so happy to hear you're all right. I can't wait for you to get home," Camille sniffled.

"Me too," J.R. said hoarsely. "Here's Dad." He handed the phone back to Chad.

Chad took a huge breath. "We should be home within the next two hours."

"I'll call Russell Wainwright and ask him if he can come over to check him out."

"I'm going to meet up with Larry and switch cars. Be careful," Chad said before Camille gave her usual send-off.

"Larry?" J.R. asked in a very odd tone.

"This is his car. He drove mine to Due Process. We'll switch and head home."

J.R. looked uncomfortable. More uncomfortable than he had just a few minutes before. "Why did you switch cars?"

"Because I wanted an all-terrain vehicle. When they said a

shack in a field, I didn't know what I would be driving on. Larry offered to meet up with us at Due Process."

J.R. had no response to that.

"You okay?" Chad glanced at his son.

"Yes, but they said not to tell anybody."

"They said not to tell the police. And we didn't."

"But why did you call Larry?"

Chad thought his son's reaction was a bit odd. "Listen, we needed help. He was the only person I could trust."

"But what if they find out?" J.R. looked disturbed.

"Who?"

"The police?" J.R. asked.

"I don't know how or why they should. And you shouldn't be thinking about anything except getting a good dinner, a hot shower and a comfortable bed. You can tell us about all of this whenever you are ready. Okay?"

"Sure." J.R. stared blankly at the passing trees.

Chad knew his son was terribly traumatized, so he kept the conversation to a bare minimum. It only took a few minutes to arrive at Due Process. Larry was waiting in the parking lot, leaning against Chad's BMW. He was beaming as they approached him. "J.R.! Good to see you!"

J.R. shrugged. "Yeah. Thanks."

Larry gave Chad a sideways look. Maybe it was the ordeal, but J.R. didn't seem very happy to be safe and in the company of people who cared about him. But then again, no one knew exactly what he had been through. Only time would tell, and only if and when he was ready to reveal the details.

Chad and Larry gave each other a bear hug. Larry was more reticent with J.R. He extended his hand instead. They shook, but to Larry it felt as if he had a dead fish in his hand instead of the grip of a fit eighteen-year-old. He comforted himself knowing he'd helped his best friend get his son back. Whatever happened next was out of his control.

Chad and J.R. got into the BMW and Larry into his Range Rover. They waved each other off and headed in different directions.

Dr. Russell Wainwright had been the Pierce family physician for twenty years. They were also social friends and on a first-name basis. He was always willing to make a house call for Camille, Chad or J.R. Camille wasn't very forthcoming with information but told him J.R. had gone camping, gotten lost and was suffering from exhaustion. She then phoned Chad to tell him to tell J.R. that was the story they were relating to anyone who asked.

Chad relayed the information to J.R., who didn't take it very well.

"Dr. Wainwright? Why?" He was almost sneering.

"To make sure you're okay."

"I'm fine." J.R. would have been on the verge of curling into a ball had it not been for the seat belt.

"Son, is there something you're not telling me?" Chad glanced over.

"No. I'm fine." He sounded like a spoiled brat.

Once again, Chad chalked it up to distress. Maybe Russell could prescribe something for him. Something to help move him past this very dark place.

The silence in the car was deafening. Chad could not understand why his son was so quiet. One would think he would want to spill his guts about the entire situation. But no. Not yet. Chad glanced at J.R. again. "Music?"

"Sure. Whatever."

Chad pressed the button on the radio and kept changing the stations until he found some cool jazz. Maybe that would put a bit of calm in the atmosphere.

They drove in silence for over an hour until they were on

the viaduct to the Lincoln Tunnel. J.R. finally spoke up. "Thanks, Dad. I appreciate what you did."

Chad let out a huge sigh of relief. He felt as if had been holding his breath since they'd gotten in the car. "Anything for you, son."

The outbound tunnel was backed up. Chad thought they would never get to East 36th Street. "Would you call your mother and tell her we're running a bit late? Maybe another fifteen to twenty minutes."

J.R. took the phone from the console and hit the button that said Home. Camille answered after the first ring. "Hey, Mom, we're running late. Traffic. Dad says another fifteen to twenty minutes."

"Okay, sweetie. Anything in particular you want for dinner?"

"Nah. Whatever," J.R. said blankly.

"Okay. See you soon." Camille gave the phone in her hand a strange look. What could have possibly happened to her son over the past few days? She felt a shiver up her spine. Chad hadn't mentioned any physical injuries or marks. Camille realized J.R.'s behavior had to be caused by serious emotional distress. They would handle it. They would do everything possible to bring J.R. back to his old carefree, determined self. After all, he possessed a lot of his father's charm. Camille was hopeful it wouldn't take long for J.R. to put all the pieces back together.

A half hour later, Camille heard the buzzer from the gate. She opened the front door with a flourish. She felt as if the weight of the world had been lifted. Standing outside was Russell. "Thank you so much for coming." She gave him a peck on the cheek.

"Of course. Besides, I only live a few blocks away, although I'm thinking of retiring and moving someplace with less concrete and more lakes."

"Fishing, is it?" Camille knew the doctor was fond of fly-fishing.

"Yes. And I feel as if I'm not getting enough of it."

"I understand. Even after all these years, I still miss the farm in Connecticut." She showed him into Chad's study. "Can I fix you a drink?"

He checked his watch. It wasn't quite cocktail hour yet and he still had a patient to examine. "Sparkling water?"

"With lemon?"

"Yes, please."

Camille excused herself and headed to the kitchen, then returned with a bottle of Perrier and some lemon wedges. She set down the tray on the coffee table.

Dr. Russell Wainwright settled into one of the club chairs. "Tell me, what is this all about? I thought J.R. was in school in Massachusetts."

"Yes, he was, but he decided to go camping and got separated from his friends. He was lost in the woods for two days."

"No BlackBerry? Cell phone?"

"They aren't allowed at the school. Besides, there's no reason in this day and age that kids should have them." Camille wasn't sure if she was proud of how easily she was able to come up with these lies.

"I don't disagree, but it's not going to be too long before everyone has them."

"What a dreadful thought," Camille said.

"Technology is running full speed ahead in every industry. That's another reason I'm thinking of retiring. Specialized medicine is becoming more popular, and if I want to keep up, I'll have to invest in a new EKG machine and an entirely new computer system."

"I know what you mean about computer systems. It's been the bane of Chad's existence since 2000 and the Y2K debacle."

Their conversation was interrupted by the sound of the front door opening. Camille ran toward it, leaving the doctor behind. She wrapped her arms around her son. He stiffened in her embrace. "What is it?" Camille took a step back.

"Nothing, Mom. Sorry." He moved closer and gave her a hug.

"Let me look at you."

She began to tousle his hair, which brought on a loud, "Stop! Please! I'm okay. I'm just tired and hungry."

"Didn't they feed you?" Camille was horrified at the thought.

"Yeah, Burger King."

"Did you decide what you want for dinner tonight?"

"Anything that doesn't come in a box and a paper wrapper."

"Ha!" Camille laughed out loud. J.R. was beginning to sound like himself. "Pasta? I'll order something from San Pietro. I promise it won't come in a box."

"And some burrata, too," J.R. added.

Camille and Chad were relieved their son was beginning to resurface. "I'll ask Gerardo to have the chef make a special antipasto. In the mood for ravioli?"

"Sounds good to me," Chad chimed in.

"Yeah. Sounds good," J.R. agreed, though with little enthusiasm.

"I'll phone them now. Somebody should be in the kitchen. I'll ask them to have it ready around five thirty." Camille went to the back of the house to use the kitchen phone.

J.R. turned to climb the stairs but was halted by his father. "Dr. Wainwright is in the study."

"Can I take a quick shower first?" J.R. paused on the staircase.

"Of course." Chad tried to look deep into J.R.'s eyes, but they seemed blank. His mood was testy. Chad could sense some irritation. Annoyance. Maybe even anger? *What could those people possibly have done to him? Why doesn't he seem relieved he's safe at home?* Chad grimaced at his thoughts and proceeded to his study, where Russell Wainwright waited. Chad poured himself a Scotch and glanced at the doctor. "Would you like to join me?" Chad realized his hands were trembling.

"Not at the moment, but please don't let me stop you." He paused. "Not that you would." He tried to make light of what was an extremely awkward situation. The young man he'd glimpsed heading up the stairs didn't look like he'd spent two nights in the woods. Weary? Sure. Disheveled? Absolutely. Disoriented? Certainly. But surly, curt and almost rude? The doctor reminded himself that no one knows what goes on in other people's lives. Sometimes even the participants have no idea. They're mired in fear or denial. He hoped that wasn't the case with the Pierce family. They were fine people. Kind. Generous. Russell restarted the conversation. "Did J.R. tell you anything about his time in the woods? What did he eat? How was he able to find his way back?"

Chad knew he was on a slippery slope. He had to keep up the façade that J.R. had simply gotten lost in the woods and was not the victim of a kidnapping. "He really had very little to say." Chad took a pull from his glass.

"Perhaps he's embarrassed. You know as well as I do that young men that age place a lot of emphasis and importance on their virility."

Chad gave a brief chuckle. "Aren't we like that at every age?"

The doctor snickered in return. "Good point."

Camille placed the call from the kitchen and ordered their dinner. She thought about the two men in the study and the one upstairs. Even though she played a part in every major decision made by the family, she had a feeling the two men should have a private talk. Guy talk. She thought it might seem a little suspicious if she was hovering in the study over her son getting lost and then finding his way back. It was also better to have just one person continue the tale and not run the risk of two people possibly contradicting each other. It was better if there was only one voice.

She heard the shower turn on in J.R.'s bathroom. Maybe a nice, soapy cascade of warm water would lighten her son's mood. A familiar environment. She gathered the dinnerware and a few serving bowls. It would be another hour or so before dinner would be ready, but she decided to busy herself setting up the patio for dinner.

Camille went back into the study to ask if the doctor wanted to join them for dinner. She hoped he would say no so they could have an intimate family meal, but she didn't want to be rude, especially when he'd made a special trip to check in on J.R.

"Well, it sure sounds delicious, and I appreciate the invitation very much, but I think the three of you should enjoy one another's company without an interloper."

"Interloper?" Camille was genuinely stunned. "Not in the least!"

Russell gave her a wide-mouthed grin. "How about a rain check?"

"Any time." Camille returned to the patio and picked a few flowers from her garden and some herbs with which to make a centerpiece. That was another thing she had learned during her travels abroad—that it was okay to mix herbs with flowers for the table. It gave the bouquet more texture and aroma. In the winter, she liked to mix rosemary with pine branches and pine cones. The fragrances complemented one another. She held the dill and tarragon up to her nose and inhaled their scent. It also reminded her how much she missed being outdoors. Their lives were so busy, they rarely took vacations, usually just a long weekend in Newport, but that, too, didn't happen frequently. Maybe once or twice between April and September. She thought of what Chad had said earlier about taking a holiday. It was time. They'd pick a place the whole family would enjoy. She'd let J.R. make the first suggestion.

About thirty minutes later, J.R. lumbered down the stairs as if no one was waiting for him. "There he is." Chad attempted enthusiasm, but even he could hear the strain in his own voice. "I'll give you two some privacy," he said to J.R. and Russell, closing the sliding doors that separated his study from the main entry. He walked to the patio, where Camille was sitting at the beautifully set table. He came up from behind and kissed her softly on the cheek. She raised her hand to touch his face.

"Do you think this nightmare is really over?" She sounded wary.

"I hope so, sweetheart." He sighed.

Intuitively, Camille knew there was an unspoken "but" at the end of his sentence and so asked, "But?"

"But I don't know. Didn't he seem a little . . . off-putting?"

"Well, for someone who simply got lost in the woods, I would say yes. But for someone who was abducted and held against their will, I would say he's probably just processing all of it."

"Is that what your therapist would say?" he asked sincerely.

"Jean? Probably." Camille didn't frequent her therapist on a regular basis. Only when she was feeling overwhelmed or slipping into a bit of depression. "Chad, I've been thinking. I know I'm beginning to have some mood swings. Seeing J.R.'s shift made me realize I'm doing the same thing."

"You've been fine, honey. Once in a while you seem to lose your patience, but it's not on a daily basis."

"Well, the depression and feeling overwhelmed is not who I am. They say menopause can cause both issues."

"Whoa. Where did this come from?"

"My mood swings, darlin.' Let's face it—I am at the dreaded hormone horror's doorstep."

Chad was perplexed at this sudden turn in the conversation.

"J.R. and I could probably use a refresher therapy session. Well, at least I know *I* could. Especially after these past few days."

"You know what's best for you. As far as knowing what's best for J.R., we might know what that is, but getting him to follow our guidance is a completely different story."

"That's very true. But sending him to school in Massachusetts paid off for him academically."

"He hasn't graduated yet." Chad looked out into the distance. "And after this, he may never graduate."

"Don't say that." Camille was surprised her husband would even suggest such a thing.

"Let's see what Russell has to say after checking J.R. You make an appointment to see Jean. Ask her if she can give you some insight about J.R. and his experience. If anyone knows about post-traumatic stress, I am sure she does."

Camille looked up at Chad. "Maybe we can get a group rate." She smirked.

Chad was happy to see Camille's dry sense of humor return.

"But seriously, Chad, all of this has made me think about a lot of things."

"For example?" He sipped his Scotch.

"No woman wants to admit she is getting old. Older. At least not in our youth-worshipping society."

"Oh, my. Where is this going, honey?"

"Just hear me out. You know I've had a privileged life. I've been lucky. We've been lucky."

"I can't argue with that," Chad concurred.

"Maybe it is my age, but I see more and more of it as I get older. Women are treated differently because of their ability or inability to bear children."

"Isn't this a bit heavy for right now? Given we just rescued our son."

"No. That's what led me to thinking about all this. What am I doing working at the museum? Of course, I love curating exhibits, but it's always something someone else wants me to do."

"And?" Chad encouraged her to continue.

"Facing this life-changing experience, dealing with J.R.'s and my own emotions . . . I believe a woman's change of life is viewed as a stigma."

"What on earth are you talking about?" Chad was genuinely baffled.

"I have an idea. I want to help women in this new chapter of their life. Act Two. Act Three, even. So many women have even more to offer at a mature age. Their experience. Their wisdom." She paused. "But where are the opportunities for them to continue to flourish? To give more and get more?"

"So you've come up with a plan?" Chad was guessing he was on the right track.

"Yes! I am going to form a support group for 'women of a certain age.' " She used air quotes around the last bit. "I am going to start a foundation where women can learn to paint. Or continue to paint. Or sculpt. Even be mentors to aspiring artists."

"Camille, I must say that is a brilliant idea."

"I thought so." She gave him a rascally grin. "But first, we will plan a holiday as you suggested. We'll let J.R. pick the spot. Then, when we get back, I'll speak to my father about starting up my crazy idea."

"Honey, I am so happy you are looking ahead in such a positive way."

"We got our son back, Chad. Everything else will be as easy as eating an ice cream sandwich." Camille had always favored that expression. Life could be tricky, like trying to keep up with an ice cream cone as it melted and began to run down your wrist. But an ice cream sandwich was so much easier to enjoy.

"You never cease to amaze me." Chad sat back in the chair across from her. He looked at the outdoor clock hanging on the brick façade. "I wonder how much longer Russell is going to be with J.R."

Within a few minutes, footsteps were heard coming from the front of the house. J.R. had a smile on his face. Camille and Chad were thoroughly relieved.

"He's fit as a fiddle, as they say." The doctor patted the young man on the shoulder. "Nothing is broken. A few minor cuts we patched with some iodine."

"Yeah, he tortured me," J.R. broke in.

"Hardly," Russell protested. "I gave him a B_{12} shot to perk him up a bit. I think a little rest and some good food should have him up and running like normal in two to three days."

J.R. jerked his head. "Two to three days? I feel great now."

"That's the B_{12} kicking in, son. You just take it easy. I don't want to make any more house calls this week. Lake George is beckoning. I only have a few short weeks in which to get some bass."

Chad walked the doctor back to his study. He pulled his checkbook from the desk drawer. "I can't thank you enough, Russell. What do we owe you for today?"

"I was serious. A rain check for San Pietro. Or Patsy's. I haven't been there in ages either."

"You got it, my friend." Chad hesitated, not wanting to violate any HIPAA confidentiality laws. Russell knew Chad was chomping at the bit. "He's fine. A bit traumatized, but he's okay physically. I'd suggest therapy, but kids his age tend to think that's only for crazy people."

"Camille and I were discussing that a few minutes ago. She suggested a family discount." Chad chuckled.

"Give him a few days. Let him talk about it when he's ready. And if you find his behavior is erratic, call me and I'll recommend someone he might be more inclined to see."

Chad walked him to the door, and they shook hands. "Thanks again, Russell. I cannot tell you how relieved we are."

"Glad to be of help." Dr. Wainwright walked across the brick courtyard and out the gate.

Chad returned to the patio, where Camille and J.R. were sitting. She was reminiscing about her days at the farm, hoping she might get some feedback from J.R. about taking a trip. "Hi, honey. I was just telling J.R. about the Connecticut country house."

"Yeah. Sounds like it was a nice place to visit." J.R. was in a much better mood than he had been only an hour or so before.

Camille was just about to blurt out something about taking a trip, but Chad caught her eye in time. *Too much too soon.* "I have to pick up dinner. J.R., want to take a quick ride with me?"

"Nah. I'll hang out here with Mom. It's peaceful." He interlaced his fingers and rested the back of his head on his hands. "Mind if I have a beer?"

The two adults looked at each other. "I don't see why not." Chad looked at Camille in a pleading manner.

"Please. Do whatever you like. Tonight is your night." Camille tousled her son's hair. J.R. flinched and jerked back.

"Sorry, honey. I didn't mean to . . ."

"It's okay. I'm still a little jumpy." J.R. was quick to recover.

"We have a few kinds of beer in the fridge in the butler's pantry," Camille said, referring to a small area adjacent to the kitchen, where they had an additional refrigerator just for beverages, cabinets for dishes and a number of kitchen appliances on a countertop.

Chad followed J.R. into the kitchen. "I'll be back in twenty minutes."

J.R. twisted the top off a dark stout beer and guzzled it down like a pro.

"Easy there."

"No prob." J.R. wiped his mouth with the back of his sleeve.

Chad cringed at his son's lack of etiquette. *So much for boarding school.* That thought led Chad to another. When would J.R. be ready to return to school? Or would he ever be ready? The past four years had been challenging enough, and now they faced another obstacle.

With these worrisome thoughts bouncing around his head, Chad walked over to Third Avenue and hailed a cab. "Just doing a few short blocks, round trip," he told the driver.

"No problem, man," the ponytailed driver replied as he looked into the rearview mirror. Chad gave him the address and they were in front of the restaurant in seven minutes.

Manolo, the maître d', met Chad at the door with two large shopping bags. "*Buona sera!*" He handed over packages containing the most luscious-smelling food.

"Thanks. I hope it makes it home," Chad joked.

"I'm sure. You don't want to get on the bad side of Señora Pierce. But I have to say, I don't think there is a bad side." He smiled and waved.

"You are correct, my friend. Ciao!" Chad was feeling more as if life had returned to normal. He had a sense of elation. *Or maybe it was the aroma of the garlic.* He got back into the cab, where the driver also commented on the pleasant scent emanating from the back seat.

"Now I know why people go there. Wow! If it tastes half as good as it smells—Ooo-wee."

Chad reached into one of the bags and pulled out a hunk of the homemade bread. "Here. Go buy some good salami later and make yourself a sandwich. That's the best I can do or my wife will kill me."

"Hey, man. I appreciate it." The driver reached back over the open plexiglass and grabbed the offering.

Within minutes they were back at Sniffen Court. Chad gave the cabbie an extra-large tip. "For the salami. Go to Citarella. It's the only place I trust with cured meat now that Balducci's has closed."

"Yeah, man. That was a bummer. I loved their sandwiches."

Chad gathered his bounty, said good night and made his way to the front door.

Camille greeted him, along with Lucy and Ricky. Even though you were not supposed to feed dogs human food, Camille would often spoil them with a little ravioli. She thought it was hilarious when they finished with red beards.

"Where's J.R.?" Chad was quite anxious to find out the details of his son's dreadful experience.

"On the patio?" Camille took one of the bags. Chad followed her into the kitchen.

He tried to keep his voice low. "Has he said anything?"

"No. We just talked about the farm in Connecticut." Camille pulled a bread basket from the butler's pantry. "I did most of the talking, really."

Chad's brow furrowed. "As much as I want to be 'in the moment' and enjoy the homecoming, it's a bit unnerving, wouldn't you say?"

"Dr. Wainwright said he was physically fine and found no evidence of abuse. But J.R.'s not opening up yet. We need to give him some time. He must have had an awful shock."

"I know you're right, but I'd like to stop the hamster wheel in my head asking why and how all of this happened."

Camille tilted her head. "He'll get there. He seems a little more relaxed now."

"For once, I don't object to his drinking." Chad snickered.

"He's only had one so far." She elbowed him as she made her way to the farmer's table, where Chad was laying out the food. Changing the subject, Camille took in a big inhale. "This smells absolutely scrumptious."

J.R. walked into the room and began to inspect the platters. "And it looks freakin' delicious, too."

Chad bit his tongue. He had long tried to impress upon his son the importance of good grammar and minimal expletives, but this was the twenty-first century and a lot of things had gone away, including respectable manners. Plus, he was letting J.R. unwind.

Camille placed a stack of the Italian VIETRI Lastra dishes on the table. She particularly liked this company and their handcrafted artisan approach to dinnerware, using durable clay and high-quality glazes. Their motto was to provide inspiration during the sacred time at the table. The imperfectly round dinner plates were a light aqua color that emphasized their artistry. She loved using them for casual family dinners. Then it dawned on her that they hadn't had one in many months. At least not all three of them together.

J.R. picked up a dish and began piling on the food. His ravioli was snuggled next to the prosciutto that covered the burrata cheese, while the chicken meatballs bullied the calamari to the edge of the plate. He ripped off a hunk of ciabatta bread and sauntered out to the patio.

Camille and Chad gave each other an approving nod. "Now, if we can only get him to talk," Chad said, lowering his voice so it was barely audible.

Camille rolled her eyes and tilted her head toward the

door. "Go. Sit down. I'll be right out." Camille plated her food with enthusiasm, but not with the same level of gusto as her son. Not that she didn't want to shove everything into her mouth; she hadn't eaten a proper meal in days, but the enjoyment of it was stifled by the fear and dread of what might still come. Still, tonight was going to be a celebration. Even if it was low-key.

As Camille approached the patio table, Chad began to pour three glasses of a nice Brunello di Montalcino. He had opened the bottle before he left to pick up dinner, giving the wine a chance to breathe. When he was younger, he thought that was all just a bunch of malarky. But as he became more sophisticated, his interest in wine also grew. He wasn't a connoisseur by any means; Scotch and cognac were his areas of expertise. Gerardo once told him, "If you like it, it's good." He also explained that a good, aged bottle should be decanted to introduce oxygen into the wine. So the word "breathe" wasn't simply a throwaway, highfalutin phrase. It was also a method used to eliminate sediment from the bottle. That was about all Chad knew when it came to wine. He relied on Camille, for the most part. She was good at giving instructions and he was fine taking them from her.

Chad raised his glass. "Here's to us."

"All of us," Camille added.

J.R.'s contribution was a big, "Yep."

Chad raised his eyebrow slightly at Camille. *It's better than nothing*, he thought.

After gobbling down a half dozen of the buffalo mozzarella slices and mushroom ravioli, J.R. cleaned his plate with the big wad of bread. At least he looked content.

Before anyone could say anything, J.R. asked, very casually, "Dad, could I borrow the car tomorrow?"

Chad did a double take. "The car?" He didn't want to sound accusatory, but J.R. hadn't pieced more than three sentences together since he got home, and now he wanted to borrow the car? A strange request, but he replied, just as casually, "Sure. What do you have in mind?"

"Just a ride out in the country. Mom was really talking it up when you went to get the food, so I thought I'd give it a try."

Everyone at the table knew full well J.R. had plenty of "country" where he went to school, but they weren't going to question him. Maybe he needed some space and fresh air after being cooped up for three days. Their town house on Sniffen Court was not known for its outdoor space. They had one of the few units with a patio. Back when they began renovating the stalls into town houses, some people opted for more indoor living space. The previous owners preferred a small, modest patio. Camille was happy with their choice. She might have gone mad without it.

Chad continued the conversation. "Sure. What time do you want it? I'll phone the garage and ask them to have it ready for you."

"Thanks." J.R. hesitated, then asked, "Do you think I can have some cash? For tips?"

Chad had handled so much cash in the past forty-eight hours, it hadn't occurred to him that his son's pockets would be empty. All that money floating around. Out there. Somewhere. Chad reached into his pocket and retrieved a money clip. He peeled off several twenties, tens and fives. A total of one hundred dollars. It struck him that it was one tenth of one percent of what he had recently collected so frantically and delivered. The gap was remarkable. Did his son have any idea what they had just spent? Chad thought J.R. must have known what the kidnappers asked for. He was right there. Or did they keep him in another room when they made the calls? What about when they let him croak out a word or two? Could he have heard anything?

More questions ran through his head: *What does he re-member? Where did they abduct him? Did he recognize any sounds? What kind of room did they keep him in?*

Chad knew at some point they would have to notify the authorities. But not until J.R. gave them some real information. What was the point in notifying anyone if you had no information to give them? He also didn't want to force J.R. to talk about anything he wasn't comfortable with. *But for how long? How long was this incident going to remain a se-cret?*

"Do you have a destination in mind?" Camille asked in a relaxed manner. She was sensing Chad's wariness and weariness.

"Not really. Maybe a few hours upstate. Something with mountains," J.R. replied.

"Will you be back in time for dinner?" Again, Camille kept her voice even. Regular. She, too, was anxious to learn about her son's experience, but J.R.'s body language was very clear. He wanted no intruders. Into his head, or into his plans. Whatever they were.

"Mmm . . . maybe. What time will dinner be?" J.R. pushed himself away from the table.

"Seven?" Camille half-stated, half-asked.

J.R. thought for a moment. "That should work." It seemed as if he had something particular in mind, but clearly wasn't going to share it.

"Anything in particular you'd like for dinner?" Camille asked.

"I could go for a good steak." At least J.R. seemed to know that much. "Twice-baked potatoes? Please?" Now he was being a bit more charming. Maybe it was the half glass of wine.

"Consider it done." Camille smiled and patted J.R.'s arm. He instantly recoiled from her touch.

"What is it?" Camille was stunned. This was quite the mood swing.

"Sorry, Mom. Still a bit jumpy." J.R. let out a sigh.

"That's understandable." She paused. "You know you can tell us anything, right?"

"Yep." He pushed out his chair farther. "I'm going upstairs, if that's okay."

"Sure, honey." Camille's gaze followed him as he disappeared into the kitchen.

"At least he brought in his plate," Chad said with a touch of impatience.

"It's only been a few hours," Camille reminded him.

"And he wants to take off tomorrow to go for a drive." Chad shook his head. "Something isn't right."

"I know," Camille said pensively. "But there is little or nothing we can do about it right now—except for you helping me clear the table."

Chad got up and began to scrape the traces of marinara sauce off the dishes before carrying them into the kitchen.

Camille pulled out a few more containers from one of the bags. "Gerardo snuck in some tiramisu, a decadent, chocolate-looking thing and what smells like a lemon ricotta cake."

Chad was happy with the surprise desserts. "Well, who could say no to all that?"

"See if J.R. wants some," Camille said as she plated the sweet delights.

Chad took the stairs two at a time. It was his way of keeping in shape. Or so went the family joke. In reality, Chad was in good shape. He went to the gym two to three times a week—just enough to keep from getting flabby.

He called up to his son, "J.R., want some dessert?"

No response.

"J.R.?" Chad knocked on his son's bedroom door. He called out again, this time trying the knob. It was locked.

Chad's reflexes were on high alert, and he began pounding on the door. Within seconds J.R. appeared with a headset plugged into his ears and a terrified look on his face. Apparently, he had been listening to music on his iPod and hadn't heard his father. He was gasping for air.

"What's wrong?" Chad asked. J.R. was almost hyperventilating. "Sorry if I spooked you, son. You didn't answer, and after these past couple of days . . . I panicked." He held on to both sides of the doorjamb. He didn't know which of them was breathing the heaviest. "We've all been a little jumpy."

"It's okay, Dad." J.R. stepped out of the way and motioned for his father to step inside the room. "I want you to know how much I appreciate what you did to get me back home." He looked like he was on the verge of tears.

Both sat down on the bed. Chad put his arm around his son's shoulders. "We would do anything for you."

J.R. bowed his head. "I know." The atmosphere in the room brightened.

"I think a ride in the countryside tomorrow will do you some good. Gerardo's apparently not happy with our weight, so he packed some dessert for us. Could I interest you in a little tiramisu? I think there's chocolate mousse and lemon ricotta cake, too."

"Sounds good, but I'm kinda full. I really stuffed my face with those ravioli. But thanks." J.R. paused, hoping his father would take the hint and scram. And he did.

"Okay. Get some rest. There's nothing like a nice, fresh set of sheets at the end of the day."

"That's something Mom would say." J.R. smiled, still waiting for his father to move along.

"Right." Chad knew he was on the brink of overstaying his welcome. He went back to where Camille was sitting on the patio with a cup of decaffeinated cappuccino and an espresso for Chad.

"No dice on the dolce?" Camille said, using the Italian word for dessert.

"No dice."

"So what do you think?" Camille stared out absently at the brick-walled terrace.

"About?" Chad asked, though he already knew what she meant.

"Our son." She turned to him. "I said it earlier. Something doesn't seem right. And now he wants to take a drive in the country?"

"Weren't you the one who encouraged it?" Chad added a demitasse-size spoonful of sugar to his coffee.

"What was I supposed to say without sounding paranoid or suspicious?"

"You're right. Right about a lot of things. Only time will tell."

The next morning, J.R. grabbed a muffin from the pantry and left the house without saying anything to either of his parents. Camille was still in the shower and Chad was in his study with the door closed when J.R. departed He flipped a backpack over his shoulder and walked toward the parking garage where they kept the family cars. J.R. used the cash his father had given him the night before to tip the parking attendant, hopped behind the wheel and left for parts unknown.

Chad and Camille began the day with their normal routine—though "normal" felt like a lifetime ago. Chad went into the kitchen, where Camille was pouring a cup of coffee and Mildred was pulling out the cleaning supplies.

"J.R. already hit the road, I see," Chad said in a lighthearted tone. He didn't want Mildred to think anything was amiss.

"It must be nice to have him home for a few days," Mildred called out from the laundry room.

"Yes, it is." Camille looked at Chad and repeated her words more slowly. "Yes. It is."

The rest of the day went along like most. J.R. returned to the town house around six, but had little to say. "Thanks for letting me use the car. The drive to New Paltz was a breeze. No traffic and the local roads were nice."

"What made you decide to go to New Paltz?" Chad asked. It had never been on J.R.'s radar before. At least not that anyone knew or heard of.

J.R. had a bit of a sheepish look on his face. "A girl."

Camille's face brightened. "And who is this girl?" she asked playfully.

"Someone I met during one of those weekend get-to-know-you type of things."

"Like an orientation?" Camille asked.

"I guess. Her parents brought her brother up a couple of weeks ago. He's thinking of going to school there. She was asking me all sorts of questions. We hung out for a few hours, and she said if I was ever in the New Paltz area to look her up. So I did."

"And?" Camille's interest was piqued.

"And not much." J.R. opened the refrigerator door, giving the inside of the fridge a once-over. "What's for dinner?"

"You said you wanted steak, so that's what's on the menu. And your stuffed potatoes," Camille answered. She wanted to know more about this young mystery girl. "What's her name?"

"Huh?" J.R. acted as if he had lost the thread of the conversation. "Oh, Jessica."

"Do you like her?" Camille was now prodding for more details.

"She's okay, I guess. She's nice." He gave what was becoming his regular shrug response to anything and everything.

Chad decided it was time to change the subject. "I'll get the grill going. Still like it medium rare?" He looked at J.R.

"Sure." Another shrug. "I'm going to go wash up." He turned and left his parents standing in the kitchen, blinking and wondering what that was all about.

"Just leave it." Chad could read Camille's mind.

"Yes. I know. But New Paltz?" She tried to shake off her confusion.

Chad imitated his son and shrugged. "By the way, Larry called this morning, wanting to know if we had any information about what happened."

"What did you tell him?"

"Exactly what we know. Absolutely nothing." Chad began to uncork a bottle of Pinot Noir. "He thinks we should notify the FBI."

"But why?" Camille looked toward the hallway, making sure J.R. wasn't within earshot.

"There is a possibility the New York State Banking Department may make an inquiry if they discover all the withdrawals."

"So?" Camille said.

"So, they may notify the IRS. We really don't need anyone probing into our business and our accounts."

Camille stopped short. "Chad, is there something wrong?"

"No. But do you realize how much time it's going to take to do all the paperwork they'll require to cover our behinds? There'll be lawyer fees, accounting fees, all for them to turn up nothing except we're out a million dollars. And we have no way to prove where the money went."

"You have the recordings from Larry, right?" Camille was thinking on her feet, as usual.

"Yes, but that could have been a setup. We really need to

think about this, Camille. It is serious business, from the very beginning to now."

"Well, we'll just have to talk to J.R. and tell him we need to get everything out in the open so we can move forward with our lives, our business and our mental health."

"You're right. We'll do it over dinner." Chad gave her a reassuring hug. "And we won't let him slide. If he had the fortitude to go visit some girl he hardly knows, he can sit through an important conversation."

J.R. was turning the corner from the stairs into the main hallway. "Who are you talking about?" he asked with a stern look on his face.

"Son. We have to talk about this." Chad was firm but calm.

"I'd rather not." J.R. went to the butler's pantry and pulled a beer from the beverage fridge.

"I'm not trying to be insensitive or impatient, but . . . Come on—let's go sit down and do this." Chad carried the bottle of wine and Camille followed with two goblets.

Chad pulled out a chair for Camille, and then for J.R., who was standing in a protest position. Chad gave his son a look that needed no further explanation. Chad was relatively easygoing, but when J.R. first started messing up in school, he took a firmer approach. He took away J.R.'s car and credit cards and stripped down his designer wardrobe. No need to spend a lot of money on clothes when you wore a uniform to school. And now, Chad was once again in "firm" mode. The kidnapping had to be dealt with. Now.

Camille tried to loosen her shoulders. She was so tense, they felt as if they were stuck to her ears. Chad's tension matched hers, but both knew they had to remain objective. Focus on the facts.

Chad looked directly into his son's face. "Start from the beginning."

Camille patted his hand. "Take your time."

J.R. took a swig of his beer and began his account of what had occurred. Sometime in the middle of the night, two guys entered his room. They were wearing ski masks. He figured they were a little older than he. Maybe in their twenties. At first, he thought it was some kind of prank, but then they put a cloth over his nose and mouth. He went on to say he felt a little prick on the side of his neck, but it all happened so fast, he wasn't sure which came first, the cloth or the prick. Both were probably at the same time. The cloth would keep him quiet while they injected him with a sedative. He wasn't sure how they got him out of his room from the second floor. It would be easy enough if the two men put one of J.R.'s arms around each of their necks and took him down the rear stairs, then out the back of the building. It was desolate out there. There were no security cameras in the back of a private school surrounded by hundreds of feet of wrought-iron fencing. His roommate must have slept through the whole thing. He then remembered being jostled awake sometime later. There was duct tape over his mouth and wrapped around his wrists.

Camille twisted her napkin at the thought of her son being bound and gagged. She had to ask. "Did they hurt you?"

He raised both his arms, exposing his skin from fingers to elbows. No sign of ligature marks. "No, they didn't hurt me. I think they just wanted me to know I wasn't going anywhere."

"When you opened your eyes, what did you see?" Chad asked.

"I was in the back of a van. The kind they use for deliveries. No seats. Just a metal floor. Anyway, there was a curtain between the front seats and the back, so I couldn't see them." J.R. took a deep breath. "Can we put the rest of this on hold until after dinner?"

"Of course!" Camille cooed.

"Sorry, son. I didn't mean for this to become an interrogation."

"No prob, Dad. It's good to get it out."

"I am glad to hear it." Chad got up and lit the grill, while J.R. went inside to get another beer.

Camille was so relieved, she thought her legs were going to turn into rubber. *Sometimes you don't know how much tension you're holding until you let it go.* "Huh," she said to herself with surprise.

"What?" Chad asked.

Camille shared her revelation with him.

"You should make a T-shirt." Chad smiled as he began working on the steaks.

"Even better. I'll make a wall hanging and give it to Jean to put on her office wall."

"Brilliant." He turned to her. "You'd better copyright it!"

J.R. returned with a pilsner glass and his bottle of beer. "Figured I should drink like an adult." He hesitated before he poured it. "You don't mind, do you?"

Chad raised his eyebrows. "Take this one slowly. Enjoy it with your dinner."

Camille was moving back and forth from the kitchen to the patio, placing the side dishes of vegetables and potatoes on a small buffet table. Chad pulled the steaks off the grill, and they took their places at the table. This was their second family dinner together since they had been reunited. And it was good.

When they finished their meal, Chad gently urged J.R. to finish his story. "Ready for more?" He knew Larry was right; they should speak to the FBI, but J.R. had to be a willing witness.

Maybe it was the enzymes from the prime steak, or the two glasses of beer, but J.R. quickly spilled the rest of his tale of tribulation, starting from when he regained consciousness. He figured they drove about an hour. The timeline certainly fit with the distance of the drop in Colts Neck. At least somewhere close by would be a good guess. He described a crummy motel room where they kept him locked in the bathroom. He didn't know how many days went by because there wasn't a window and he lost track of time. He said he never saw their faces. When it came time to feed him, they wore masks, only opened the door a couple of inches and tossed him a bag of fast food. He wasn't sure if they had a gun, so he didn't try to make any moves. Then he mentioned the two calls when he'd muttered into the phone.

Chad stopped J.R. "They used the motel phone to call me?"

"I guess. What other kind of phone could they use?"

"Maybe a cell phone." He made a mental note to ask Larry about the cell towers in Monmouth County. There should be a record. But if the kidnappers were smart, they would have ditched the phones by now. Larry said it could take a couple of days to get the information from the mobile carriers. That was one area Larry hadn't taken a dive into. Yet. Technology surely was a fast-moving fire.

Camille was the next to ask a question. "How did you get to the gas station?"

"They put a hood over my head and kept me in the motel bathroom while one guy left and the other stayed with me. Then the first guy came back all excited. He said something like, 'It's all here.' The second guy told the first one to shut up. Then they tied my wrists and guided me back into the van. We drove about ten minutes and they left me on the side of the road and told me to keep walking in the direction of the gas station." J.R. took a very long breath. "And that's what happened."

"Do you have any idea who they were? Did they have accents? Foreign? New England? Southern? Jersey? New York?" Chad asked with intensity.

J.R. frowned. "Nothing that stood out. You know, same as how we talk."

Chad got up and put his hand on J.R.'s shoulder. "Son, I know this wasn't easy for you to talk about."

"Yeah, but it's better. Now I can believe it's over."

Camille hugged her son while Chad gave her a look. "What?" She winced.

"J.R., we may have to talk to the FBI about this."

J.R. backed away. "They said no police. I heard them!" He was on his feet and beginning to pace. "Dad, you can't do that."

"J.R., it's over. You're home safe now. But there could be repercussions regarding the withdrawals I had to make."

"What are you talking about?" J.R. asked in an accusatory manner.

"The bank has to fill out forms whenever anyone withdraws over ten thousand dollars."

"What?" J.R. obviously had no idea.

Chad described how he had to make a number of withdrawals to meet the kidnappers' demands, which meant the paperwork would be going to the Departments of Banking and Insurance. Chad explained, "Considering the family is in the banking business, it could appear to be something . . . unseemly."

"Huh," was all J.R. could say, but it wasn't in the same tone as Camille's "huh" earlier. Not the least bit revelatory, but more resigned.

"Let me make a few phone calls tomorrow to see how we can handle this without it turning into another horror show."

Over the next few days, Chad spoke with Larry and his connection at the FBI. After several conversations, they decided it would be best if an agent came to the house and took a statement from J.R. and Chad. At least he would be in a comfortable environment rather than an intimidating, government-secured building.

J.R. begrudgingly met with Agent Lantana in Chad's study. He repeated the details of his abduction as Camille and Chad sat off to one side of the room. They didn't want to be intrusive, but J.R. didn't object to their being there.

J.R. slowly recounted his ordeal, and Lantana had some simple questions, similar to what his parents had asked. "Did you notice any particular sounds? Smells? Feeling hot or cold?"

J.R.'s answers were the same. He didn't remember or reveal much of anything.

Lantana was satisfied the information was enough to create a file. One never knew what could come of it later. The money could show up if one of the kidnappers was dropping a lot of cash. Especially in twenty-dollar bills. ATM machines had $200 limits on withdrawals, except for the casinos in Atlantic City. Or one of the abductors could be stupid enough to spill the beans.

J.R. got out of his chair. "Can I go now?"

"Yes. Of course," Agent Lantana said casually and handed J.R. his card. "If you remember anything else, please give me a call."

J.R. tapped the card in his hand. "Yeah. Okay." He turned and went to his room.

Camille went into the kitchen to get some coffee. She hoped this would be the last time she would need to shuffle Mildred's schedule. Not that Camille minded making a pot of coffee. They could not afford for any of this to get out. The fewer people involved or within earshot the better, but today they had to add one more person to the very short list of "need to know."

Chad explained to Agent Lantana about the number of withdrawals he'd made and handed him copies of all the bank receipts. Lantana took copious notes without any reaction. When they finished, Lantana looked up at Chad. "You were very lucky. Statistically, seventy-four percent of children under the age of eighteen are dead within hours of their abduction."

Chad thought he was going to vomit. Lantana made a mental note of Chad's response. The agent could tell this man was not trying to hide anything. Lantana continued, "However, forty percent of the victims are returned after the ransom is paid." He stopped for a moment. "Like I said, you were on the better side of the statistics."

Chad was relieved he hadn't known during the ordeal just how dreadful the odds were. Had he known, it would have been extremely difficult to meet the demands with a cool head. Chad was happy Camille had left the room a few minutes earlier. She would have been hysterical if she had known. It was better she didn't know, and there was no point in telling her now.

Camille returned with a tray of coffee and scones and placed it on the cocktail table in front of the small leather sofa. Lantana smiled at Camille. "Thank you very much. This is quite a treat for me." He took the cup from Camille's outstretched hand. "Most people I interview don't offer me so much as a glass of water. Not that I'm complaining. Dealing with the government can be intimidating, and they can't wait for me to leave."

Chad sat up in his chair. "Do you think this will go anywhere?"

"What do you mean?" Lantana asked.

"An investigation?" Chad asked.

"To be honest, Mr. Pierce, we have more caseloads than Bayer has aspirin. This situation would be deemed 'resolved.' We have no suspects, no location. Basically, we have nothing to go on, and it would not be a productive use of the agency's time."

"Speaking of time, I am going to have to get to my office," Chad said. "But please finish your scone and coffee."

Camille took a seat across from Lantana. Chad hoped she wouldn't ask for statistics. Lantana could tell from her husband's reaction that hers wouldn't be good either. He had gathered ample enough information, as little as there was; he saw no need to continue the interview. He tried to make small talk instead: "How do you like Sniffen Court? How long have you lived here?"

Camille could sense the agent was trying to move away from the reason for his visit. "So tell me, Agent Lantana, how many cases like this have you been involved in?"

He hesitated before answering. "A few dozen."

"And how many were resolved in a positive way?" Camille asked, then raised her cup to her lips.

"Probably half." He was getting uncomfortable. Despite being a fed. "I really can't discuss any details," he said, pulling the confidentiality card.

"I understand," Camille said coolly. "I guess we'll never know who those people were. Are." She gave an ironic snort. "Two people terrorize a family and walk away with a million dollars." Camille instantly realized she might sound accusatory. "Of course, *we* chose not to contact the authorities. I guess my point is, your world can be tossed upside down, and then it goes on." She shrugged. "What I am trying to say is, there are two people out there who are whooping it up without considering what they put us through." She set down her cup. "And life goes on."

"Yes, it does." Lantana copied Camille's gesture and placed his cup on the table. "Thank you very much for your hospitality. Here is my card. Please call if you come across anything."

Camille took the card and placed it on Chad's desk, where another one of Lantana's cards already sat. She wondered if anything would ever come of all this. Camille walked Lantana to the front door.

"Thank you again for coming here. It took a lot of stress off our shoulders." Camille shook his hand.

"Anything for Larry." He smiled and walked toward the wrought-iron gate onto 36th Street.

After two weeks of recovering from his ordeal, J.R. returned to Briarcliff Academy but failed to show up for classes. J.R.'s parents agreed the trauma was still having an impact on him. There was only one month left on the academic calendar. It would be a terrible waste if he didn't graduate. His parents therefore made arrangements with the school to allow for "special circumstances," providing tutors so J.R. could complete his lessons from home. Five weeks later, he was issued his high school diploma. J.R. was a very fortunate young man to have parents like his.

Chad and Camille were delighted and began to bring up colleges to consider. J.R. had been accepted to three small private colleges, but he wasn't emotionally ready for college. He needed to take some time to regroup and instead asked if he could travel. His parents reluctantly agreed to this, figuring he still needed time to process the ordeal of being kidnapped. After a year of traveling abroad, funded by his parents, Chad arranged for J.R. to work as an administrative assistant in the construction loan department of the bank. It wasn't a big job, but if J.R. took it seriously, he could work his way up to higher management and make a career of it. He didn't want J.R. to be a ship without a rudder, and J.R. was willing to "give it a shot," as he put it. It was time for him to act like an adult.

Over the next decade, Camille developed her organization for Women of a Certain Something. Starting a foundation from scratch took careful planning, but Camille was meticulous. Chad navigated the financial free fall of 2008 and developed a program of free seminars to help people get back on track after being tossed on the wild sea of economics. His need to prove himself had evaporated after he successfully handled the return of his son. He was finally comfortable in his own skin. There was nothing left to validate.

During his time abroad, J.R. polished his charm, style and ambition. He proved to excel at all three. Once he began the job at the bank, he observed his father and the executives' manner of doing business. J.R. may not have been a model student in school, but he was a quick study when it came to the game of life. He saw what was possible if he worked the system. Not necessarily in an immoral way, just understanding the way things were done—using the people you know to get you where you want to go. And doing it with aplomb.

J.R. continued to develop his network. He impressed his immediate supervisors and moved up the ladder quickly. Within a few short years, he was an assistant loan manager, and gradually gained possession of a fine automobile, had his own platinum card, a modest co-op in the Financial District and enjoyed luxury vacations. Chad kept an eye on the business and saw that J.R. was earning his keep at the ripe young age of twenty-five. Chad remembered being his son's age. It was obvious J.R. had inherited a good part of his DNA.

J.R. also enjoyed the posh parties of the upper crust and made sure he was always on the guest list of any gathering that could create an opportunity for business. He preferred a rich lifestyle, which meant he had to be productive at his job, much as he hated it.

After screwing up his education, the traumatic ordeal during his senior year in high school, then traveling abroad to "clear his head" and skipping college altogether, he had landed in a good place. Chad was disheartened his son chose not to continue his education, but that didn't mean he wouldn't amount to anything. Chad had the means to create opportunity for his son. What J.R. did with it was up to him. Chad couldn't do it for him. J.R. was smart enough to know his career path was up to him. Chad Pierce Jr. had his sights set on success and he was not going backward.

Camille was constantly involved in fundraising events and always encouraging J.R. to attend. He loved the idea. It allowed him to broaden his network without having to pay $1000 per ticket. At one of the social gatherings, J.R. was introduced to Lindsay Elizabeth Marshall. Lindsay came from a wealthy lumber family. J.R. thought it would be a perfect connection for someone who managed commercial construction loans. They would certainly know people in common. Then there was Lindsay. She was tall, with a model's figure and a face that would be at home in any women's fashion magazine, especially *Vogue*. When they first met, she was wearing a Dolce & Gabbana black minidress that showed off her long legs down to her mesh, pointed-toe ankle boots. Her makeup was professionally applied and her waist-length, white-blond hair was draped over one shoulder. J.R. was almost speechless when they were introduced. She was a knockout and a bit of a snip. But that wasn't going to stop him from kicking his charm through the stratosphere. First rule: Make them laugh. Laughter releases the neurotransmitter dopamine in the brain, producing a sense of euphoria. That was one of the few things he had learned in biology, and J.R. was on a mission to push the throttle on Lindsay's endorphins. He kicked up the charm several notches and cajoled her into going on a date with him.

One date led to another as he jumped through hoops to impress her and monopolize all of her free time, even though Lindsay was a socialite and had no job to speak of. Her skills involved making purchases at the shops on Madison and Fifth Avenues. She was spoiled, but J.R. knew how to handle her. Between his six-figure salary and bonuses, he figured he could wine and dine her to her satisfaction. He was his father's son when it came to wooing a young woman.

He took her on long, romantic weekends to the Bahamas, Vermont, and Lake Tahoe; expensive dinners in New York at Per Se, Eleven Madison Park and the very exclusive Kappo Masa on Madison Avenue. After several months, J.R. decided he shouldn't waste any more time and asked Lindsay to marry him. He wasn't going to let this one get away. Much to his delight, she said yes, and wedding plans were in the works within a short time.

Lindsay's parents managed their expectations of their offspring early on. Lindsay had no ambition except to be a wealthy wife whose vocation was spending said wealth. In many cases, their circle of friends were creating a new generation of pampered, trust-fund-entitled descendants who had no interest in maintaining the family businesses. Considering the options, the Marshall family was happy their daughter was marrying a solid businessman rather than a rock musician or a failed poet. There was much too much of that going around just then.

Camille was optimistic about her son's future. She was delighted he had overcome his lack of ambition, his traumatic experience and his aversion to commitment. He had been a very happy bachelor up to the age of twenty-five, when he met Lindsay. Camille was acquainted with Lindsay's family through their philanthropies. The union of these two powerful dynasties would provide a lot of social clout when it came to raising money for their various charities. That was the upside for Camille. And J.R. was happy. Lindsay was the opportunity of a lifetime for him—if they could stick it out. Sometimes the rich found plenty wasn't enough and infidelity struck, or just plain boredom and discontent.

The wedding was covered in all the lifestyle sections of the major newspapers, including an article in *Cosmopolitan*. It was the perfect subject for a magazine that gave women the green light for practically everything, often using the phrase *You Can Have It All*. And it didn't hurt that both J.R. and Lindsay were both exceptionally good-looking. They were being referred to as the "It" couple. About six months after the magazine article was published, Lindsay was approached to be part of *The Real Housewives of New York City*. She was ecstatic—almost apoplectic—at the idea, but Camille and Chad shut it down in a heartbeat. In this day and age, there was too great a chance that J.R.'s kidnapping would become public knowledge. Before, people didn't have ready access to computers and the internet; now, there were many ways to dig up dirt. J.R. had never revealed his abduction to Lindsay. Only a handful of people were privy to the family's ordeal, and she was the last person you could trust with a secret. When J.R. broke the news that under no uncertain terms was she going to expose their families to the mockery and criticism of appearing on a reality show, Lindsay had a hissy fit. Fortunately, Lindsay's family agreed with the Pierces, and they sent the pouty wife on a spa vacation to Cabo San Lucas for a week.

At the beginning of their marriage, Lindsay wasn't interested in having kids because she didn't want her body to change. Then she wasn't interested because kids would take up too much of her time. Even the suggestion of having two nannies—one for daytime and one for nighttime—did not appeal to her. It was still too much of an inconvenience and distraction from her daily activities. At thirty-five, she would not even consider an attempt at childbirth. Not so much because the physical risks increased with age; she just wasn't thrilled at the idea of chasing after little kids when she should be thinking about liposuction, breast augmentation, Botox and every other kind of youth-preserving procedure.

J.R. was perfectly fine with Lindsay's obsession with her appearance. He enjoyed having a hot, trophy wife. Camille had once thought his traumatic experience would change his obsession with spending money and being frivolous. Maybe give him some humility? Unfortunately, that wasn't the case. She often thought Lindsay's influence was enhancing his bad traits.

Thankfully, money was never an issue between J.R. and Lindsay. They had separate checking accounts and one house account to which each was responsible for making monthly contributions. But with her trust-fund allowance, Lindsay was able to continue her favorite pastimes such as shopping, gossiping, and spending days at the spa, while J.R. was free to spend his salary on whatever he wanted. When they got married, Lindsay's parents paid for their 3,000-square-foot loft in Tribeca, which allowed J.R. to sell his co-op in the Financial District, depositing the profit into his personal account. Checks and balances were in check and balanced.

Camille wisely kept her opinion of Lindsay to herself. As long as J.R. was content, his almost fifteen-year marriage to Lindsay was none of Camille's business. Camille recognized that Lindsay was not much different from the girls she grew up with. But this was a new generation of entitlement. And as social media grew, so did people's self-obsession. It was an epidemic. Camille regretted that she and Lindsay never bonded. Lindsay wasn't mean or nasty, just one-dimensional. She preferred the company of her equally vacuous friends instead of conversations with wise, accomplished, educated, creative and thoughtful women. Lindsay was shallow and didn't seem to have any interest in digging deeper.

Camille and Chad were living a full life, filled with fundraising events, dinner with good friends, long weekends in the mountains or at the beach. Camille and Chad maintained a good balance of work, play and relaxation. The only disappointment for them was the lack of grandchildren. J.R. and Lindsay enjoyed whatever was on the fun du jour menu. And so the family continued to flourish financially, and life was good.

PART TWO

Chapter Four

A Piece of Furniture

Buncombe County, North Carolina
Present

L una Sage Bodman was bright and charming, with a hint of mischief in her eyes. Her bohemian wardrobe, wire-rimmed glasses and long, light brown hair, usually fashioned in a slightly messy braid, were the first suggestion she was a bit eccentric. At least that was what she preferred to be thought of instead of a weirdo. Now in her midthirties, she had possessed since childhood an innate ability to read people—a gift many found unnerving. Luna's imaginary playmates, which she'd insisted were only invisible and *not* imaginary, were the cause of much teasing and mocking. That was until she scared the pants off someone by saying something only that particular person would know. For instance, there was the time when she was around ten years old and a neighborhood wiseass named Jack Martin threw a rock at Luna, yelling, "Freakazoid!"

Luna picked the rock from the ground and slowly tossed it back and forth in her hands. "If you don't shut up, I am going to tell your father you nicked money out of his wallet. A five if I am correct." Jack's face went pale. There was no way she could have known that. There was no way *anyone* could have known it. Jack's father always carried a lot of cash, and one afternoon, while he was doing yardwork, Jack snuck into his parents' bedroom and riffled through his father's dresser drawer, pulling out one of several five-dollar bills.

Luna stared him down. "You gotta problem with that?" She took a few steps closer. Jack backed away. "I didn't think so." She turned and tossed the stone over her shoulder.

Luna's older brother, Cullen, had been playing soccer a few yards away when he saw Jack take flight. Cullen was much more of a regular guy. He could have walked out of a Gap ad. He and Luna were as different as night and day, but as tight as a Palomar knot. Cullen jogged over to his sister.

"Are you okay?" He placed both of his hands on her shoulders.

"Yep." She twisted her mouth in a satisfied expression.

"At it again, eh?" Cullen smiled. Though he wasn't much of a believer in anything bordering on the paranormal, he did believe his sister had some type of a gift. Some people called it empathy. Cullen called it "a Luna thing."

As they grew older, Cullen witnessed more and more of Luna's ability to read people. Not always in a psychic way, but in her own way. When they went off to college, Luna studied psychology, with an emphasis on paranormal psychology. Cullen took the steady route and worked in the financial department of a large land development firm.

When their parents decided to retire from their antiques business, Cullen decided it was his opportunity to break away from the nine-to-five, stiff-shirt atmosphere, a move that came much to everyone's surprise. Except Luna's. She knew her brother had a creative streak. She could sense it.

She could see the joy in his face when he tinkered around with some of the pieces of furniture his father discarded, bringing them back to life. Rather than continuing to just sell antiques, Cullen incorporated his love of restoring furniture into the family business.

After graduating college, Luna took a job at the local Children's Services office, working primarily with foster kids and adoptions. Her innate abilities proved helpful when it came to investigating the backgrounds of potential parents and families. It also offered her the opportunity to do occasional freelance work with the US Marshal's Service Missing Child Program.

Around that same time, Elle Stillwell, a local former art professor, began her quest to build an art center where artists could create, display and sell their work. The Stillwell Center became widely known as one of the largest working art centers in the country.

With the restoration business growing, and Luna's freelance work thriving, Cullen and Luna applied together for spaces at the Stillwell Center. Cullen's vision was to have a showroom of restored furniture with a workshop in the back, and Luna would maintain a coffee shop next to his place called the Namaste Café. Luna also had a knack for design and became an asset to Cullen when clients were redecorating or remodeling their homes. It was a good partnership and welcomed by Elle Stillwell.

Luna enjoyed it when Cullen received a new shipment of discarded furniture. She would always sit with it, touch it, smell it and talk to it to see if she could get any kind of vibration from the piece. Cullen got used to her "aura checking" and humored her with each new delivery. On one particular afternoon, a very worn-out armoire arrived in Cullen's workshop. Luna was in her café, but something beckoned her to her brother's shop. She wiped her hands on a towel and put up the sign with an arrow that read "Come Next Door." Then she made a beeline through the showroom, practically crashing into a young couple looking at a newly refurbished dining room table. Cullen apologized for his sister's flurry. Luna made her excuses, too. "Sorry, sorry. But I know Cullen just received a shipment. I've gotta see what came in!" The couple smiled at the young woman's excitement. Cullen smirked and continued to explain the steps he'd taken to restore the table.

Luna continued to the rear of the showroom, which led to the workshop. She was like a little kid who'd just been given a new toy to play with. She walked around the armoire a few times, running her hand over the front and then the back. After scrutinizing the piece, she opened the door, wiggled inside and pulled the door shut. She closed her eyes and within seconds heaved a huge gasp. She quickly pushed against the door of the armoire, but it wouldn't open. She started banging and calling for Cullen, but he was busy with the customers in the showroom. Luna took a few slow breaths, trying to remain calm. She could hear her dog, Wylie, sniffing around outside the armoire. "Wylie, go get Cullen!" she commanded. The dog gave a quick woof and then trotted off to fetch his owner's brother.

When Cullen saw the dog coming toward them, he could tell something was amiss. He excused himself from the couple and followed the dog. While Luna waited to be rescued from the dark cabinet, she ran her hands along the inside. She could feel something in the wood. Something rough. When Cullen jerked open the door, Luna tumbled out, hair flying in different directions and her glasses askew. Luna calmly brushed herself off and asked for a flashlight, a piece of paper and a pencil.

"What are you doing?" Cullen sounded annoyed as he stuck his hands on his hips. He was usually patient with his sister's high jinks, but today she took him off guard. He hadn't even looked at the armoire yet. He had signed for the delivery and then gone out to meet the clients in the showroom. He grumbled under his breath.

"I think someone wrote something in here. There are grooves in the wood," Luna explained.

Cullen rummaged through the drawer of his workbench and handed her the items. "Try to stay out of trouble for a few minutes, please? I'm about to close a deal."

She gave him a salute. "Aye, aye, Captain." She squeezed back into the armoire and began to do a rubbing. She gasped again and unfolded herself from inside the piece of furniture. She was sitting on the workbench when Cullen returned with a check in his hand and a concerned look on his face.

"Are you okay?" Cullen noticed Luna was unusually quiet.

"Look!" She handed Cullen the paper, which appeared to read *HELP!*

"Now that *is* strange. Even for you." He grinned. "It doesn't seem as if that person needs help anymore." He peeked inside. "Unless it's a termite."

Luna gave him a little slap on the arm with the back of her hand. "When did you become a comedian?"

"When I started hanging around you and Chris." Cullen was referring to Luna's romantic interest, Marshal Christopher Gaines, who Luna had met two years before during the search for a missing child.

"Again with the jokes." Luna shook her head, leaned over and smoothed the piece of paper. " 'HELP!' That's it. Nothing else." She peered closer. "I wonder when this was written." She picked up the rubbing and held it to the light, searching for any more clues.

"Decades ago. That piece of furniture is pretty old. Seventy, maybe eighty years."

"Where did it come from?" Luna was still focusing on the paper.

Cullen placed the check from the sale of the table in a strongbox, then went to the wall in the back where he kept his clipboard. "I bought it through one of the auctioneers who sold off some inventory from a commercial sale. You know, the leftovers. Stuff nobody wants, even for free. They can't even give it away."

"Then they find a sucker like you who will buy it!" Luna chuckled. This was the core of Cullen's business. He restored furniture whose next stop was either the dump or a firepit. He did remarkable work, and his reputation had grown ever since he began at Stillwell Center.

"Well, I pay practically nothing for the castoffs and turn them into gems." He jerked his thumb toward his showroom. "That dining room table I just sold? I bought it for twenty-five dollars. And that check I just put in the box? Seven hundred fifty-five dollars, and they bought some chairs to go with it." Cullen knew his time was valuable, so he would calculate the number of hours he spent on a piece and multiply it by seventy-five dollars. Some weeks were more fruitful than others, but he loved what he did. As long as he could sustain his modest lifestyle and pay the bills, he was content.

He flipped through the list of items that had been delivered. "This thing cost me fifty dollars. After I'm done with it, some other sucker will pay hundreds of dollars for it. Maybe even a thousand! So there, Miss Smarty-Pants."

Luna stuck out her tongue. Even at thirty-five, she still acted like a little sister. "So, how can we find out exactly where it came from?" She squinted at the paper with the traced writing.

"I'll have to call the salvage company, but they might not know either."

Luna pouted. "Please? Pretty please?" Again with the little-sister approach.

"Why, oh why, do I let you talk me into stuff like this?" Cullen said as he reached for the phone and dialed the number on the invoice. "Good afternoon. This is Cullen Bodman from the Stillwell Center in North Carolina. We received a shipment today containing an old armoire. Would you happen to know where it originated?" Cullen listened. "I see." He repeated what he heard. "From New England. Any particular state in New England?" He made a face and shrugged at Luna. "No, I understand." Cullen knew Luna would not let it rest, so neither could he. "Any chance you could give me the name of where it was picked up?" He scribbled something down. "Longmire Educational Salvage Company." He continued to write. "I see. They dispose of old desks and such?" He tried to sound interested and engaged. It wasn't often you could get someone on the phone who was willing to be helpful. "I see. Yes, thank you very much. You have a blessed day, too."

"Well?" Luna was practically jumping up and down.

"A place in the western part of Massachusetts." He handed her the paper. "She didn't have the number handy, so now it's your turn to call."

Luna pouted again. "Fine." She snatched the paper out of his hand, went over to his laptop and typed in the name and state. In a few seconds, Longmire Educational Salvage appeared on the screen. Just as they were told, it was in the western part of Massachusetts. Luna pulled up a chair and dialed the number. Three rings later, a voice answered.

"Hello, my name is Luna Bodman. How are you today? No, no, this is not a spam call! I promise! My brother bought some pieces of furniture from a salvage company." She looked at the invoice and read aloud, "We Sell Junk." She rolled her eyes and gave Cullen a look that said, *You have got to be kid-*

ding me. "Yes, that's the name." She gave a slight giggle. "Imagine that." She listened for a moment. "They said they got the merchandise from your company." She listened again. "It's an armoire." Another pause, and then Luna had a brainstorm. "Oh, I know it's very hard to track it down, but we found a note inside and thought maybe the original owner would want it." She lowered her voice in a conspiratorial whisper, "It looks like a love letter."

The person on the other end must have said something to make Luna laugh. "Right? We wouldn't want the husband or wife to know if it wasn't from either of them!" She cackled before getting serious again. "But what if it is something sentimental? Maybe a lost love letter." Luna was grasping at straws now. Then her face brightened. "Sure, I can hold on. Thank you so much."

Cullen sighed and shook his head. If there was one thing you could say about her, Luna could be very convincing. And technically, she wasn't lying. Sorta.

About a minute passed and then Luna shrieked as she scribbled something down on the paper. "Thank you so very much. I am sure this will come as a surprise to someone!" She giggled. "Yes. Thanks again." She hung up the phone and handed the paper to Cullen. It read, *Briarcliff Academy.*

Chapter Five

The Invitation

Stillwell Center
The following day

Elle Stillwell entered the center with her two dogs, Ziggy and Marley, at around six thirty a.m. They were usually the first to arrive. Heidi, the baker who ran the Flakey Tart, would be right behind them, carrying trays of aromatic baked goods that could get you fat just by smelling them. Shortly thereafter, Alex, the dog sitter, would open the patio area that led to the gardens and the dog park at the back of the complex. Elle referred to him as the dog whisperer, even though Cesar Millan traded on that moniker.

Alex had a special knack with animals. He once worked at an animal hospital but left when Elle offered him a job to run the dog park at the center. The idea of playing with and enjoying pets was much more appealing to Alex, and he jumped at the opportunity. Elle wanted people to be able to bring their canine companions along and let them run, relax and play while their humans relaxed, browsed and enjoyed the art center. Elle's idea was that the center should be a gathering place for people and their pets. Kids, too, as long as they behaved. And when they didn't, somehow they would end up in the garden area, out of earshot of the rest of the clientele.

From her glass-enclosed office on the second floor, Elle watched the vendors and artists begin to open their kiosks and stalls. She took immense pride in the center. When she'd first applied for the land use permit, she was met with a lot of resistance. Not because she wanted to develop a hundred acres into an art center but because no one thought it would bring anything of value to the county. Asheville was already a thriving community. Why did they need a massive, 75,000-square-foot building on the outskirts of town? But when she brought the drawings and the 3D model to the zoning board, they were stunned.

The schematic showed a private road leading from the main highway to a dramatic piece of modern architecture in Frank Lloyd Wright's Prairie style, with an emphasis on simplicity and nature. The plans showed how it would be equipped with renewable energy, and solar panels were incorporated in the design. Instead of the monstrosity some feared, it was a work of art. All of it. From the indoor landscaping in the atrium to the signage and floor tiles—everything was handcrafted or designed by one of the local artists.

When she offered use of the atrium free of charge for community fundraisers, not one of the old codgers on the board could turn her down. Not if they didn't want to get kicked out of their church or other benevolent organizations. Elle had thought her plan through down to the hand-dryers in the bathrooms, which were set at various heights so anyone could access them. The two-story, 75,000-square-foot center had a large, landscaped atrium surrounded by spaces that ranged from artisan cheese, wine and pastry shops to ones occupied by painters, sculptors, glassblowers, potters and origami instructors. This unique and creative atmosphere opened out to acres of meticulously kept grounds that included the dog park where visitors could leave their pets in the care of the resident dog whisperer while they enjoyed the distinctive and innovative space.

It was also open to the public on Thursday evenings for music events. Not raucous concerts, but jazz combos, string quartets and an occasional folk singer. The mood was mellow and inspiring at the same time. A wine tasting was held once a month by The Wine Cellar in conjunction with The Cheese Cave, both vendors at the center. The artists would bring some of their pieces into the atrium, where guests could sip and nibble and be surrounded by internationally renowned talent.

Elle checked the calendar to see who would be performing that coming week. It was Charlie Clark's jazz ensemble. Elle hoped Chi-Chi would sing a few songs. Lebici "Chi-Chi" Stone was a beautiful, striking Nigerian woman. Aptly named, she made unique jewelry from stones brought back from her home country by her brother. Her shop was called Silver & Stone. After a local celebrity was photographed wearing one of her pieces, she was contacted by the features editor of *Vanity Fair*. As soon as the article came out, Chi-Chi was inundated with requests from all over the country. She wasn't used to operating at such a hectic pace, but she accepted the requests gladly, working well into the night. Elle and Luna had finally convinced her to take on an apprentice.

Elle thought back to the first year the center opened. She recalled the story of how Cullen and Chi-Chi became close. It didn't take long before it became obvious that Cullen was sweet on her. And while it wasn't as obvious to most other people that Chi-Chi was rather keen on Cullen, it didn't get past Luna's radar. Chi-Chi and Luna had a spiritual connection, and they became fast friends. Chi-Chi would often join

Luna and Cullen for casual dinners. Luna's antenna was always up when it came to her brother. She knew he would never take the initiative. Once, when the three of them were having dinner, they were discussing a trip Luna planned to take to Charlotte for the weekend. She teased Cullen and Chi-Chi about what they would do without her for a few days, and then suggested they go out together. As sassy as her suggestion was, it was the natural thing to do. And it was just like Luna to blurt something out of the blue. Plans were set and the two soon had something to look forward to while Luna was away. Something both were excited and anxious about.

Cullen wanted it to be a special evening and booked a table at a fine French restaurant. Both were all atwitter. Neither could figure out what to wear until Luna came to their rescue, assuring both they would look fabulous. Cullen was taken aback when he picked Chi-Chi up for their date. She looked regal. Stunning. He was walking on air when they got to the restaurant. The champagne was chilled, the entrée divine. The evening could not have been lovelier. At least until halfway through dinner, when Chi-Chi excused herself from the table during one of the music breaks. She was gone much longer than Cullen thought a woman would need in the ladies' lounge, and he feared she had bolted. Crazy thoughts zipped through his head until he saw Chi-Chi walk up to the microphone. The recognizable introductory chords to "Sweet Love" began, and Chi-Chi started the first line of the song. People quickly turned in their seats to see if it was actually Anita Baker, the singer who'd made the song popular in 1986. But the woman looked more like Sade Adu, the Nigerian-born Brit whose big hit was "Smooth Operator." The restaurant clientele was baffled and confused, but no one was more surprised than Cullen. He practically fell out of his chair. He was so verklempt he fumbled with his cell phone and called Luna, who was supposed to be having a romantic weekend with Chris Gaines. He held up his phone in the air so Luna could hear her friend singing in the background. Other guests decided to do the same. For a moment it looked like a private concert, with cell phones clicking photos and recording the music. Ever since that evening, people took every opportunity to cajole Chi-Chi into singing at least one or two songs.

And ever since that evening, Cullen knew he was in love.

Elle sighed and smiled at the activity in the atrium. It had been almost two years since the center had opened, and Elle had found a new family in Luna, Cullen, Chi-Chi, and Chris Gaines, when he was in town. The center was infused with good feelings, camaraderie, companionship and friendship.

Elle turned toward her desk and began to go through a stack of mail she had left from the day before, including a beautiful linen envelope with the initials *CTP* engraved on the back. She recognized the return address of Sniffen Court. Elle used her pearl letter opener to expose the letter's contents. Attached to an invitation was a personal note that read:

> *My dearest Elle,*
> *It has been far too long since we spent time together. I was so very happy to hear about all the wonderful things at the art center. Bravo! I hope to visit soon. You may recall me talking about my organization for women over fifty who never explored their creative souls. I discovered so many things change in our lives at that time, and I believe we should not be set adrift. I call it Women of a Certain Something. Right now, I have a dozen women who have created wonderful pieces of art. We are having a gallery opening next month in SoHo and I would love you to come. Please be my guest at the Four*

*Seasons Downtown. I have a block of rooms, so please
bring Luna and Cullen, the brother and sister you've
spoken so highly of, and their friend who makes that
fabulous jewelry—Lebici?*

*It will be so much fun to spend time together. Truth
be told, I would love your opinion on my protégés.
Please say yes!*

Big hugs and much love,
Camille

The invitation was printed on a trifold, heavy-stock glossy
paper illustrated with samples of the artists' work. Elle was
intrigued and delighted. Of course she would go to the
gallery opening. She couldn't wait to tell the others.

She went to the balcony and looked over the railing. Luna
was opening the Namaste Café. Elle could see her firing up
the coffee makers. Heidi Dugan, from Flakey Tart, brought a
basket of goods over to Luna, who also sold them to customers. But every morning Luna plucked a scone for Elle, a
croissant for her brother and a muffin for Chi-Chi. Today,
Luna decided on a slice of crumb cake for herself. She looked
up from the tray and waved to Elle, motioning for her to
come down. It had become their morning ritual. Before the
center opened to the public, Elle, Luna and Chi-Chi would
have their coffee and a breakfast treat together. Luna would
make coffee for her brother, but he was relegated to his
workshop. Mornings were for girls only. Cullen would pretend to pout and march off to his corner of the building. He
appreciated the times when Chris Gaines was in town. At
least then he had someone to talk to.

Elle spotted Chi-Chi floating across the atrium in one of
her traditional kaftans. Her long black hair was pulled back
in a straight ponytail. Elle marveled at how stunning a
woman she was. Luna, on the other hand, was cute. Pretty.

She had a Reese Witherspoon kind of look, except with long, light brown hair with a few blond streaks. Chi-Chi saw the direction Luna was looking and gave Elle a wave as well. The two met up at the open glass panel where Luna's best furry friend, Wylie, sat thumping his tail.

"He wanted to say good morning before he met up with Alex." Luna gave Chi-Chi a hug and then bestowed one on Elle. Chi-Chi squatted down and looked into Wylie's eyes. "*Ti o dara ajas.*" It was Chi-Chi's morning greeting, which meant "good dog" in Yoruba, her native language. Elle did the same but spoke in English.

Luna gave Wylie a nudge. "Okay, pal, you can go see Alex." Wylie sprang up and trotted toward the automatic doors.

"How is everyone today?" Luna asked as she brought several cups of coffee to the table.

"Very good." Chi-Chi bowed her head.

"I, too, am very good." Elle could barely contain her excitement. "I have some wonderful news!"

"What?" Luna's hazel eyes grew wide under her wire-rimmed glasses.

"Do tell." Chi-Chi placed her hand on Elle's.

"My friend Camille is having a gallery opening in SoHo next month."

"She is the one you set up with her husband, correct?" Chi-Chi was trying to remember the details.

"Not exactly. He came over to the table where we were having dinner, and I invited him and his friends to join us. He was clearly interested in Camille, and she had just come off a very bad, mortifying relationship." Elle recounted how and when she'd first met Camille.

"Right!" Luna slapped the table lightly. "He had a flower and told her how beautiful she was, or something like that."

"Correct!" Elle smiled brightly. "I may have mentioned she started a mentoring program, where she helps women of a certain 'something.' " Elle made air quotes around "something." "She now has twelve artists who will be showing their work, and . . ." Elle took an extra-long pause for dramatic effect.

Luna could sense it was something big and turned her face to Elle. "*And?*"

Elle sat back primly. "And . . ." She paused again. "She invited all of us to go to the opening."

"Oh, how lovely," Chi-Chi said in response, never anticipating Elle's next sentence.

"Indeed. She is putting us up at the Four Seasons Hotel."

"For real?" Luna's eyes got even wider.

"Yes. She said to invite your brother also."

Luna had a mixed reaction to that. "Bummer." Then she looked at Chi-Chi. "I mean, it could have been just us girls, but I guess it will be fun to have him there, too." She tapped Chi-Chi's knee with her own. "Sounds great!"

"It will be wonderful," Chi-Chi said with much more grace than Luna.

Luna rolled her eyes. She knew Chi-Chi and Cullen hadn't slept together. Yet. Chi-Chi was very traditional, and Cullen had absolutely no issues with that. He enjoyed her company immensely, and the limited physical contact they did have was warm and sweet.

Luna looked around the table. "Well, *I'm* not sharing a room with him."

Elle burst out laughing. "He'll have his own room, and so can you, unless you want to share."

Luna thought the invitation was very generous; there was no reason for Camille to pay for another room. "Of course we'll share, right, Chi-Chi?"

Chi-Chi smiled. "Absolutely. You do not snore, do you?" she kidded her friend.

"Not that I know of, or that anyone's pointed out to me." Luna gave a devilish grin.

"What should we do about the center?" Luna asked. They had backup interns who worked as information guides when the center was busy. Some were apprentices with the artists. There would be people to keep the shops open, but Chi-Chi wouldn't be able to work on her jewelry, Luna couldn't do readings and Cullen wouldn't be in his workshop.

"The opening is on a Saturday," Elle explained. "We can fly up that morning. The center is closed on Monday and Tuesday, so we're only asking for coverage for a day and a half." She looked at Chi-Chi. "And you need a little R and R. We could all use some fun and a change of scenery."

Luna clapped her hands in agreement. "Yes!" She walked over to the wall and picked up the intercom that connected her café to Cullen's workshop. "Bro! We're going to the Big Apple! Come on over here!"

A few minutes, Cullen appeared, wearing his work apron. "What are the three of you conspiring about?"

"No conspiracy, Mr. Smarty-Pants." Luna rested her elbow on the table and placed her chin on her fist. "We are going to New York City." Then she made a sweeping circle around the table. "All of us. Including you."

"Wait. What? New York? When? Why?" Cullen was visibly bewildered.

"My friend Camille Pierce is having a gallery opening for twelve artists she's been mentoring. Kind of 'the next chapter' for women. Especially for those who always had a desire to paint, draw or sculpt but never had the time."

"Sounds interesting." Cullen pulled up a chair and jiggled his way between Luna and Chi-Chi. "But how did we get invited?"

"Camille and I have known each other for a very long time. I met her in 1983, when I was doing art tours in France. She's a couple of years younger than I am, but she was coming off a bad relationship and needed a sympathetic ear. We shared the same passion for art, and the trip was a great distraction for her. By the time the six-week immersive course was over, we were mates. We agreed to meet up during the summer, and a couple of the other women thought a reunion would be fun. Camille was so gracious and invited us to stay at her family's estate in Newport for the America's Cup."

"Yeah! That's when Elle played cupid," Luna burst in.

Elle smiled and continued to give Cullen an abbreviated recap of that now infamous evening in Newport, and how Camille had met her husband, Chad Pierce.

"Elle Stillwell—aren't you the instigator?" Cullen said when Elle was done. He folded his arms and rested his back against the chair.

"Never you mind. Anyway, she is offering for us to stay as her guests at the Four Seasons in SoHo. Camille and I always remained in touch, and she wants my opinion of the artists' work."

"Well, if that's not a good reason to go, I can't think of one," Cullen said emphatically.

"Splendid! Shall I tell Camille to reserve us three rooms?" Elle asked.

Luna's thoughts were elsewhere. She would love to have Chris go with them. He'd gone to college in New York and could show them around. *Would it be too much to ask? Too cheeky?*

"Luna?" Elle broke the silence.

"Of course!" She twisted her mouth the way she did when she was about to say something even more out of the ordinary than usual. "Do you think I could invite Chris? He could share a room with Cullen." There it was. Out in the open. And nobody flinched. "So, you guys wouldn't mind? Do you think Camille would mind? Am I being too pushy? Am I asking too many questions?"

Elle chuckled, Chi-Chi snickered and Cullen rolled his eyes.

Elle replied. "No, no, no and yes."

Everyone burst out laughing. Then Cullen put on a straight face. "But you didn't ask me if I would mind sharing a room."

"Your vote doesn't count," Luna teased. She knew Cullen was very fond of Chris, and they could have some guy time together. It had been over a year since Chris stayed at Cullen's house. It was always a group gathering when Chris was in town. At least, when he wasn't alone with Luna.

"Well, it doesn't matter if my vote doesn't count." Cullen was acting like the bossy big brother. "I still say yes."

Chi-Chi clapped. "It will be a fine weekend."

"I'll send Chris a text and see if he wants to go," Luna said.

Cullen jumped in and grabbed her phone. "That is no way to invite someone for a weekend in New York." Then he pushed the Speed Dial button. Luna gave Cullen an I-might-like-to-kill-you-now kind of look. Chi-Chi and Elle were always amused at the siblings' banter.

Marshal Chris Gaines answered on the second ring. "Lunatic. To what do I owe the pleasure?"

Luna could visualize his long, dark eyelashes surrounding those twinkling. deep blue eyes. "Marshal Gaines. Would you be interested in joining our little clique on a trip to New York City?"

Chris was taken aback. The two of them had developed a romantic relationship, but he still got butterflies when he heard Luna's voice—and the feeling was reciprocal.

Chris Gaines was bigger than life to Luna. Strong, intelligent and handsome, with looks he'd inherited from his Brazilian mother. He was self-assured without being obnoxious, but most of all, he was kind. His work at the US Marshal's office dealt with missing children. It was one of the most sensitive positions in the bureau, helping people frantic about their children. He was divorced and had joint custody of his son, Carter. Chris checked his calendar. "When is this escapade supposed to take place?"

"In four weeks." Luna held her breath.

Fortunately for Chris, that particular weekend was when his son would be with his mother. "That would work out just fine. I don't have Carter that weekend."

"Super-duper!" Luna could barely contain her excitement. "Elle's friend, Camille Pierce, is reserving rooms at the Four Seasons Hotel in SoHo."

Chris let out a low whistle. "That's a pretty pricey place for a guy on a government salary."

"That's the best part. We will be staying as Camille Pierce's guests. You and Cullen can share a room."

Chris had mixed feelings about her announcement. If he and Luna could stay together, it would make for a much more romantic interlude, but even if they stayed in separate rooms, the trip would still be special. "That sounds great."

"We'll check flights on our end," Luna said.

"Just get me the dates and flight info. The office in New York has been bugging me about going up there for a few days. There's a new computer program they want me to learn, but I've been putting it off. It's been softball season for Carter, and I didn't want to miss any of his games. Especially being the coach. But we play the last game week after next. Once I get the info from you, I'll make my arrangements. They'll be happy they won't have to put me up in a hotel."

"Excellent." Luna began to relax. "This should be a lot of fun."

Chris laughed. " 'Fun' with you can mean almost anything. I've gotta go. Talk to you later."

When the call was over, Luna instinctively raised her hand for a high five from everyone. "This is sooo exciting!"

Elle glanced at the big clock in the atrium. "Okay, kids, time to go to work." She pushed herself away from the table.

"A morning delight, as usual. I'll have my travel agent check on flights and will let Camille know how many we will be. Enjoy your day, everyone." She placed her coffee cup and plate in the sink at the end of the counter.

"I'll get those. You have important work to do," Luna said.

Elle turned before she walked out and said, "Don't forget to give me all your information. Date of birth, name exactly as it appears on your passport and any frequent flyer numbers." She gave a little wave.

Cullen was heading toward his showroom. "See you guys, later. Lunch? One o'clock?"

"I don't think I will have time," Chi-Chi said. She had a lot of orders to get out and the clock was ticking.

"I'll bring you something," Luna offered. "Now, go. Get busy." She chuckled as she patted Chi-Chi on her fanny. It was something the two women had started doing and it had become part of their routine. At first, Chi-Chi was a little taken aback by the intimate physical contact, but it didn't take long for her to accept the gesture as part of the affection they had for each other.

With all the excitement of the upcoming trip to New York, the new—rather, old—armoire was put on Luna's back burner.

Later that evening, Chris Gaines phoned Luna at home. Her mind immediately went to "He's going to cancel," but she shook it off. She of all people should not be taking a wrong turn when it came to positive thinking.

"Hey, what's up?" Luna's smile could be felt through the phone.

"Hey, you. I have an odd question."

"Uh-oh." Luna was half serious.

"Did you say that woman's name was Camille Pierce?"

"Yes, that's her name. Why?"

"Something about that name. Pierce," Chris said, thinking out loud.

"It's not an unusual name."

"True." Chris shrugged to himself. "Maybe it will come to me."

"So, what else is on your mind, Marshal Gaines?"

"Uh, what should I pack? Is this a formal event? A tuxedo type thing?"

"I doubt it. It's in SoHo, and it's artists. Although I suppose some of the benefactors might be dressed in monkey suits. I think that cool, charcoal-gray Joseph Abboud suit with a black shirt and a gray tie would be very appropriate. Oh, and a pocket square. Very hip, man." Luna chuckled, visualizing him looking so very handsome and sexy.

"Good idea. I better check it out. I haven't worn it since the anniversary party for the art center. I hope it still fits," he said sheepishly.

Luna wasn't going to try to be funny and crack a joke. She knew Chris was in excellent physical condition. There wasn't an ounce of flab on his toned, athletic body. "I'm sure it will." Their mutual affection radiated across the airwaves.

"What else is on the agenda?" Chris asked.

"We haven't gotten that far yet. Just the gallery opening on Saturday night. It starts at seven. Then Camille wants us to have a late dinner at the Tribeca Grill. She booked a private room for ten o'clock. I think Elle said it was just Camille's family and us. Maybe ten to twelve people."

"That works for me. At least my suit won't go to waste."

"Yes, Mr. Funny Man." Luna smirked into the phone.

"What about the rest of the weekend?"

"Not sure. I should have more details tomorrow. So, are you going to go up a day or two early to learn that new program, or are you going to do it Monday and Tuesday?"

"Are you guys planning on spending four days there?" he asked.

"Again, I'm not sure. The center is closed Monday and Tuesday—but then again, so are all the theaters, museums and most restaurants in the city. So maybe we'll fly home on Monday and then have a chance to regroup on Tuesday, before it's back to work."

"Sounds like a good plan. So maybe I'll fly up Friday morning."

"But I thought you said the Bureau would be glad they're not putting you up in a hotel."

"Well, they're not gonna put me up at the Four Seasons. That's for darn sure. It won't be a dump, but it's not going to be a five-star hotel either. I think I can live through one night."

"Good. Then you can meet us at our hotel on Saturday."

"Great. I've gotta go. Carter has to finish his homework and I have to check it over."

"Okey dokey. Have a good night." Luna didn't want the conversation to end, but she appreciated how involved Chris was with his son's education and extracurricular activities.

Luna stretched across the sofa. Wylie was on the floor in front of her. "So, what do you think? You gonna be a good boy while we're away?"

Wylie put both paws over his eyes. That was his way of showing disapproval. In dog speak, it meant "not really."

"Hey, what about if you, Marley, and Ziggy spend the weekend together? I'll see what Elle has planned. Probably Alex, but I don't think he'd mind. And I'll give him extra cash."

Wylie gave a woof of approval. Luna checked the clock. It was still early enough to call Elle.

"Hello, Luna," Elle said after she picked up Luna's call.

"Everything all right?" She wasn't used to getting regular phone calls from Luna in the evening.

"Oh, yes. Fine. I was wondering about our doggies. Who is going to take care of your fur babies?"

"I asked Alex if he could stay at my house. Do you want to bring Wylie here? There's plenty of room, and they all love each other. Including Alex."

"That would be swell. Thanks, Elle. That will make Wylie very happy. See you tomorrow."

"Righto. Sleep tight." Elle ended the call and smiled at Ziggy and Marley. "You are going to have a sleepover with Wylie in a couple of weeks." The dogs looked as if they understood every word she said. Elle smiled. She was truly happy. When her husband, Richard, first passed away, she had felt lost. Lonely. Then she discovered how much money she had, and it changed her life in many ways. She didn't go on a spending spree. At least, not the kind a lot of other people would have, buying a new car, a new house or taking lavish vacations. No, it had been a chance for her to fulfill a fantasy she'd always had—creating a center where artists could work on their crafts in an affordable environment where they could also be exposed to the community.

She had felt inspired, motivated and stimulated. It was a new beginning. Each morning after she walked the dogs, she sat down at the kitchen table and worked on rudimentary drawings of the center. The more she drew, the more it began to take on a life of its own. When she had a clear idea of what she wanted, she knew it was time to find an aspiring architect and an engineer. When word got out about this hairbrained scheme, a landscape artist offered to do the work for free if the center paid for the plants and trees. Finally, the dream was realized with the bonus of fine friends and colleagues. They looked out for one another and became Elle's extended family. Even Ziggy and Marley had gained a friend.

Elle sent Alex a text letting him know he'd be watching three pooches instead of two.

Alex sent a reply: **Cool beans.**

Elle knew that was slang for excellent in Britain. But here? She snapped her fingers and then remembered. Yes, it was from a TV show, *Full House*. Someone must have picked up the phrase, and whammo, it became part of the lexicon. Well, as long as Alex didn't feed the dogs beans, everything should go smoothly. She giggled at the pun.

Chapter Six

Big Plans

Present day

Camille was delighted when Elle phoned to let her know she would be coming to New York with a few friends. As much of a social butterfly as she was, Camille always felt more comfortable around people she knew well. Camille spent much of her time organizing charity events that required a lot of diplomacy and tact. Chairing and hosting events was always stressful, and she had to put on the "good" face for photographers and anyone covering the social calendar. Now, with social media and everyone owning a cell phone, one had to be very much on guard. A simple frown could create ridiculous chatter like "Socialite Scorns Husband at Gala." Not that anything like that had happened to her, but she'd seen it happen to many of her friends. Everyone in her circle had a publicist they could call to quash the rumors. She sometimes thought how fortunate it was there had been fewer platforms on which to spread gossip and lies when J.R. was abducted. Thankfully, the ordeal had only lasted a few days, and no one got wind of it. The FBI had kept their word and the documents were as good as sealed.

Camille checked the guest list. At least a hundred people involved in the arts would be attending, from reporters to critics to agents. It could be a breakthrough for any one of the women; women who once led ordinary lives, working, raising a family and only dreaming of being creative. It was almost her version of *America's Got Talent*, except with brushes, paint, charcoal, pastels and clay. It was an experimental program, most of which she funded herself. Some of her peers thought she was wasting her time and money on people who never "gave it a shot." Camille's argument was "they never had one." Granted, the women had to show some innate talent and the willingness to hone their craft. Neither was a problem when Camille was interviewing them. She had decided on working with twelve women at a time. Camille wouldn't necessarily be teaching, but she would be mentoring and grooming them, and personally paying for their classes if donations were slim, which they often were. She hoped the women would develop into talent worth showcasing. Whether or not anyone gained fame or recognition, the program was a labor of love and would, hopefully, result in a sense of accomplishment and creativity for all involved.

As in most such programs, participants came and went. Interests peaked and waned, but the most recent group had shown great promise, and Camille had decided to challenge them to put together enough art for a show. It took five years for the dozen women to have five complete works each, ranging from oil, pastels, pen and ink and collage to sculpture. It was a diverse collection with the theme "My Journey." Camille was confident the work would be well received and hired a PR firm to send out press releases. She wanted the show to be an inspiration to all women to follow their passion, whatever it was, and no matter their age or stage of life.

One early evening, when Camille was sitting on the patio of their town house, she decided to add gardening and flower arranging to the next session. Those, too, were art forms, in all their natural glory. She began a notebook for that purpose, but for now she had to focus on the upcoming debut. One of the press releases was titled, "Art and Age. It doesn't matter." Another was titled, "Creativity Has No Clock." With the number of baby boomers and empty nesters, inquiries for future programs were flooding in. This was something she would be sure to discuss with Elle. Maybe she would like to start an offshoot of the group at her center.

When Camille was working on large projects like this, she would often hire a student from NYU, Pratt or Parsons to help out. For approximately six weeks, the student would work as an intern and received college credit and a small stipend. For this particular project, she needed someone who was well organized and understood something of the New York art world, whose participants varied from hipsters to traditional procurers of fine art. Rarely did its many factions intersect. Her exhibit would be for those who had an interest in modernists and contemporary form, so she needed a hipster type with management skills. She found the perfect candidate in a third-year student at Pratt. Keith was African American, gay and married. He had spent a few years in the corporate world before he realized it wasn't the life for him. He was older than most of his peers, which gave him a leg up when it came to understanding the business side of creativity. Making a living at art was not easy.

Camille heard the bell that signified someone was at the gate. Mildred let Keith in and poured two cappuccinos for him to take up to Camille's office.

"Morning, dahling." Keith batted his eyes and gave Camille a grin once he was upstairs.

"Same to you, dahling," Camille answered and plucked the coffee from the tray. Keith took the seat across from the large table that served as her working desk.

"I've been thinking," Camille said as she gazed around her snug surroundings.

Keith teased her with an "uh-oh."

"Oh, stop." She grinned. "Normally, this is enough space for my work, but this show requires more elbow room. We should probably move our operation to the gallery this week. As in maybe today." She waited for Keith's expression to change. But it didn't.

"To be perfectly honest, I was going to suggest the very same thing. It's getting a bit tight in here." Keith made a gesture, pumping his elbows on each side.

"I'm glad you agree." She opened her notebook. "Where are we with the installation?"

"Next week," Keith said without referring to his notes.

"Caterer?"

"Waiting for you to approve the final menu."

Camille pulled out the pages from The Central Catering Company. She handed them over to Keith. "Smoked salmon canapes, miniquiche, shrimp and then you pick the rest. The budget is thirty-five-hundred dollars for food and thirty-five-hundred dollars for champagne and cocktails. I don't want an open bar. Let's do one vodka-type cocktail, maybe mint and cucumber, and one bourbon. Or a whiskey sour. Whatever is popular now." She continued to tick off the beverages. "White wine. Un-oaked Chardonnay, champagne. You can stash a bottle of Macallan for my husband and his friends. Food and beverages will be passed. No table setups. We want people to enjoy the art; it's not a food festival." She smiled at Keith, who appeared cool, calm and collected. In one short week, Keith had shown his dexterity at planning and executing. He reached into his sleek messenger bag, pulled out his tablet and quickly typed in Camille's suggestions.

"You need to speak to Dexter at the hotel and give him the names of my guests." She handed another sheet of paper to him. "Two doubles, one king, adjoining if possible."

"Car service?" Keith asked.

"Yes. As soon as I get their flight information." Camille began to pack her journal, notebook and folders into her tote bag. She liked to write everything down on paper and then enter it into her computer. She believed it was easier to remember something if you went through the exercise of writing. "I suppose we should start packing up a few things to bring to the gallery. You have the keys?"

"I do." Keith jiggled them. "Let's get packing." He stood up and pulled all the various folders from vendors together and placed them in a Bankers Box. Camille grabbed the plans for the layout of the exhibit and placed them in a tube, and off they went to the car that was waiting for them on 36th Street. Normally, they would have taken a taxi, but Camille's tube of drawings needed a bit of coddling. It had taken her weeks to lay out the exhibit. Theme, flow, size, lighting, color. Display pieces. Movement. Many things had to be considered, especially because the space she was leasing had not previously been used as a gallery. She was literally starting from scratch.

As they drove down Lexington Avenue, Camille confessed her butterflies to Keith. "I don't think I've ever been this nervous about anything." She took a deep breath. "Maybe my wedding."

Keith chuckled. "This *is* like a wedding. There's lots of planning involved. At least you don't have to worry about pleasing the in-laws."

Camille laughed. "Yes, but I will have to keep some people away from one another."

"You just point them out to me and I'll run interference," Keith offered.

"You have been a godsend," Camille said with a very big smile. "You seem to know the next steps before I say them."

Keith laughed. "Parties are my thing."

The car pulled in front of a building on Mercer Street. Brown paper covered the windows of an unoccupied first floor. There was a lot of commercial space on the side streets that were being used as pop-up stores. Camille had leased this space with the understanding she would commit to four months upfront, at which time they would renegotiate. This was considered "a limited showing," but with publicity and public interest, she anticipated it could become ongoing. Camille paid the rent in advance. They needed a month to get the place set up and organized. After the grand opening, the gallery would remain open for a minimum of three months. It was a sound and logical plan. Besides, the landlord was no dummy. He knew the Pierce name well.

"J.R. and Lindsay live around here? Right?" Keith asked as he retrieved two Bankers Boxes.

Camille tilted her head south. "A couple of blocks over."

Keith knitted his eyebrows together. "Is she helping you with any of this? I mean, I don't want to be nosy."

"Of course you do." Camille gave him a sly grin. "Lindsay is otherwise occupied." She smirked. That was all Keith needed to hear and see. Camille went on to say, "Besides, she could never do the job you're doing. Her head would spin right off her shoulders if she and I had the same conversation you and I had in my office this morning." Camille lowered her voice. "You don't want to inundate her with too many sentences at the same time."

Keith thought he was going to spit. "Oh. My. God. That is just too funny!"

"And if you ever repeat it, I will deny it, and I will have to kill you," she chided.

"Mrs. Camille Pierce. I would never. Besides—who would believe me?" Then Keith lowered his voice. "I'm sure it wouldn't take long to figure out."

Camille giggled, then put her free hand over her mouth. She looked up and down the sidewalk. "I never say anything about anyone. I don't know what came over me."

"Oh, don't be silly. Everyone can be a little impish now and again." Keith bobbed his eyebrows up and down. "Plus, I can be a very bad influence." He gave her another eyebrow bob.

"Oh, just what I need." Camille rolled her eyes. She inserted a large key into the main lock and then handed the key to Keith. She pointed to the safety locks at the bottom of the door. Then she pointed to the locks at the top. "You're taller, and much more flexible."

Keith guffawed and winked. "Don't tell anyone."

The driver helped with the boxes and Keith searched for light switches. He and Camille both recoiled when the space was illuminated. "Ew!" they said in unison. There was some kind of sticky residue on the floor, crumpled paper strewn everywhere, empty cans scattered about, and the place smelled like sour beer. She and Keith had seen the space only weeks before.

"Pop-up party," Keith said with confidence. He immediately pulled out his phone and called a cleaning service. He gave them the approximate measurements of the space, including the small office and bathroom, and offered a cash incentive. The cleaners promised they would be there within two hours.

Camille walked around the large room. It looked completely different from before. She was muttering to herself.

What a mess. She wondered if the management agency was aware of the condition. She would surely send them the bill for the cleaning service. She was just about to say something to Keith when he said, "On it. I'll take some photos, too."

Within several hours, the place looked more inviting. Camille rolled out the floor plans on a large, cafeteria-style table. They began to map out the locations of the display walls by laying masking tape on the floor.

"The electrician will be here tomorrow morning to set up the lights," Camille noted as she jotted it down in her notebook.

"Do you want me to meet him here? I am sure you have a few other things to do," Keith offered.

"Perfect. I still have to confirm travel arrangements with Elle and her crew."

Camille checked her watch. It was just after five p.m. She pulled out her phone. "Hello, J.R.? I'm in your neighborhood. Keith and I started working on the space today. Care to have an adult beverage with your dear mother?"

"Hey, Mom. I'd love to, but I have a meeting at five thirty, so I won't be home until seven-ish. Someone from my old school phoned and said he wanted to chat it up with me. You know, reminisce."

Camille stiffened. "Are you sure you want to do that?" She remembered all too well what a bad senior year he'd had.

"Yeah, why not?" he replied as he examined his reflection in a mirror. "He can see for himself that I wasn't a total failure." He checked his cuff links.

"Okay, dear. Well, then, enjoy showing off." And she knew he would. "Oh, what is Lindsay up to? Do you think she might want to meet at the High Line?" Camille knew the answer would be no, but she wanted to be polite.

"She's got some kind of something somewhere. You know Lindsay." J.R. looked in the mirror again. He should probably shave, but he rather liked his rugged scruff. J.R. was a very handsome thirty-eight-year-old. He'd inherited both his mother's and father's good looks and imitated his father's charm. He still had a full head of hair, very little gray, and was fit. Buff. As much as he enjoyed having a hottie for a wife, he knew he had to keep up.

"Okay, honey. I'll catch you at the end of the week." Camille turned to Keith. "Would you care for a cocktail?"

"That would be lovely. Where to?" Keith replied.

"The Grand Bar and Salon," Camille answered.

"I love that place," Keith squealed. "Such a throwback to real cocktail lounges." He tapped his cheek. "I think I'll have a traditional whiskey sour. After I taste it, I'll decide if we should go in that direction or to a Manhattan for the opening." He pondered. "You know, I discovered a secret ingredient to add to Manhattans."

"Do tell." Camille smiled.

"You add a squeeze of fresh orange and then use the peel as a garnish."

"Sounds delish. I think I'll order one of those." She threaded her arm through his. "Shall we?"

They walked to the corner and turned left on Grand Street toward the SoHo Grand Hotel.

Gregory, J.R.'s assistant, stuck his head in J.R.'s office. "I'll be heading out soon. Do you need anything?"

"Don't think so." J.R. leaned back in his X-Chair. "Who did you say was stopping by? Someone from my old school?" J.R. couldn't recall the name as Gregory checked J.R.'s calendar.

"Henry Johnson," Gregory replied.

A slight shiver went up J.R.'s spine. *Did he mean Hank?* J.R. wondered to himself. Was it the same guy who had also dropped out a few months before him? He winced. He figured there were plenty of Johnsons in the world, so perhaps not.

"Everything all right?" Gregory asked.

"Did he say he went to Briarcliff?" J.R. had been to several schools, so it could have been any one of them.

"No. Just said you and he were classmates."

A sense of disbelief passed over J.R. Hank Johnson was a flash from the past. A past he would surely like to forget. Could it be the same person? He hardly remembered anyone's name, not to mention what schools they'd attended. "You said five ?" He looked down at his leather desk diary.

"Yessir. Do you want me to wait? It's only another fifteen minutes."

"If you don't mind?"

"Not at all." Gregory turned and went back to his desk, outside J.R.'s office.

"Gregory?" J.R. called out. "Please close my door." J.R. began running through his many thoughts. *Why now? Hadn't they parted ways years ago?* He considered pouring a tumbler of Scotch but decided against it. He'd rather be on edge than too laid back.

In a few short minutes, J.R.'s intercom rang. He picked it up. "Yes, Gregory?"

"Mr. Johnson is here to see you."

"Give me one minute, then bring him in." J.R. was deciding if he should be standing or sitting. Sitting at his desk might be more impressive. Even imposing, if he had to take that kind of posture. *Jacket or no jacket? Sitting, no jacket. Standing, definitely jacket. Or maybe no jacket and standing casually, confidently gazing out the window that overlooked Madison Square Park.* He jumped at the knock on the door. He'd been so immersed in his thoughts, he no longer had a choice. *Sitting, no jacket* was the winner.

J.R. pushed back his chair as he stood to welcome a most unwelcome guest. He offered his hand. "Henry Johnson." He said it as coolly and smoothly as possible.

"J.R. Pierce." Henry shook his hand a bit longer than J.R. was comfortable with. "Well, look at you now. All grown up." Henry's smarmy character was slightly different from twenty years before. He had more attitude now.

Henry—or Hank, as he was once called—had been raised by his aunt and uncle, who really had no use for him. They had enough money to send him to a private school, not so much because they cared about his education but to get him out of their hair. He was a terrible student and dropped out two months before J.R.'s incident. Hank didn't want to go back home any more than his aunt and uncle wanted him there, so he didn't tell his relatives and hung around town, doing odd jobs and working part-time at a gas station. He'd been over eighteen, so his guardians no longer had any say in his life choices. He just hadn't been ready to tell them yet. He surely didn't want to go back and work in his uncle's septic cleaning service. Talk about gross. He'd rather be covered in grease.

J.R. gestured to one of the sleek, modern armchairs surrounding a matching sleek, modern cocktail table. The sitting area looked more like a lounge than a lending office. Granted, they dealt with large sums of money.

Hank plopped into the light gray armchair. He stroked the sides. "Nice. Leather?"

J.R. leaned against his desk, wondering what this guy was doing in his office. "Yes. Italian."

Hank looked down at J.R.'s feet. "Shoes too?"

J.R. took the opportunity for levity. "Yes, I wear shoes, too. I've come a long way."

Hank gave a snicker. "I see you have." His eyes surveyed the room, taking in the original art and pieces of sculpture. "Oh, I remember. Your mother was into art stuff. Right?"

J.R. knew this conversation was not going to end well. He could feel it in his bones.

"Yes. She procured those pieces before the artists became famous."

" 'Procured'?" Hank stroked his chin. "Interesting word."

J.R. gave him a sideways look and then headed toward the console where he kept his liquor. "Procured. Yes. What of it?" He opened the cabinet before Hank had a chance to reply. "Drink?"

"Don't mind if I do." Hank rearranged himself in the very comfortable chair. "Yeah. Procured. Doesn't that mean 'taken'?"

J.R. knitted his brow. "It means 'acquired.' With care. Effort." J.R. didn't think this was going to be a lesson in vocabulary. He juggled a few bottles. He didn't want to waste the good stuff on this guy. "Scotch? Bourbon?" He looked over his shoulder.

"I'm sure you got some good bourbon there. I'll take it straight. Or 'neat,' as you fancy people might say."

J.R. decided not to comment. There was an air of resentment. Jealousy. He poured two fingers' worth of bourbon into the sleek Norlan rocks glasses. As he approached Hank, he could feel something coming on. Might as well get this over with. No sense in pretending he cared about Hank's health, family or whatever. Because he didn't. "So, what brings you here?"

Hank saw right through him. "Aren't you gonna ask me how I'm doin'?"

"Sorry. Been a long day." *And it's getting longer by the minute*, he thought. "So, how are you? What have you been up to? Still living in Massachusetts?"

"Yeah. When my aunt died, my uncle wasn't doin' well, so I moved in with him."

J.R. cringed at the thought. He wondered if the place smelled like someone who owned a septic cleaning service. He took a pull of his drink, his eyes looking directly over his glass. "He still alive?"

"Nah. He passed about a year ago."

"What happened to the house?" J.R. wasn't really interested but played along.

"Well, ya see, it's like this." Hank moved closer to the edge of his chair. "Uncle Ernie, well, he wasn't the best businessman. It's a shame, too. Most of his customers paid cash. He coulda done something with the money, but ever since they put up that casino in Foxwoods, he was burning through whatever cash he had. Then he mortgaged the house. By the time he died, the sheriff had the place up for sale."

J.R. wondered why Hank hadn't tried to help out his uncle, but he didn't want to ask. "What did you do next?" J.R. took another sip. The warmth of the amber liquid was comforting.

"Well, that's why I'm here."

And there it is, J.R. thought to himself. He wasn't going to ask because he knew Hank would tell him anyway.

"Ya see, J.R., I was looking in the newspaper a couple of weeks ago and saw your name and some photos of you and your family. You had your bombshell wife at your side, and your old lady and old man were at some shindig for some museum. That's the first I seen how good you're doin'. It's been a long time. I knew your folks had money, but I guess I wasn't payin' much attention to exactly how much. I was too busy trying to get cigarettes and beer." Hank chuckled at himself. "Anyways, I remembered the time when you asked me to pick you up at some Goodwill furniture place."

It was Longmire, you nitwit, J.R. thought. "Yes, I remember." He set down the glass on the cocktail table but remained standing. "I also remember paying you one thousand dollars for that particular ride."

"Yes, sir. And you did." Hank smacked his lips. "Three

days later. But ya see, here's my situation. I'm broke way down to the bone and I could use a little help."

"I see. Well, I am a loan officer. Maybe I can pull a few strings." J.R. knew there was no way he could get the bank to sign off on a guy like this, but he had to keep the conversation going. He wanted to get whatever this was over with. And as soon as possible.

"Nah. I don't need ya to get me a loan, J.R." Hank sat even further forward on the edge of the chair. "I need ya to get me some cash."

"I'm not following you." J.R. knew exactly where this was heading, but wanted Hank to spell it out: b-l-a-c-k-m-a-i-l.

"I figured there was some reason why you needed that ride to Farm Neck, New Jersey."

J.R. wasn't sure whether he should correct him or not, but he did anyway. "It was Colts Neck." He folded his arms, intentionally not making it easy for Hank.

"Yeah, wherever. I'm figurin' you wanted me to give you a ride because you didn't want anyone to know where you were going."

"So, what of it?" J.R. said coolly. "What if I had a date?"

"Kinda late in the night, wouldn't you say?" Hank took a swig and handed his empty glass to J.R. "A teeny refill, if you please." He made a gesture between his thumb and forefinger, indicating another two inches of liquor.

J.R. took the glass and walked slowly to the credenza. Without turning around, he asked, "Why does it matter what I was doing?"

"Heck, I don't give a rat's tail, but I remember you never paid me for gas."

J.R. jerked his head around. "Say what? Gas?" He was agape.

"Yeah. The grand was for the work, but cost of materials, man." Hank held out his hand and took the tumbler from J.R.

He continued to feign confusion. "Materials? You were driving one of the cars from the garage."

"Correct. And I coulda gotten into a lot of trouble, takin' it off the lot."

"Yes, but you didn't." J.R. felt the heat rise up the back of his neck.

"No matter. I need some money, J.R., and by the looks of it, you have some to spare."

J.R. wondered what Hank would do if he refused to pay him.

"Before you start thinkin' I don't have something I could share with other folks . . ."

J.R. put up his hand. "Enough. Exactly what is it you want and why should I give it to you?"

"Another grand would be nice." Hank smacked his lips again. "And why? Well, I was still in touch with some of the boys at school when someone told me you went missing for a few days and then went home. Nobody knew nothing. Nobody but me. I know you were somewhere you were keeping a secret." He sat back again. "Correct me if I'm wrong."

J.R.'s mind was racing. He had to get rid of this guy. But if he gave him the money, would he come back for more? He had to know what Hank thought he had on him.

"I was seeing someone. Someone my family didn't want me to be associated with."

"So then how come when you finally went back to Briarcliff, you left after a week?" Hank asked slyly. "And your folks shelled out some green so you could graduate?"

J.R. was surprised Hank had as much information as he did. Should he plead a nervous breakdown? Obviously, the girlfriend angle wasn't getting him anywhere. "They threatened to stop my monthly allowance if I didn't stop seeing her. I was livid, had a hissy fit and stopped eating." J.R. couldn't believe how well he was manufacturing this story on the spur of the moment. *A new talent: extemporaneous lying.* "That's when they decided I should stay home and continue my studies with tutors." He took a sip and dug deeper into his fable. "Man, you cannot imagine how suffocating it was, being around my parents twenty-four-seven. Don't get me wrong. The town house was pretty cool, except I'd get cabin fever. Anyway, I ultimately ended the relationship. It wasn't worth the angst and it was geographically untenable." J.R. was spreading a layer of manure so deep, he was surprised they couldn't actually smell it. "Long-distance relationships are really challenging, and I was already challenged." He shrugged and made a what-can-you-do kind of face.

Hank's head was bobbing around. "Well, it looks like everything turned out all right in your life, J.R."

"Yes. I'm very grateful." *Wow. That was probably the first time he'd actually said those words in maybe . . . years?*

"Well, then, as the Good Book says, 'Do unto others.'"

J.R. couldn't stand it any longer. "'Tis better to give than to receive."

Hank pointed a finger at J.R. "Righto." He slugged back the remaining bourbon. "Tomorrow? Say around this time?"

J.R. did not react immediately. "How about this—I am going to loan you the money." He put up his hand, anticipating Hank's objection. "We will just *call* it a loan in case my accountant asks."

"Oh, come on, man. Don't give me that bull. You probably have that much on you right now."

"You think I'm foolish enough to carry one thousand dollars cash around? In New York City?" J.R. shook his head.

"You know it ain't gonna be no loan. 'Cause I don't plan on payin' it back."

"Exactly." J.R. refolded his arms. "I repeat, we will just call it a loan." He narrowed his eyes.

Hank jumped up. He was beaming. "Cool, man. And I promise, you won't ever see me again."

"Promise?" J.R. knew it was more of a request, and with no guarantees. He made some notes in his desk diary. "Tomorrow. Five thirty. Meet me at McSorley's pub."

"Not very highbrow of you." Hank gave him a once-over.

"Well, I'm not going to hand over a grand in a place where I might be recognized. Besides, McSorley's is a landmark."

Hank put both hands on the armchair and lifted himself up. "Whatever. See you there. And this time, throw in a few Ulysses S. Grants and a couple of Franklins. All those twenties were a pain in the butt."

"For someone who is having money issues, you sure know whose face is on what bill." J.R. was growing impatient, but he couldn't show his hand. He didn't know how far this was going to go or where it could lead.

"Yeah, well. I'd rather be the windshield than the bug, but sometimes it's the other way around." Hank clicked his tongue. "Had my ups and downs." He turned toward the door and said, "Hasta la vista," then gave a two-finger salute.

J.R. poured another splash of bourbon into his glass and sat back down behind his desk. He'd never thought someone would rake up his past. But desperate people did desperate things. He hoped he wouldn't become one of them. As long as this guy kept his word, he could put the kidnapping behind him. Again.

He shot back the bourbon. He wasn't going to worry about it. Guys like Hank were small-time losers. One thousand dollars would be a windfall for him. Then, there was the possibility he would blow it on booze, drugs, gambling or women. J.R. rethought that. No woman would want to be with a creepy guy like Hank. Maybe for money, but certainly not for his dazzling personality. He let out a big whoosh of air and looked down at his hands. They were shaking. He couldn't remember the last time he was on edge like this. He opened a drawer and pulled out a large leather checkbook. He made the check out to cash and planned to stop at the bank on his way home from his office. *What should I put in the notation?* The usual: *Petty cash. Tips.* No one would question it. Satisfied he was in control of the situation, J.R. put on his jacket and locked the inner door to his office. On his way out, he noticed one of the assistants busily working at her desk. *Had she noticed he was still here? Did she see the creep come and go? Should he say good night?* Better if he did. No need to act suspicious. Even if she'd seen the extortionist, she wouldn't know who he was or why he'd been here. She was too far along the corridor and away from the corner to see who came and went from J.R.'s office. Hank could have been there to see someone else in the executive suites. J.R. walked closer and cleared his throat. The assistant jumped.

"Mr. Pierce, you startled me!" She was almost embarrassed.

"Sorry. You're working late tonight, Margie." J.R. smiled at the newbie.

"Yes, a lot of contracts are coming in and I have to log them. Must be the interest rates," she mused.

Or the tax breaks, he thought. The city and state were giving away tax credits like candy on Halloween. They needed to continue to rebuild and renew the city. There were monolithic skyscrapers growing all over Manhattan, but many were only partially occupied, and the older buildings were in much need of repair. There was a big push to save centuries-old neighborhoods and the local shops. Incentives were in abundance. The only hitch was you needed a lot of money to begin with. *Money makes money.*

"Don't stay too late. And remember to order a car to take you home." J.R. may have been spoiled, but he wasn't a brat when it came to his staff.

"Yes, thanks, Mr. Pierce. Have a good night."

J.R. took the elevator down to the lobby. He sighed as he looked south toward the Flatiron Building, one of the most iconic structures in New York City. The triangular-shaped building at the crossroads of Broadway and Fifth Avenue was completed in 1902. J.R. snickered, remembering that the original architects neglected to provide space for ladies' restrooms, so management had to designate different bathrooms on different floors. *Brilliant. Yes, much has changed, and much has not.*

J.R. decided to walk the thirty plus blocks home. He strolled down Fifth Avenue and through Washington Square Park, where there was always something going on. Jugglers, dancers, fire-eaters (when the FDNY wasn't looking), guys selling nickel-bags of pot, unicyclists. It was a circus at almost any time of the day. Once he crossed the park, he was on LaGuardia Place, surrounded by the buildings of NYU. The crowd was an eclectic mix of students, businesspeople and local neighborhood folks. He walked several more blocks through SoHo until he came to Franklin Street, where he and Lindsay lived. He checked his watch. Forty minutes to walk two miles. Not bad. He wasn't even winded. He'd thought the walk would calm him down, but he couldn't sit still. He took a quick shower, put on some casual clothes and decided to walk to Raoul's for dinner. That would take another fifteen minutes. Maybe he would be able to relax by then.

Just as he was about to leave, Lindsay came in.

"Hey, honey!" she squealed, wrapping her shopping bag–filled arms around his waist. "Where you off to?" She untangled herself from his hug.

"Thought I'd go to Raoul's tonight. I have a hankering for jumbo lump crab beignets." Then he snorted at his own use of the word "hankering." Unfortunately, it was an inside joke he could not share.

"What's so funny about crab beignets?" Sometimes Lindsay would catch a few things.

"Nothing. I just don't think I've ever used the word 'hankering' before."

"Huh. I don't think you have either." She plopped the bags onto the white sofa. "Want some company?"

J.R. hesitated. *Did he?* Not really, but if he said no, she would get suspicious. "Sure thing. Are you ready to go now, because I am famished. I walked home from the office."

"Wow. Impressive," she said in her squeaky tone. "Just give me five minutes to refresh." She sauntered down the hall to their massive bedroom. It was big enough to be a studio apartment for one person. She flung open the built-in wardrobe cabinet. It, too, was larger than some living rooms in New York. If you even *had* a living room. Truth of the matter was that most apartments in New York looked more like *Seinfeld* than *Friends*.

Lindsay decided on a pair of skinny jeans, a white T-shirt and a short, red leather jacket, with Jimmy Choo high-heel, red patent leather sandals. She brushed some purple eyeshadow on her lids and then lipstick to match her jacket and shoes. The crisis came when she couldn't decide which handbag to use. She called out, "Honey? What handbag should I bring?"

J.R. thought how lucky she was that picking out a handbag was the biggest challenge of her day. Being one who was also stuck on labels, J.R. had a good idea of her accessory inventory. At least he knew who her favorite designers were. "What are you wearing?" He mockingly squinted his eyes, as if he could see through the wall.

"Jeans, tank, red leather jacket," she called out from the master bathroom.

"The Hermès Bridado backpack." *Why did he know that? What was up with his constant need to show off the extent of his handbag knowledge?* He remembered when he was

younger, his father was the same way. *Only the best.* Then
something changed, and his father wasn't as obsessed with
brands, labels and the trappings of money. Then it hit J.R.
like a brick. The change happened after the abduction. *But
why?* That was a subject he was not about to broach. Not
now. Not ever. With some luck, the subject would be reclosed
after five thirty tomorrow when he met good old Hank
again.

Lindsay bounced down the hall. She hadn't changed a bit
in thirteen years. Same body, same face. J.R. could not com-
plain. At least, not for the moment.

Dinner was superb. Authentic French cuisine, along with a
wonderful bottle of 2010 Aile d'Argent Blanc du Château
Mouton Rothschild from Bordeaux, France. "The vintage is
the same year we were married," J.R. said as he swirled the
light, lemon-colored liquid in his glass.

"Aw, that's sweet," Lindsay said. "So, how was your
day?" She always asked.

"Good. Fine." He indicated to the sommelier it was acceptable to pour. He turned his attention back to Lindsay.
"And yours?" He would much rather hear of her inane antics
than think about his last appointment.

"Briana and I met at the Sisley-Paris Spa at the Carlyle,
then we went to the Met for an hour." She sipped her glass of
wine. "Yum."

"You never go to the Met." At least not that he could recall.

Lindsay perused the menu and peeked her head above it.
"I wanted to see the Gala dresses on display."

Now, that made more sense to him. "Speaking of art, you
know my mother is having a show in SoHo in a couple of
weeks."

"Yep. The twenty-fourth. Or was it the fourteenth?" She
kept reading the list of entrées.

"It's the twenty-fourth. Lin, can you please make sure you put that on your calendar? It's very important to her, and she has some friends coming in from out of town."

"Of course. I shall be your perfect date." She didn't bother to move the menu to say it to his face.

"As you always are." He stared straight at the menu she was holding up in front of her.

Lindsay recognized a few of the other diners in the restaurant and waved a hand covered in bling. For no apparent reason, J.R. found himself adding up the amount of money Lindsay was wearing: $900 shoes, a $4,000 bag, at least $25,000 in jewelry. The engagement ring he'd bought for her was at least $15,000. Jeans? Probably $500, $300 for the tank top, and a guess of $7,000 for the jacket, and at least $700 in lingerie. He lost track of the total. It had to be over $30,000. And that guy was looking for a mere grand? J.R. was glad Hank had never seen Lindsay in person. He would have upped the ante by several thousand. But then again, what did he even have over J.R.? A lie? Big deal. At least that was all Hank thought it was. Or so J.R. hoped.

They decided to skip dessert and get some ice cream on the way home. As shallow as Lindsay was, at least she was perky and fun. She asked for one small scoop of pistachio with some of those "cute sprinkle things!" They opted for cups instead of cones. The sidewalks of New York were not known for their smoothness, and Lindsay was wearing five-inch-high sandals. Like most men, J.R. liked to *see* his wife in high heels, but they surely weren't practical. One slight misstep and that beautiful Saint Laurent jacket would be an ice cream sundae.

At the Stillwell Center, Chi-Chi was working well into the night. There were several pieces she had to finish before she left for New York. She also wanted to make something for

Camille as a show of appreciation for her generosity. She guessed her taste was classic. Simplicity and elegance.

Most of Chi-Chi's work was bold. It was wearable art. She decided on a thin bangle bracelet with a polished amethyst embedded in a simple design. It was elegant yet casual and could be worn any time of the day. She was in the back of her shop, putting on the finishing touches, when she was surprised by Cullen.

"Oh, my goodness. You scared the daylights out of me!" She put her hand to her chest.

Cullen sheepishly held out a bag. "Sorry. Didn't mean to startle you. I brought you something to eat."

"You are a love. Thank you." Chi-Chi patted a stool for him to sit on. She peeked inside the bag. "You are too good to me." She opened the wrapped sandwich. "What about you?"

"I already had something."

"Why are you here so late?" Chi-Chi bit down on the ham and brie sandwich.

"Oh, that sister of mine." He feigned a sigh. "She wants to find out more information about that new armoire."

Chi-Chi dabbed her mouth. "I thought she was going to put that on hold until we got back."

"As if. You know Luna. She is like a dog with a sock in its mouth."

Chi-Chi snorted. "That is funny. Did she learn that from Wylie?"

Cullen laughed. "No, I think she taught it to him!"

"What are you going to do about the armoire?"

"She wants to call Chris to see if he can try to get finger-prints from it."

"That's a tall order, isn't it?" Chi-Chi asked.

"Could be. I don't really know, but if Chris thinks it will make Luna happy—or I should say, placate her—he'll go through the motions."

"But doesn't that mean he would have to ask someone in a lab to do the work?"

"I suppose." Cullen shrugged. "Anyway, she wants me to use special gloves and take the piece apart." He twisted his mouth to the side, the same way Luna did when she was in deep thought.

"What are you planning to do?" Chi-Chi continued to enjoy her sandwich.

"I hope I can stall her until we're back from New York."

"Sounds like you could use some help?" Chi-Chi asked.

"Don't I always when it comes to my little sister?" He cracked a smile.

"I have an idea. I am so busy, but my apprentice can't work late. I'll ask Luna to help me with the packaging and shipping. That should get her out of your hair." Chi-Chi crumpled the napkin, put it in the bag and tossed it in the trash.

"You are brilliant." Cullen stood and kissed her on the forehead.

"And we shall keep this little secret between us." Chi-Chi broke into her beautiful smile.

"I owe you," Cullen said. Another excuse to take her out for a romantic dinner. Cullen was thrilled their relationship was growing. But slowly. Very slowly.

Luna must have sniffed out a conspiracy because she seemed to have shown up out of nowhere. "Owe you what?" She stuck her nose in their direction.

"He asked me to make something for Camille. I was planning on giving her a bangle with an amethyst, and then I thought maybe I could make a set of bracelets with a different stone in each. She can stack them up or wear each one individually. Mix and match." Chi-Chi was on a roll. "Elle said she likes elegant but simple. See?" Chi-Chi handed Luna the bracelet she was working on. "I still need to polish it, but you get the idea?"

"Beautiful. I think it's a stupendous idea!" Luna held up the bracelet to the light so the amethyst shone.

"I'll make one with aquamarine, one aventurine, a watermelon tourmaline and a clear crystal. I should call Elle to see if she wants to join us, or if she has a different idea in mind."

"Oh. What about Chris?" Luna said thoughtfully. "I'm sure he'll want to chip in, too."

"All you will have to pay for is the materials. Somewhere between one hundred and one hundred-fifty dollars each." She paused. "Is that okay?"

"Sure! Fine with me. I'm sure Chris won't have any objections. Besides, it will save him the trouble of figuring out a gift." Luna chuckled. She leaned back to check the clock in the atrium. "Wow. It's nine o'clock already. Do you think Elle is still up?"

"I am certain this can wait until morning." Cullen was getting fidgety and wanted to put the plan in motion. "Chi-Chi has a lot of work to do."

Chi-Chi sighed. "I do. And Marie can't work late, so I'll be doing all the packing and shipping myself."

Cullen took a beat before saying, "Luna? Why don't you give Chi-Chi a hand? You said you didn't have any freelance work, and you can see your clients during the day."

"Well, sure!" Luna was more than happy to accommodate her friend. "Just tell me what you need and I'll get to it!"

Cullen hoped Luna had put the armoire out of her thoughts for the time being. He knew he had to stop thinking about it himself before Luna started to read his mind. Again.

Luna twisted her mouth. "What about that armoire?"

"What about it?" Cullen pretended it had no special meaning.

"When are we going to try to track down whoever wrote that stuff?"

"Oh, please, Luna. That can wait."

"But what if it's recent? What if someone was locked in there at the Longmire place? What happened to that person?" Luna looked genuinely concerned.

"Well, there isn't much we can do about it right now." Cullen sighed. "Besides, Chi-Chi needs your help more than some elusive stranger. Then again, maybe it was just a prank."

"Huh." Luna was a little deflated. "All right, but promise we'll get on it as soon as we come back from New York."

"Promise." Cullen held out his pinkie.

"Pinkie swear!" Luna was buoyant, a rather natural state for her. When she wasn't meditating, she was like a bag of bubbles.

Chi-Chi grinned at her two best friends. She wished she and her brother were more playful, but in many ways her relationship with Abeo was not very different from Luna and Cullen's, except Chi-Chi was the more serious of the siblings. Chi-Chi was often talking Abeo out of a sticky situation, like the brushup he'd had with Jennine May, the owner of Clay More Pottery. Jennine had a reputation as a man-eater. She reminded people of the character Blanche from *The Golden Girls*. She actually wore similar outfits that resembled lingerie. Even in public. She took a bit of getting used to, and any man over the age of twenty-one needed to be on high alert when he was around her. One weekend, Abeo arrived earlier than expected, and Chi-Chi was not about to change her plans with Cullen to spend time with her brother. It had been their first official date. Abeo was left to his own devices and found himself literally in the clutches of Jennine. He blamed it on the champagne, but it wouldn't take much for Jennine to pounce. The next day, he was terribly embarrassed, and Chi-Chi had to lie to Jennine and tell her Abeo had to leave abruptly. She didn't tell Jennine he was actually hiding out in Chi-Chi's house.

"Okay, you two. Leave me to my work." Chi-Chi pretended to scold them.

"Don't you need my help?" Luna asked.

Cullen's eyes grew to the size of hockey pucks, giving Chi-Chi a pleading stare.

"Yes, I do. You can stay. Mr. Bodman, I am going to have to bid you adieu for the evening. Thank you again for the delicious sandwich. Between the two of you, I will be getting fat."

"Highly unlikely." Luna snickered.

"But I truly appreciate your kindness and looking out for me," Chi-Chi said in her endearingly formal manner.

"Always a pleasure." Cullen pretended to tip his imaginary hat. "See you tomorrow." He turned and let out a sigh of relief. Chi-Chi would keep Luna occupied long enough to put off any detective work she was planning.

"So, tell me where to start." Luna walked over to a long table under a row of wooden compartments with shipping cartons, silver gift boxes, tissue, a bolt with liquid silver beads, brown paper, bubble wrap and labels. A postage machine sat at the far end.

"These three pieces need to be gift boxed with the description card and tied with liquid silver strings."

"I think I can handle that." Luna put on a pair of cotton gloves so as not to get fingerprints on the jewelry. "Huh."

"I know that 'huh.' What is on your mind?" Chi-Chi asked but kept working.

"Fingerprints," Luna said. "I told Cullen I wanted to ask Chris to dust the armoire for prints."

"And what did Cullen think of that?"

"What do *you* think?" She carefully wrapped one of the finished pieces in fine tissue. "All of my ideas seem crazy to him." She sighed.

"Oh, I think that is just his way of protecting you."

"From what?" Luna turned toward Chi-Chi.

Chi-Chi burst into a big grin. "From you!"

"Everyone is a comedian." Luna made a face.

"I think Cullen may feel you are asking the fine marshal to do something that is, well, not part of his job." Chi-Chi knew she had a point.

"I know, but who else could I get to dust for prints?"

"Don't they have a do-it-yourself-detective kit?"

"More jokes." Luna smirked.

"No. I am serious. I am sure you can purchase something."

"Yes, but I would still need a lab and a database to figure out whose fingerprints they are."

"Isn't that what you call trying to find a needle in a cornfield?"

Luna burst out laughing. "Needle in a haystack."

"Yes, I can never figure out your similes and metaphors. We have plenty of our own," Chi-Chi said. Then she asked, "Music?"

"Sure. What do you have in mind?"

"Of course something mellow, but not enough to put us to sleep." Chi-Chi thought for a moment. "I am a big fan of smooth jazz."

"Yes, we figured that out the first time you went out to dinner with Cullen." Luna chuckled.

"George Benson? Grover Washington Jr.? Bill Withers?"

"Any of them. They have such staying power."

"Yes. Imagine—'This Masquerade' was recorded in 1976."

"Geez, I wasn't even born then." Luna gently tied a ribbon of liquid silver on one of the packages and clipped onto it a charcoal-black card with the initials "S&S" embossed in silver.

Chi-Chi chucked. "Me either." She walked over to a small, compact stereo system sitting on a shelf on the opposite wall. She clicked a few buttons, plugged in her phone and the intro to George Benson's first major hit began to play. Both women immediately began to sing along.

"As sad as these lyrics are, the song is still painfully romantic," Luna mused.

"Speaking of romantic . . . How are you and the good marshal doing?"

"As in what? I don't keep any secrets from you."

"No. You only keep them to yourself," Chi-Chi teased. "Have you told him how you feel?"

"Have you?" Luna said, referring to her brother with a slight tone of accusation.

"Okay. Okay. We can talk about me after we talk about you."

"I really like him. A lot. I get all butterfly-y when I see his name pop up on caller ID. What do you call that?" Luna pulled out a sheet of bubble wrap.

"After all this time, I would not call it a crush, even if it feels like one," Chi-Chi advised. "You truly care about him. And I know he cares about you."

"I think it's the distance. Not the emotional distance, but the miles. He lives over two hours away. Sometimes I think that's what keeps it exciting. We're not in each other's hair all the time."

"True."

"Besides, what do I say? Hey, Christopher, want to go steady?"

Chi-Chi let out a big snort. "You, my friend, could get away with something like that."

Luna giggled. "Hmmm. Well, let's see how this trip goes. You can tell a lot about someone when you are in a different place."

"Wait—you are the one who can read people." Chi-Chi stopped what she was doing to give Luna a pointed look.

"Yep. Except when it comes to my own life." She sighed. "I suppose that's how I'm supposed to learn life's lessons. If everything was easy to read, what fun would it be? When it comes to other people and things, I get a vibe, and then I try to fit the pieces together."

"Yes, and I have seen you do it. Many times." Chi-Chi went back to hammering a piece of silver.

"And so, what about you?" Luna prodded.

"I am going to follow your lead and wait until we are back from New York City to make any decisions."

The next morning, Elle, Chi-Chi and Luna met up at the café. Each spoke the Nigerian greeting for good morning, "*E kaaro*," followed with "Namaste," a Sanskrit greeting that meant, "I honor you."

Luna brought over a tray of their usual coffee and scones to the small table where Chi-Chi and Elle were sitting. She pulled out a chair. "So? What's the latest?"

Elle was all atwitter. "I phoned Camille, and she is thrilled all of us are coming to New York. I made some inquiries about flights." She tapped her finger on the table. "First option is we get up early to catch a nine ten flight from Charlotte to Newark. But I'll get a car service, so we don't have to be fully awake to drive. It will take two hours to get to the airport, so we should leave around five thirty."

"In the morning?" Luna faked a yawn.

"Yes, my dear, but you can sleep most of the way. We'll wake you when we get to the airport. You'll just have to stay awake long enough to get through security. Then you can sleep on the plane. It's a two-hour flight."

Luna stretched across the table and laid her head on her arms. "What's the second option?" Clearly she wasn't liking the first.

"There's an eight forty flight in the evening that arrives at around eleven. With any luck, we'll get to the hotel by midnight." Elle tapped two fingers this time.

"I can live with that." Luna sat up taller. "We'll have to close up early."

"Or have two of the interns sit in. It's a Friday night, so it will be busy. Your apprentice can manage any sales you have, right?" Elle asked, addressing Chi-Chi. Then she turned to Luna. "Sabrina knows how to operate your coffee machines, and Cullen can put up a sign like Jimmy Can-Do." Elle pointed to the sign sitting on an easel outside the shop that sold items made from beer cans. The sign read:

WE HONOR THE HONOR SYSTEM. IF YOU WANT TO PAY BY CREDIT PLEASE LEAVE YOUR NAME AND CONTACT INFORMATION AND THE ITEM NUMBER YOU'RE TAKING. SOMEONE WILL CONTACT YOU. OTHERWISE PLEASE DEPOSIT CASH OR CHECK. THANK YOU.

"He can change the wording a bit. I don't imagine anyone would be trying to haul away a piece of furniture on their own," Elle added.

Luna chimed in. "Good idea. There are price tags on the pieces, and he can lock up anything that could grow legs and walk off. So I vote on taking a late flight on Friday night. Then we can sleep in on Saturday and have the whole day to enjoy and prepare for the opening." She looked at Elle. "We should pay for the extra night."

"Camille offered four nights. I don't suppose it matters which four nights," Elle replied.

Chi-Chi looked at both women. "Well, this sounds like a perfectly reasonable plan." Then she giggled. "Maybe I should ask my brother Abeo to cover for me."

Elle and Luna howled. "Who will protect him?" Elle gasped.

"He's a big boy now. Plus, he owes me several stones. I shall call him and tell him he must come here and mind the shop." She said it with great authority. Then she finished with a sheepish grin. "And he won't have his sister prying him out of who knows what."

The other women laughed. "We should get busy. We have a lot to do over the next couple of weeks," said Elle.

* * *

J.R. walked onto the sawdust-covered floor of McSorley's Ale House a half hour early for his appointment. He wanted to get a seat with the best vantage point, and he was early enough to have his choice of tables. In a few short minutes, the place would be packed with exhausted office workers, blue collar workers and an assortment of tourists. He motioned for one of the servers and ordered a Redbreast fifteen-year-old Irish Whiskey. "Neat."

It wasn't long before Henry "Hank" Johnson sauntered into the bar. He was straining his neck to peer over the crowd that had quickly descended upon the old ale house. J.R. caught his eye. Hank slithered through the throng of the thirsty and weary and made his way to the table where J.R. was waiting. J.R. was not in a good mood. This man had walked back into his life, made demands and thrown him off schedule. Demanding $1,000 to keep his yap shut after all these years was bad enough. J.R. wasn't about to just hand him an envelope. That would be too obvious. The plan was for J.R. to put the money in a messenger bag and leave it on the floor next to his chair. When it was time for them to leave, Hank would take the bag with him. It was one of the oldest handoffs in the books. J.R. was also annoyed at how clichéd it all was. He tossed back the whiskey seconds before Hank squirmed into the wooden chair across from him.

Hank held out his hand. J.R. knew if he didn't act civilized, it would piss off Hank, and he didn't want to start anything. What he wanted was to *end* everything. So he begrudgingly shook his hand.

"How ya doin'?" Hank asked.

J.R. reminded himself to be polite. "Okay. You know. Same old thing."

"Well, that's just it. I don't know." Hank was twirling a toothpick in his mouth.

Really? J.R. thought to himself. *If you're going to be a criminal, don't be a stupid criminal.* And Hank was looking pretty stupid.

"No. I guess you wouldn't." J.R. sat up straight. "I know my life looks easy, and for the most part it is. I've been lucky to have decent parents. But don't think I don't work at it every day."

"You sayin' I should feel sorry for you?" Hank smirked and snapped his fingers at the waitress.

"No. Not at all." J.R. was clinging to every molecule of decency he had in him. If he could, he would grab the guy by his collar and throw him into the alley. "Look, we both know why we're here. Can we suspend the cordial banter?"

"Tsk-tsk." Hank clicked his tongue. "Whatever you say, boss."

J.R. didn't remember Hank being this much of a creep. But people changed, and they had only been eighteen when they first met. J.R. pointed to the bag on the floor. "It's all there." Then he pulled out a one-hundred-dollar bill and placed it under the saltshaker. He pushed his chair back and stood, slightly looming over Hank. "I have a meeting in a half hour. Have another drink on me." J.R. wasn't sure if that would please Hank or provoke him. For the moment, he didn't care. He just wanted out.

PART THREE

Chapter Seven

Putting It All Together

New York City
Friday

M arshal Christopher Gaines reached out to his superiors at the field office to notify them he was finally going to learn the new computer system. They were even more pleased when he told them they wouldn't have to pay for a hotel. The travel arrangements were made, and he planned to fly up to New York on the earliest flight that would get him into Manhattan by eleven. The course would take a total of six hours. He would do as much as he could on Friday and then return to the headquarters to finish on Monday. Because the rest of the crew wouldn't be arriving until late Friday, he would try to finish everything that evening and meet up with them at the hotel for a nightcap. The trip was a few short weeks away and he was ready for anything. And with Luna and her pals, anything was possible.

The trip was a long time in the planning, but the day finally arrived. Marshal Gaines reached his destination, the field office in New York, while Luna, Cullen, Chi-Chi and

Elle were preparing to leave that evening. Chris reported to the security office, checked in and went to a waiting area on the second floor. There were several chairs and a table with the day's newspapers. It was refreshing to see real newspapers. He'd left his phone with security until they cleared it, so he couldn't read the news there.

He thumbed through the *New York Times.* An article about Camille's opening was on the front page of the Arts section, titled "Art Has No Age." He snickered. Camille was part of the New York art world and from a prominent family. It was natural for them to run an article about her.

Camille Pierce. Again, the name rattled in his memory, but before he had the opportunity to read the article, an agent summoned him into a large computer laboratory. There were several cubicles in a very chilly room.

"I'm Hector," the agent introduced himself. "I'll be walking you through the program. I know it seems silly to do it in person with all the technology available, but people always have so many questions, and sometimes things progress more efficiently in a classroom-type atmosphere."

"Yes, I agree," Chris answered. He was still kind of old school in some ways.

As expected, the program was complicated. "Until you learn it," Hector encouraged. "Most people can do this in a few sessions. I recommend taking breaks to give your brain a chance to 'file' away the information." He used air quotes for "file."

Chris chuckled. "And how many times have you used that pun?"

Hector snickered in response. "Too many to remember." He motioned for Chris to take a seat in front of a large monitor. Hector took the seat next to him in front of an equally large monitor and began the tutorial. They were at it for several hours and had taken a few breaks when Chris realized it was almost five p.m.

"I have dinner plans with one of my former professors. Do you mind if we reconvene later? Or tomorrow?"

"Later is fine with me. If we can get through all of the protocols, we'll both have the weekend off."

"Sounds like a very good plan of action." Chris stood and stretched. "What time do you want to meet up?"

"Seven thirty? Eight?" Hector suggested. "I'm going to grab a bite in the cafeteria, so whenever you're ready, just send me a text. They'll give you your phone back when you leave the building. You can text me just before you get back."

"Terrific. I appreciate your flexibility." Chris held out his hand.

"I appreciate your wanting to bang this out before the weekend!" Hector gave Chris a firm handshake in return.

"Okay. See you later." Chris moved toward the elevators and pushed the button for the lobby. Luckily, the FBI offices were only a ten-minute walk from the hotel and an eight-minute walk from the Odeon, where he was meeting Professor Robert Hasselberg. Chris was the first to arrive at the neon-lit, retro café. It was a shining light amid the dark streets of Tribeca in the 1980s, just before the revival of the neighborhood. Many luminaries such as Andy Warhol, Robert De Niro and John Belushi could be spotted back in its early days, when it signaled a new chapter of New York's nightlife. It would soon shape the culture of Tribeca and SoHo. It set the bar for being hip. Chris enjoyed the history of the restaurant, particularly its roots in the days of unadulterated sex and drugs. He snickered that this place, once known for its debauchery, was a quick walk to FBI Headquarters. *Right under their noses.* But that was the eighties.

Chris entered the famous foodery, took a seat at the bar to

the left of the maître d's station and ordered an iced tea. As much as he wanted a glass of Cabernet, he decided iced tea would be the better choice. There would be plenty of time later for a cocktail. The food was always impeccable. The French menu provided just enough of a selection to please most palates, and his was craving steak tartare. He figured a good dose of red meat would keep his blood flowing and his mind alert for the rest of his training. He spotted his former professor entering the restaurant. Chris was happy to see the older gent looking spry. It had been almost a decade. People could change in the best and worst ways in ten years.

"Christopher Gaines!" the professor exclaimed. "My, have you grown up!" He chuckled. "A marshal, no less."

The men shook hands and patted each other on the back.

"Yes, sir. A full-fledged US Marshal."

The men were ushered to their table as they chatted. "So, what brings you here?" asked Professor Hasselberg.

"The field office wants me to learn a new program the FBI has initiated for recovering kidnappings and missing persons."

"You mean two different branches of government are working together? Wonders shall never cease."

"Ain't that the truth." Chris relaxed into his chair. "It's surprising, but they actually have task forces now to help each other out."

"Amazing," Hasselberg remarked. "And you're in the missing children's department?"

"Yes. Sometimes it's good and sometimes our work does not have a happy outcome. That's the worst part of my job. Computer systems are a nuisance, but dealing with bereaved parents is horrible."

"I can only imagine," the professor said as he perused the menu.

Chris continued, "But I am also here for a little R and R. Some friends were invited to a gallery opening and I am the lucky recipient of a room at the Four Seasons."

"Oh. Fancy."

"I suppose it is. I'll be sharing that room with a friend from Asheville. He and his sister have a shop in a very large art center in Buncombe County, and the woman who owns the center is friends with the woman who is sponsoring the opening."

"I never took you for the artsy type," Professor Hasselberg joked. "I don't mean to say you're not sophisticated."

Chris laughed. "I wouldn't go so far as saying I'm sophisticated. Let's just say I'm not a hayseed or a Bubba."

"What kind of art installation is it?" the professor inquired.

"It's a show for women artists." Chris thought for a moment. "Let me see if I have this right . . . A benefactor named Camille Pierce started a program for women of a certain age to pursue their dream of being an artist."

Hasselberg immediately placed his hand on Chris's arm. "Did you say Camille Pierce?"

"Yes, why?"

"Do you remember the class you had in unsolved kidnappings?"

Chris snapped his fingers. "Yes!" he almost shouted. "I *knew* that name was familiar. When Elle, the woman who owns the art center in Asheville, mentioned Camille's name, I thought it rang a bell."

"It was one of those unsolved cases that was resolved without the aid of law enforcement."

"Right." Chris was thinking back now. "There was an abduction, but the family decided to pay the ransom and not notify the authorities."

"Yes, and then, after their son was returned, they decided

to speak to the FBI and go on the record. Pierce was concerned all the money he withdrew would send up red flags."

"Wow. Talk about a coincidence." Chris's mind ran rampant, anticipating Luna's reaction to this newfound information.

"A coincidence is a significant coexistence of circumstances or events that have no obvious connection with one another, "the professor said in his most professorial voice. "Or, as Albert Einstein said, 'Coincidence is God's way of remaining anonymous.' " He shrugged. "It all depends on what side of spirituality you're on."

Chris broke out into a huge grin and chuckled. "This woman I've been seeing, Luna Bodman, is one of those 'woo-woo' types."

"You? Mr. Feet on the Ground?" He looked incredulous.

"I know, I know. But I must say, she has something special about her."

"She must if she's garnered your attention."

"Seriously. I met her when a young girl went missing. She signed up for the search party, and we happened to be paired off. She and her dog, Wylie, took me to where the little girl was hiding." He tapped his finger on his chin. "It was quite remarkable. Since then, she's worked on a few cases with our field office." Chris grinned. "She's spooky, but in a good way."

"You seem to think very highly of her and her special talent."

"I do. And she is fun and funny."

The professor smiled. "You seem happy."

"I am. Carter is doing well in school, and he's becoming a decent softball player."

"Sounds like things are going well for you, Christopher. You've made me very proud," the professor said as he peeked over his horn-rimmed glasses.

"Thank you, sir. You were very inspirational."

"I take it that it's Luna you are meeting later?"

"Yes. Her brother and I get along very well. He's a good mate, for sure. Very different from his sister, though. Very buttoned-up. But not in an uptight way. I think he feels he has to be the straight arrow of the family." Chris chuckled.

"There has to be at least one with their head screwed on right." The professor grinned, but then his expression grew reflective. "Camille Pierce, husband of Chad Pierce Sr. Their son was . . . is Chad Pierce Jr." He paused. "It was during your first year at John Jay, I believe."

"Yes, it was." Chris hesitated, but then asked, "Do you think I could take a look at the case history?"

"I don't see why not. I have a class tomorrow morning. Why don't you stop by my office and we'll check the archives?"

"Still in the same place?"

"Oh, yes. I could never move. Too many books to pack." He laughed.

Chris was in a grand mood. He had finally put the name and the events together. Now the question was whether or not he should tell Luna. He figured he would decide after he looked over the old files.

Chris picked up the check for dinner and they agreed to meet the following day at noon. "I'll bring lunch," Chris promised.

It was around ten p.m. when Chris finished his crash course in data entry. Afterward, he walked to his hotel. He couldn't stop thinking about the Pierce kidnapping. He smirked as he thought about the next night's introductions: *"Nice to meet you. Weren't you the guy who got kidnapped twenty years ago?"* He knew it was going to be difficult to keep any of this to himself. He knew Luna would get a vibe off Chad Jr. She had some kind of radar. He also knew he would have to keep her grounded—otherwise she would want to look over the files, too, and that was definitely not going to happen. But she would pick his brain nonetheless.

He stopped in the lounge of the hotel for a nightcap and waited for the rest of the crew to arrive. He checked his watch. Their flight should have landed by now. Traffic would be light, so the ride from Newark to downtown shouldn't take more than a half hour. He was deep in thought when he heard the familiar voices of Luna, Chi-Chi and Cullen. "Yoo-hoo! We're here!" Elle lagged behind and gave a wave. Hugs, kisses and handshakes went around as everyone began to speak at the same time.

"How was your trip?"

"How was the class?"

"Did you finish?"

"Where did you have dinner?"

Chris held up both of his hands. "Trip was good. Finished the class. It was boring as hell. The Odeon." He held Luna's hand for an extra minute. "Have you checked in?"

"Yes," Cullen said. "We had the bellman drop our luggage and headed here straight away."

Chris motioned for the bartender. "What is everyone having?" They gave him their selections as Elle and Chi-Chi each took a seat.

Luna stood as close to Chris as she could without looking too obvious. She just *loved* his vibe. Except for that moment. Something was up, but she knew she couldn't get all "spooky" or weird on him. Maybe later, but probably tomorrow. If she could manage to wait to ask him, "What's going on?" She never had a lot of patience when it came to waiting for something. But when her "sensors" were ignited, there was little that could stop her. *Maybe the glass of wine will help*, she thought to herself.

There was lots of chatter. Their excitement was contagious, and their conversation grew to a dull roar. Elle was the first to cover her mouth with her hand. "Ssshhh. We're bothering the other guests." She looked over at an old gent with a sour look on his face. Then she broke into a smile and gave him a toodle-oo kind of wave. His head jerked back, but then he grinned. "Looks like the old gal's still got it," she remarked with pride. That, too, created a bit of hilarity.

When the laughter eased, they discussed what was on the agenda. Elle said they should have breakfast at the hotel restaurant or order room service, then plan to take a stroll around the neighborhood. The gallery opening started at six, so they should leave the hotel around five forty-five. Elle went on to tell them about dinner at the Tribeca Grill after the showing. "I am going to meet Camille for brunch on Sunday at Penelope on Lexington Avenue. It's a few blocks from Camille and Chad's town house." She took a breath. "Then, after brunch, I want to stop at MoMA." Elle added, "Y'all are on your own, unless you want to meet me at the museum."

Chi-Chi offered, "Why don't we play it by ear? We have a lot on our agenda for the next twenty-four hours." Chi-Chi hoped she and Cullen would have a little alone time together. Maybe take a walk on the High Line. Something. But just the two of them. She gave Cullen a look she hoped would get the message across. He tried to stifle a smile. Mission accomplished.

Luna immediately tuned into what Ch-Chi was suggesting. She, too, would like to spend Sunday with her romantic interest. Alone. Anywhere. Just the two of them. She looked over at Chris and casually asked, "Anything you'd like to do?"

"Brunch sounds good." He figured he was in the city that practically invented Sunday brunch, so why not do it?

"Brunch?" Luna was expecting something like Chelsea Piers, where you could play sports.

Chris smirked. "Do you not think I'm refined enough for a Sunday brunch in New York City?"

Luna snorted. "Sorry. My bad. I forgot you went to school here."

"Speaking of which, I am meeting one of my former professors tomorrow at noon. I should be back in plenty of time to clean up my act before the gallery opening."

There was something in his voice that made Luna think the meeting had to do with whatever was on his mind. She had to push. Just a little. "Oh? Anything special?"

Chris could tell—she knew. No point in lying. "An old case we discussed during my first year."

"Anything interesting?" Luna couldn't help herself.

"I don't know yet. That's why I'm meeting with him." *Okay, so it was a little bit of a lie.*

Luna wasn't satisfied, but she didn't want to risk pushing too hard. *It's not easy being me.* She chuckled to herself. "Okay. Sunday brunch. I'll let you decide." The lack of an invitation to Chi-Chi and Cullen was not lost on anyone. Chi-Chi and Cullen were grateful they hadn't been put in the position to say no, for they did not want to have to say yes.

By the time they finished their cocktails, everyone was ready to hit the sheets. On their way to the elevators, Luna decided to be a bit cheeky. Maybe that would get Chris to spill whatever it was that was on his mind. She threaded her arm through his and leaned into him. "So, did ya miss me?"

Chris was taken aback. It wasn't the overt attention that rattled him, but her attempt to soften him up. He realized she knew something was on his mind without his speaking a word about it. As much as it gave him the willies, he liked the feeling. Their mental connection was a kind of intimacy that had nothing to do with sex. "Like missing a migraine." He bumped her in response.

"Such a sweet talker." Luna knew it wouldn't take much prodding and prying to get him to spill. When it came to his work, he was all business. As tough as it was, Luna knew she had to be patient. This was a big adventure for all of them, and she didn't want to ruin it by pushing the wrong buttons. When they arrived at their rooms, everyone gave one another hugs. They decided to order room service for breakfast and placed their order for the next morning.

Once they were in their shared room and behind closed doors, Luna was the first to speak to Chi-Chi. "You want to spend Sunday with Cullen, don't you?" The question wasn't accusatory. It was a confirmation.

Chi-Chi blinked several times before answering. "Well, yes. Of course I do. But I don't know what is expected of us. And I do not want to be rude."

"I totally get it. Me either. But even if Elle has plans for Sunday, there's no reason why you and Cullen can't do your own thing." She raised her eyebrows. "And the good marshal and I can do ours."

Chi-Chi gave her an affectionate slap on the thigh. "Don't you be thinking naughty thoughts."

"Oh? Me? Why would you say that unless *you* are thinking naughty thoughts?" Luna teased.

Chi-Chi giggled. She knew she was blushing.

They unpacked and placed their order for an eight a.m. breakfast. It wasn't long before they were both fast asleep.

Across the hall was a different scenario. Cullen and Chris were gabbing about baseball and tuned in to watch the thirteenth inning of a Yankee game. "I wonder if they take bets on how many innings the game will last?" Cullen mused, referring to the many extra innings the team played during the regular season.

"You know people will bet on anything," Chris replied.

Cullen stretched and yawned. "I think it's time I got some sleep. I was up at five to make sure everything was in order."

Chris turned off the TV, got into his bed and placed his hands behind his head. "I'm sure you were." He gave a little chuckle. "Good night."

Chapter Eight

The Big Day

New York City
Saturday

Luna was the first one up at six thirty. Chi-Chi was still sound asleep. Luna was glad to see her allowing herself some well-deserved rest.

Chi-Chi had been working until eleven almost every night for the past several weeks. Even with an apprentice, she was still the one who actually made the jewelry. At least she didn't have to polish the stones or prepare the silver and could concentrate on the artful part of the process. Nonetheless, she still enjoyed the art from beginning to end. It reminded her of when she was a little girl learning metallurgy by watching her father craft silver ceremonial bowls when they lived in Kano, Nigeria.

There was a soft knock on the door. Luna checked the digital clock next to the bed. It was just before seven a.m. and breakfast wasn't due for another hour. She climbed out of the plush linens, padded toward the door and peered through the peephole. It was Chris. She was surprised to see him. She quietly opened the door and stepped outside, taking care to avoid locking herself out.

"Good morning. What's up?" Luna was well aware her appearance wasn't quite what she would have preferred, but it wasn't the first time he'd seen her a little rumpled.

"Hey. I just wanted to say I was heading uptown and probably won't see you guys until just before we leave for the opening."

Luna threw back her long, loose hair. "Oh?"

Chris looked a little nervous. Luna's mind went wild. *Is he meeting up with an ex-girlfriend?* Why she was so insecure was beyond rational thought, but then again, when it came to men and relationships, everything could turn upside down in a New York minute.

"I'm meeting a former classmate." He hesitated, then realized he should be crystal clear. "Bob Brielle. We were actually roommates for a year. It's been a long time, so we're going to grab breakfast. Then I'm heading up to John Jay to bring my old professor lunch." He paused.

"And look at some old files," Luna finished for him.

Chris smiled. "I'll fill you in later. I just wanted to tell you to have a nice day and try to stay out of trouble." He put his hands on her shoulders and gave her a quick kiss on the lips.

She was taken by surprise. It was true that they'd displayed a lot of affection toward each other, and a little bit more, but for some reason she wasn't expecting too much of that on this trip. She was looking at it more like a field trip than a romantic getaway. But clearly romance was in the air after all.

"I shall do my best. Besides, Elle will be supervising my every move. And Chi-Chi, of course. I am sure you won't have to find bail money." She grinned.

He smiled, then gave her another kiss. This time it was a bit softer than the previous peck. Luna was satisfied. She

watched him casually stroll down the hall toward the elevators. She slipped back inside to find Chi-Chi sitting up in her
bed with her arms folded.

"A little nooky in the hallway?" Chi-Chi gave Luna a
raised brow.

"Ha. No, he just stopped by to say he won't be back until
later today and for me to stay out of trouble." She bounced
onto the bed next to Chi-Chi's. "As if." Luna chuckled.
"But . . ."

"Uh-oh. I know that tone." Chi-Chi looked at her sideways.

"There is something going on. I can't put my finger on it,
but under that rugged, handsome face is a puzzle."

"Men are always puzzling, *abiwá.*"

"You've got that right." Luna flipped over to her stomach
and propped herself up on her elbows. "No, I mean I can feel
that he isn't telling me something."

"But what could that be?" Chi-Chi was trying to keep
Luna from going off on some wild tangent.

"Well, duh, if I knew I wouldn't be fixating on it." She
twisted her mouth in the way she did when she was thinking.

Chi-Chi nodded her head. "This is true." She got out of
bed and proceeded to the bathroom, where she began brushing her teeth.

Luna wasn't going to be silenced by a mere toothbrush.
"Yeah, well, let's hope he tells me something by this evening.
Otherwise, I am going to be too distracted to enjoy myself."

Chi-Chi rinsed her mouth. "We are here to have fun. You
are not here to do your psychic thing."

"I can't help it. It's like a song that's stuck on one line. I
know it comes off as if I'm just being bossy or wacky, but I
get these messages and I can't just let it go." With that, she
began to sing the lyrics from the movie *Frozen* about letting
it go.

Chi-Chi threw a pillow at her. "Let it stop! Let it stop!" They fell over laughing.

"I think I'm going to wait to take my shower until after we get back from lunch. Wash off the street dust." Luna spun around and hopped off the bed. "I wonder if Elle's up. Maybe she'll want to have breakfast with us if she hasn't already." Before she had a chance to pick up the house phone, there was a knock on the door.

"Room service," a soft voice uttered from the hallway.

"Coming!" Luna went to the door and let the gentleman with the rolling cart into their room. "You wouldn't also be delivering to the room next door, would you?"

The man smiled. "Well, yes."

"Hang on a sec." Luna held up a finger and phoned Elle. She picked up on the second ring. "Good morning, sunshine!" Luna said happily.

"And good morning to you!" Elle returned the greeting.

"Room service is here and he's stopping by your room next. Do you want to join us? Like we do back home?"

"Lovely idea. But why don't you come to my room?"

Luna realized Elle's room would probably be even more posh than theirs. "Sounds good. Be right over." She asked the server to roll the cart next door and explained that she would follow in a minute or two. She signed the check and gave the gentleman a cash tip, which was much appreciated. As directed, the cart carrying stuffed French toast, poached eggs, fresh fruit and baked goods was wheeled to Elle's room.

Luna quickly pulled on a maxidress and a pair of sandals. Chi-Chi copied her casual wear and they followed their morning fare next door.

As Luna expected, Elle's room was larger than theirs, with a settee, a coffee table and side chairs. The gentleman pulled out the drop leaf of the cart, turning it into a dining table, and spread a white tablecloth on top of it. He placed the chairs around the table and began to reach under the cart for the food. He removed the metal covers from the plates and presented a superb breakfast. Elle thanked him and also gave him a cash tip after signing her bill. He bowed and thanked them profusely, backing his way out of the room.

"Looks yummy," Elle said as she sat down and took an inventory of the meal. "And I worry about my morning scone being fattening!"

Chi-Chi's even, melodious voice said with authority, "This is for us to enjoy. Not to count calories, fat grams, sodium or sugar." She bowed her head. "Let us be thankful for this bounty."

Luna, Elle and Chi-Chi held hands as Chi-Chi said a prayer in her native language. Elle and Luna followed with an "Amen."

The three women chatted about what they wanted to see and do that day, taking care not to overplan. They had to save their energy for a long and exciting night. Luna suggested taking a nap after they got back from scouring the neighborhood. Bobbed heads indicated agreement.

"We'll play it by ear, of course, but I have a feeling we're going to need to recharge our batteries. This city's pace is far faster than what we're used to," Elle remarked.

More chatter followed, including Cullen's plans for the day. "He said he wanted to meet with someone at Authentiques, and then go to Olde Good Things. Do a little research on the competition," Luna offered. Then she remembered the armoire sitting back in Buncombe County and started tapping her fingers on the table.

"What is it now?" Chi-Chi glanced over at her drumming friend.

"Just thinking about that piece that came in a few weeks ago. The one that had the word 'HELP!' carved into the wood on the inside."

Elle looked surprised. "Why are you thinking about it now?"

Luna flipped her palms open. "I. Don't. Know."

"Let us make a pact. We are not to think about what is waiting for us back at the center." Chi-Chi folded her arms across her chest.

Elle chimed in, "I totally agree." She and Chi-Chi both looked at Luna.

"Okay, okay." She put up her hands in surrender.

Chi-Chi unfolded her arms and held out her hand. Elle placed hers on top of Chi-Chi's, and Luna slowly put hers on top of Elle's. "There! It's official," Elle proclaimed.

When they finished their coffee, Chi-Chi and Luna went back to their room to get dressed and ready for their jaunt through SoHo and Tribeca. "Fifteen minutes!" Luna said as she closed Elle's door behind her.

The three met up in the hallway, each with a tote bag for collecting whatever goodies they might come across.

They walked north on Church Street, checking out some of the new, chic boutiques that were able to make a comeback after 9/11 and the pandemic. People in New York had fortitude, something Elle admired, which was why she was so fond of Luna and Chi-Chi. And Cullen.

After two hours of pounding the pavement, they stopped for a beverage at a small corner café. "So, what do you think? It's almost noon. Shall we grab a quick bite for lunch and then head back to the hotel?" Elle asked.

"Sounds good. I would like to get down to Trinity Church. Alexander Hamilton is buried in the churchyard there," Luna said.

"I thought you didn't like cemeteries. Too many voices talking to you." Chi-Chi let out a huge guffaw.

"You got that right." Luna elbowed her. "Seriously, for whatever reason, that's the one churchyard/graveyard that doesn't give me the heebie-jeebies. It's so old, the spirits are long gone. I don't understand why people visit graves. Their loved ones aren't buried in the ground. Their spirits live on.

In another dimension," Luna explained. "And they come through to send us messages and remind us of their love."

"Well said," Elle concurred. She'd had her own "visitation" with Richard the night of the art center opening. Then, when she sat with Luna a few days later, Luna described Elle's experience down to the scent of Richard's aftershave. After that, Elle didn't need any more convincing that Luna had a real gift.

"Shall we drop our things at the hotel, then head down? It's a ten-minute walk from there," Elle said.

"Sounds good to me." Luna was lugging a bag of essential oils and a variety of aromatherapy items she'd purchased. "I don't know why I didn't ask them to ship these home." She switched the tote to her other shoulder.

Elle stopped short. "Luna, you just gave me a brilliant idea! The next shop at the center should be someone who blends essential oils. Handmade aromatherapy! Why haven't I thought of this sooner?"

"I wish you had. My triceps are burning," Luna joked.

"I guess I need to check my peripheral art vision. So many things beyond the canvas or potter's wheel are artistically crafted. And I rarely think of them that way. Shame on me."

"Don't be too hard on yourself, Elle. I think you have done wonders for the artisan community. Expansion is good when the timing is right. Even expansion of the mind." Luna switched her bag on her shoulders again as they neared the hotel. The gray-vested porters swung open the massive brass-and-glass doors for them. As soon as they entered the lobby, Elle took in a large breath of air. "White tea and thyme."

"It does smell lovely in here." Chi-Chi had noticed the scent when they first arrived.

"The scent is in the air filtration system. I was thinking about doing that at the center, but I enjoy the aroma from the Flakey Tart!" Elle said.

"Yes, I agree. The Flakey Tart can make you fat by simply

inhaling," Chi-Chi said, echoing Elle's earlier concern about calorie consumption. "But I can see—or I should say smell— how scent might create a different ambience, depending on what you use."

"Another brilliant idea!" Elle was excited. "I can rotate different scents depending on what is happening. When the center's really active, I'll use lavender to calm people down."

"Please make sure you put the children's faces in front of the air vents," Chi-Chi teased, keeping a solemn expression. Kids seemed to be overly attracted to all the shiny objects in her shop.

"This has been a very enlightening trip so far and we haven't been here a full day," Elle exclaimed as they rode up in the elevator. Then they deposited their loot in their rooms and began their trek toward Trinity Church.

Chris's friend, Bob, was coming in from New Jersey, so they decided to meet on the West Side, which was also convenient for Chris. He took the A Train from Chambers Street to Columbus Circle, then walked a few blocks west to Birch Coffee, where they planned to meet. The men spent two hours sharing memories, catching up and showing off photos of their kids. It was near ten when Bob had to hurry back for one of his daughters' swim meets, which gave Chris time to kill before meeting up with his professor.

He decided to go back to Columbus Circle, cross over to Central Park and do some people watching. For Chris, it was as relaxing as it was educational. He would try to figure out what people were talking about from their body language and facial expressions. If not enlightening, it was entertaining. Just before noon, he went to Greek Kitchen and ordered spanakopita, hummus, baba ghanoush, pita and souvlaki to go. His mouth was watering as he inhaled the aroma of the food. It had been a long time since he'd feasted on this cuisine.

As Chris approached Professor Hasselberg's office, he spotted the older man busily moving piles of folders from one side of his desk to another. Chris laughed out loud. "This has not changed one bit in twenty years."

"I made them put it in my contract." Hasselberg chuckled. "No messing with my filing system." Then he pointed to a stack of books. "Look—on the other side. I have a computer."

"But do you ever use it?" Chris set the shopping bag of lunch munchies on the corner of a half-empty chair.

The professor lowered his voice. "I use it every single day. But don't let them know that. They'll have me updating, uploading, Zooming, Insta-facing, tick-clicking and who knows what else. I don't have time for all that. I really don't." He shook his head. "The older you get, the more persnickety you become about how you spend your time."

"I agree. Time is important. We need to learn to appreciate its value more often." Chris spotted the very current HP-All-In-One desktop computer. He tilted his head at the electronic device. "Then what do you use it for?"

"I use the internet." He winked. "And I use it to enter all of my notes." He placed his hand on an eighteen-inch-high mound of files. "Technology has accelerated in many ways. Clearly, many good ways. However, I believe also in unnecessary ways. Some have been hugely detrimental to our society. But don't get me started." He flapped his hands. "Come. I'm feeling a bit peckish. We can go eat in the cafeteria. This food looks too delicious to be balancing food and paper plates." He paused. "You *did* bring paper plates?"

Chris froze. It hadn't occurred to him to ask. "Well, no. No, I didn't. I didn't check the bag either."

"There are several new laws regarding paper products. They don't automatically give them out anymore unless requested, and many times you are on your own, or you have to purchase supplies from the restaurant."

Chris snorted. "Wow. Times have changed."

"Indeed they have." Hasselberg gestured for Chris to step back into the hallway and gave him a devilish grin. "But not to worry. We still have plates here."

They took less than an hour to devour the Mediterranean lunch, and then they were off to a large room with a dozen modules set up with computers. "Some of the older files are on a different server, so we often have to come in here to do research." The professor wheeled out a chair from under the desk and slid it toward Chris. "You take the throttle; I'll grab another chair."

The two men sat close together. Hasselberg leaned over Chris to type in his password. And off they went.

Chris placed the cursor in the search bar and typed "Chad Pierce Jr. 2003." The screen blinked, indicating it was looking for the file. Seconds later it appeared:

Chad Pierce, Jr.
RA-NS-NA-MNR

Chris remembered the codes they used back then. RA meant Returned Alive; NS meant No Suspects; NA meant No Arrests; MNR meant Money Never Recovered. He turned to the professor and then turned back to the screen and read the report:

Subject Chad Pierce Jr. was abducted from his dorm room at Briarcliff Academy at approximately 3:00 a.m. Abductors were wearing ski masks. He thinks he may have been drugged. Woke up later in the back of a delivery van, taken to a motel. Family was contacted to deliver $1 million in small bills to a drop point in Colts Neck, New Jersey. Shed on outlying portion of parcel known as Saker's Farm on Route 71. One hour after drop, Chad Pierce Sr. went to Newman Springs Road, where his son was walking on the side of the road. Pierce Jr. said the van stopped about a half mile away, told him to get out and walk. No bodily injury was mentioned. No other information is available at this time.

"Wow." Chris turned and looked at the professor. "So, somebody got away with a million dollars?"

"Was the kid hurt?" Professor Hasselberg asked.

"Not according to this," Chris said, pointing at the screen. "Do we know what happened to the kid after he got home?"

Chris pulled a yellow pad out from his messenger bag. There was no time to power up his tablet. Quick notes would be sufficient. "No. The family has a lot of money, and they were able to keep it under wraps. This happened twenty years ago, before everyone had access to every minuscule piece of information. Benign or otherwise. One of the many charms of Luna is that she is so *not* plugged into social media." He scoffed. "Maybe that's because she's psychic."

The professor gave him a sideways look. "You and metaphysics. An interesting combination."

"Yes, but there is a connection. Out there. For example, a gut feeling. What is it, exactly? Where does it come from?" He shrugged.

"I cannot tell you the answer to that question. I suppose the point is that there is something. We simply haven't been able to quantify it and put a scientific label on it. The word 'parapsychology' is getting a bit more legitimized, but I still think we are a long way away from understanding most of it."

"Anyway, back to the son."

"Yes, well, all I know is that he is married to a woman who comes from money, and he works as a loan officer in the commercial loans department at Metropolitan Savings and Loan. Photos of him and his wife have appeared in the Arts sections of the *New York Times*, and sometimes the *New York Post*, I'm afraid. The wife likes to party, as they say."

"And the parents? Camille and Chad Sr.?"

"They do a lot of fundraising. Well, Camille usually chairs the functions. Chad hits up his clients to buy tickets." He chuckled. "Actually, Chad runs free seminars for people who need financial help. Not necessarily handing out money, but helping them navigate their way through the pitfalls of the economy, jobs, kids, etc. Most middle-income families can't afford a financial adviser, so he does a three-hour, bullet-point session with them."

"Sounds like a nice family," Chris said thoughtfully.

"They are. Or so it seems." The professor slapped Chris on the back. "And things are seldom what they seem."

Chris wasn't sure why, but he got a bit of a chilly sensation from the professor's words.

Satisfied he had enough information, Chris thanked the professor profusely. He didn't know what he would do with this newfound material. Probably nothing. But, then again, maybe something. *Just a gut feeling. Yeah, right.*

By four, everyone had showered, and most had taken a nap.

"I don't know what's more fun, getting ready or the thing itself," Luna said as she applied foundation, something she did on a limited basis. But tonight she was in New York City, going to an art opening in SoHo, with the extra bonus of being there with her big crush. She let the foundation sit for a few minutes and asked Chi-Chi for some eye shadow suggestions. Should she keep the green theme or go more natural? Luna laughed. "This is the hardest decision I've had to make in a while!" They decided to go with soft browns and green eyeliner. Elegant and artsy enough.

For Chi-Chi, getting ready was a ritual, something she had grown accustomed to as a young girl. For this event, she chose a one-shoulder, cobalt-blue, body-conscious dress. It had a wide, sheer scarf tied to the shoulder strap, and an artfully folded *gele* head wrap to match. She was conscious of her height. She was five foot eight, only two inches shorter than Cullen, and decided on a pair of flat silver sandals. She wore chunky, sodalite earrings and a matching bracelet. She looked stunning.

Luna decided on a lime-green theme with a midcalf, sleeveless, V-neck silk sheath. It flowed beautifully down her petite, five foot four frame. She hadn't worn high heels in years and she wasn't about to go back to that torture, so she chose low, multicolored kitten-heel slides with lime-green accents. Chi-Chi helped with her hair and went for a low, side ponytail draped over one shoulder and held together with a Silver & Stone hair clip with pieces of citrine. A simple matching necklace and bracelet finished the look. She could have doubled for a famous actress at a red-carpet event.

These women were ready for a party. A very posh party.

Around five thirty, phones stated ringing as they called one another.

"Ready?"

"Ready!"

Like a well-rehearsed play, all three hotel room doors opened at the same time, revealing five dapper, stunning, gorgeous people. Gasps of delight and compliments filled the hallway, everyone careful not to kiss anyone so as not to mess up their makeup.

"Air kisses!" Elle proclaimed.

The ensemble loaded themselves in the elevator and got off in the lobby, where a driver from a car service awaited. The concierge approached Elle. "Ms. Stillwell?"

"Yes. Hello."

"Mrs. Pierce sent a car to take you to the gallery."

"What a lovely surprise." Elle motioned to the others. "Shall we?"

It was a Suburban van with retractable steps. Chi-Chi was

relieved she wouldn't have to try to climb into the vehicle in her very tight dress. Luna hoped she wouldn't get her heel caught in the step, and Elle was grateful there was an assist when dressed in an elegant, white silk pantsuit. It was almost the same color as her chin-length hair but without the black streak. She also wore one of Chi-Chi's creations, a string of onyx stones set in a silver lariat chain.

The men looked as if they had spent the afternoon perusing the pages of *GQ*, neither letting on that it was Luna who had helped them decide on their attire. Her little private joke.

The five of them could have been going to a photo shoot. In some ways they were. Surely there would be cameras, plus everyone's phones. When they arrived, heads turned as Chi-Chi stepped out of the vehicle. She looked so regal . . . so much like a queen. Luna stepped out next, the more diminutive princess. Simple. Elegant. Elle complemented them with her white hair and flowing white pantsuit. She floated like a cloud dotted with pieces of onyx.

Luna was all atwitter. She felt as if she was going to the prom with the high school star athlete and debate champion. She wasn't far from wrong. It was simply a different venue. And several years later.

Camille greeted them inside the entrance to the gallery space. "Elle! Oh my goodness! Let me look at you!" She gasped when she realized they had identical haircuts, except Camille had a platinum streak in her light brown hair.

Elle fluffed Camille's hair. "Well, look at us!" They did a shoulder brush hug so as not to ruin their makeup. Air kisses as well. Some women didn't wear makeup, or care to, but some approached it as an art. Perhaps that was why they were called "makeup artists." Even ancient Egyptians were known for their extreme eyeliner, worn as a symbol of wealth and to please the gods. In this case, it was the goddesses.

The typical hugs and handshakes were exchanged during reception line protocol. There was lots of gaiety as each member of the group was introduced to Chad Sr. and J.R. Lindsay was gabbing in a corner somewhere with one of her gal pals.

Luna was still in the giddy stage until she came to J.R. There was something about him that gave her an uncomfortable feeling. Not creepy, but not quite right either. She decided to tuck away that vibe in her imaginary, or rather invisible, psychic pocket. She knew it wouldn't take long for the vibe to start trying to wiggle out, so she distracted herself with the exhibit.

Elle was enthralled with the quality and diversity of the pieces displayed on the movable walls. Large panels on wheels separated each exhibit in a way that kept an open-space look and feel but provided privacy so the artists could speak to the guests as the music of John Coltrane played softly in the background. It was the epitome of a gallery opening in SoHo. A mixture of beautiful people and grunge.

Luna spotted J.R. talking to someone across the room. The conversation did not look friendly. She could tell by his body language that he was tense. His fists were clenched. She decided to make her way in their direction. Time for some small talk.

J.R. could barely keep his voice down. "What in the hell are you doing here?"

"Oh, excuse me. I thought this event was open to the public." Hank put his hand on his chest in a mocking fashion.

"Listen, we agreed. Once you got your cash, you would disappear."

"Huh. I don't remember agreeing to that. All I remember is that you said it was a loan I didn't have to pay back." Hank looked like a slimy greaseball with his hair slicked back. J.R. was sure it wasn't from any haircare product. He was still surprised at how much Hank had changed. Then again, so had he.

As Luna approached the two men, she felt a zap of tension between them. This was going to be juicy.

"Hey, J.R.. I'm Luna—we met briefly earlier."

"Yes, Luna. Elle's friend." J.R. wondered whether or not he should introduce the reprobate to her, but before he had a chance to say anything, Hank interrupted.

"Hey there, pretty lady. I'm Henry Johnson, but most people call me Hank."

Luna blinked several times in response. *Pretty lady?* Were men still allowed to speak like that? "Oh, thank you, er, Hank. I'm Luna Bodman. I'm here with Elle Stillwell, a friend of J.R.'s mother."

"Kinda like a reunion, huh? Well, fancy that." He jerked his thumb at J.R. "He and I are having a kind of reunion, too."

"Oh?" Luna's electromagnetic field was on high alert.

"Yep. We both attended Briarcliff Academy."

Luna thought her hair was going to stand on end. She took a short breath. "Briarcliff?"

J.R. wanted to hurry the conversation along. "Yes, in Massachusetts."

Luna imagined a bright white light surrounding her body. Otherwise, she thought she would faint right there on the spot. "Classmates?" she managed to ask.

"I guess you could sorta say that," Hank replied.

Luna could feel J.R.'s uneasiness. "I'm sorry if I interrupted your conversation."

"No. Not at all. I was just about to tell Hank I have to fetch Lindsay before she drinks all the Veuve Clicquot." He took Luna's arm and steered her away from the menace. He had to shrug off his anxiety. Hank's appearance was not what he'd expected, but he wasn't going to let anything ruin this event for his mother.

Luna couldn't help but remark, "How long has it been?"

"Since?" J.R. asked.

"Since you and Hank have seen each other." Luna was determined to get to the bottom of the situation, but she had to be careful.

"Years. Twenty, I think. He dropped by my office the other day for a few minutes, but we didn't have much time to talk."

"So you invited him here?" Luna thought they were an odd fit. Hank didn't seem very educated, and also didn't seem to care that he didn't fit in. He was crass, if she needed a one-word description.

"It was one of those situations where you can't avoid it." J.R. wasn't totally lying.

"I know what you mean." Luna reached for a glass of champagne. "I imagine you come to these types of things often."

"Only if my mother makes me." He snickered. He felt a sense of relief now that he was twenty-five feet away from the extortionist.

Lindsay sashayed over to them. "Mother makes you do what, honey bunch?" Lindsay put her arm through his, claiming her territory.

J.R. chuckled. "Come to these things."

"Don't believe him. He *loves, loves, loves* the attention." Spoken like a true bubblehead.

Luna could understand why J.R. would attract attention. He was a very handsome man. And so was Marshal Gaines, but in a different way. Chris had inherited his mother's black hair and his father's azure-colored eyes. He had a slightly exotic look. Rugged. On the other hand, J.R. was a fair-haired, Anglo male who played a lot of tennis.

Luna tried to make conversation, but she was too worked up to stay still. She had to let Cullen know about Briarcliff. She craned her neck, trying to look above all the dazzling heads. Chi-Chi was a bright blue beacon who stood out from the crowd. Cullen was at her side. Luna tried to give him a ladylike wave, but what she wanted to do was jump up and down and shout, *Briarcliff!*

After hastily excusing herself, Luna scurried over as fast as she could make her way through the servers passing hors d'oeuvres, guests, movable walls, easels and pottery. "Cullen, you are not going to believe this." She was breathless. She looked over both her shoulders, searching for the two men, but didn't see them anywhere nearby.

"Take it easy. What are you so excited about?" Cullen asked.

"Briarcliff Academy."

"What about it?"

"J.R. went to school there!" Luna could hardly keep her voice down.

Cullen jerked his head. "Seriously? How do you know that?"

"He was talking to some guy, and I walked over to them. I sensed this vibe, and, well, you know what comes next."

Cullen rolled his eyes.

"I walked over and reintroduced myself to J.R., and his friend said they went to school together at Briarcliff Academy. And, yes, before you even ask, it's in Massachusetts."

"Wow." Cullen was dumbfounded.

"What are the odds?"

"I wouldn't venture to guess."

"Do you think we should tell him about the armoire?"

Cullen hesitated. "I don't know. What would we say? 'Hey, you ever heard of someone getting locked in an armoire and carving 'HELP!' into the wood?' That would be a very strange conversation starter."

Luna twisted her mouth.

"Uh-oh. She has that look on her face," Chi-Chi said, her eyes opened wide.

"Oh no, you don't," Cullen commanded. "We will not bring up anything outside of the reason why we are here."

"How do you know the armoire *isn't* the reason we are here?" Luna raised her eyebrows.

"You're killing me." Cullen groaned. "How about this— I'll mention I recently acquired a piece from Briarcliff and go off on a furniture tangent."

"Sounds boring," Luna said.

"Okay. I'll mention the armoire, but not the message. It could have been a prank or a hoax. I don't want to make something out of nothing."

"Party pooper." She turned and went to fetch Chris.

Chi-Chi looked at Cullen. "You know your sister is not going to let this go until she is satisfied."

"I know. I know." Cullen hung his head.

"Come. Let's look at some art." She took his hand and cleared a path through the throng. It was as if she parted the sea.

On her way toward Chris, Luna spotted J.R. talking to Hank again. J.R. was staring him down. She wished she knew how to read lips. J.R. looked stern. Hank gave him a crooked smile and moved toward the exit. J.R. froze in place, watching every step Hank took until he left the building. Luna saw J.R.'s shoulders relax once the intruder was gone. Something was definitely up between those two. And it wasn't an old reunion of school chums, unless you were referring to the type of chum that was bait.

Luna caught up with Chris and snuggled close to him. "I have to tell you an interesting coincidence."

Chris's knees almost wobbled at the word. Hadn't he been discussing the phenomenon of coincidence just the night before? "Another one?"

"What do you mean, another one?"

"You notice them on a daily basis, don't you?"

"This one is very interesting."

"Aren't they all? Until *you* figure out the connection?"

"True. But listen. A couple of weeks ago, Cullen got an armoire delivered. It was pretty dilapidated. I got a vibe from it and climbed inside."

Chris's eyes were smiling at her childlike explanation.

"But then I couldn't get out!" she exclaimed. "Thank goodness Wylie was wandering back from the dog park and started sniffing the armoire. When I heard him, I told him to go get Cullen!"

"And he did," Chris replied with certainty.

"Yes, he did." Luna nodded. "But before I got sprung, I felt something in the wood. It was rough and it gave me the willies. So, after I almost fell on the floor, I asked Cullen to grab a flashlight and I made a rubbing. You are not going to believe what it was!"

"You know I will." Chris was standing in front of Luna. She had her back to the wall. He placed his arm above her shoulder and leaned in. She could feel his breath against her cheek. She froze. What she wanted to do in the moment was nuzzle his neck.

He could feel the heat coming from her. "Go on."

She wasn't sure she could. She took a swallow of champagne. "There was a word. Carved into the wood. 'HELP!' " She looked deep into his eyes.

Now it was his turn to steady himself. Again. "You said it was a coincidence." He managed to hold his composure.

"Yes. We tracked down the origin of the piece. It came from Briarcliff Academy."

That almost did him in. "Briarcliff Academy?"

Luna was getting something from Chris. A shift in his energy. Like the night before. "What is it?"

"What is what?"

"Please don't play that game with me." Luna's expression became serious. "Something has been on your mind since we got here." She softened her look. "Sorry. It's my radar."

He lifted her chin. "Don't apologize. I don't want any secrets between us. Okay?"

Luna was overjoyed that he had finally expressed something that could help define their relationship. Trust. A big thing.

"Okay. Me neither. So? What is it?"

"What I mean is, there are some things I can't talk about because they're official business."

"I'm official. Sometimes." She made a pouty mouth.

He smiled. "That's true. But not necessarily tonight. Okay?" He brushed her cheek with his thumb. "I promise I will tell you what I can when I can."

Luna filled her lungs with air. "Pinkie swear?"

He held up his other hand. "Pinkie swear."

The next couple of hours moved quickly. Camille received many accolades for the opportunities and support she'd provided to the female artists, and the women in turn received high praise for being brave enough to put their souls on display.

Those in Camille's dinner party took different cars to the restaurant. A table for twelve was set in the rear of the main dining room, which boasted the old mahogany bar from the famed Maxwell's Plum. The walls were covered in art by actor Robert De Niro's father, Robert Sr. There were place cards on each plate. Camille was seated at one end of the table, Chad at the other. She'd tried to mix up the group in order to foster lively conversation.

Platters of appetizers lined the long, wooden table, including a charcuterie board, assorted cheeses and salmon rillettes. A server came around the table with a bottle of red and a bottle of white wine. Camille didn't want to lollygag with cocktails, so she had ordered the wine ahead of time. Actually, Keith had ordered the wine. Camille appreciated everything Keith had helped her accomplish and had invited him to attend the dinner.

"Had I known, I would have ordered a more expensive vintage!" he'd exclaimed.

She adored his sassiness.

Once everyone's glass was filled, Chad stood. "To Camille. The bravest, most loyal, most compassionate woman I have had the privilege and pleasure to know."

Lots of clinking glasses and words of praise resounded.

"Hear! Hear!"

"Salud!"

"Bravo!"

Then Chad turned to Elle. "And to the woman whose keen perception helped to make it happen, Elle Stillwell."

More clinking and cheering. A conversation started about that auspicious night in Newport.

J.R. looked at his mother. Then he looked at his wife. They say men marry women like their mothers. He thought for several minutes. Family wealth was the only thing the two women had in common. Despite her affluence, J.R.'s mother was raised to be kind, considerate, thoughtful and generous in spirit as well as with her money. She was refined. Lindsay? True, she gave away a lot of things, but only after she no longer had any use for them. She had no outside interests to speak of and she did no volunteering whatsoever. It dawned on him that she suffered from what a lot of people suffered from: myopia, as in "my." *My* world. He could provide a list of reasons why he'd married her, and it had seemed like a good idea at the time. He realized his thoughts had seeped into the shadows since Henry "Hank" Johnson had reappeared. It occurred to him that he might be having feelings of guilt. Questioning his principles. How curious. He leaned back in his chair, observing the dinner guests chatting back and forth. Lindsay was touting the latest skin cream she'd purchased at Bergdorf Goodman earlier that afternoon after having lunch at Palette.

"You know, they specialize in plant-based food," she droned on.

J.R.'s thoughts meandered. *A new trend. Not a terrible one, but let's see how long it lasts. I wonder what she'll order for dinner tonight.*

"Do you have any vegan dishes?" Lindsay batted her eyelashes at the waiter, who appeared to be dazed and confused. The Tribeca Grill was not known for its veggie burgers. They weren't on the menu either.

"Madame, we have pasta," the server said.

"Is it gluten free?" Lindsey asked.

And there it is. J.R. sighed. *Yes, everyone knows you are hip to what is in vogue.*

The waiter replied, "We can accommodate you."

"Thank you. I need another minute." Lindsey stuck her head back behind her menu.

The waiter went around the table and took everyone else's order. He returned to Lindsay, who ultimately ordered the crab cake.

A crab is not a plant, J.R. mused. *She probably flunked biology.* He smirked to himself as Luna caught his eye. She grinned. She knew exactly what he was thinking.

As dinner was winding down, Luna became anxious as to when Cullen would bring up the armoire and Briarcliff. She began to give him what he referred to as "The LDS." It stood for "The Luna Death Stare." He could feel her eyes burning a hole in the back of his head. He turned slowly. Sure enough. *How does she do that?*

Her eyes widened. "And?"

He didn't have to ask what she was referring to.

"And now. Or I'll start the conversation," she half-threatened.

Cullen waited for a break in the conversation before he

leaned toward J.R. "Luna tells me you went to Briarcliff Academy."

"You know of it?" J.R. was feeling squeamish again.

"Not really, but I recently purchased an old armoire that came from there."

J.R. went pale. "Say again?" He thought maybe he was hearing things.

"Briarcliff."

J.R. cleared his throat. "You don't say. Now that it is a co-incidence." He hoped that would end the conversation. But it didn't.

Chris almost fell off his chair at the same time. That word "coincidence" brought Luna smack-dab into the middle of the conversation.

"Don't you find coincidences fascinating?" Luna was getting excited and began to rattle off a few quotes, including one by Einstein. That, too, made Chris extremely uneasy. He knew he would have to tell her. What he'd learned. But obviously later.

Luna was being cagey about the armoire. She felt J.R. had something to do with it, but this surely wasn't the time to bring it up directly. She had another idea. "Why don't you give me your business card and we'll send you a photo after Cullen turns it into a masterpiece?"

J.R. kept his cool. "Yeah. Sure. That would be interesting."

Luna wondered if he remembered carving the words into the wood. But maybe it wasn't him. Or maybe it was. She carefully took the card from J.R. and placed it deftly in her handbag.

Dinner wrapped up with an assortment of desserts, including the restaurant's famous chocolate cake, New York-style cheesecake and a Tahitian crème brûlée. Everyone bid the others adieu, promising to meet up the next day, whenever their agendas allowed. On the short ride back to the hotel,

Luna sat silently clutching her purse. Chris could tell she was concocting something in her head.

"Go on," he urged her. "Spit it out."

She looked at him. "What are you talking about?"

"What is going on in your head?" Chris encouraged her.

"I think you should dust this for fingerprints." She opened her purse and let him glance inside.

"You want me to dust his business card for fingerprints? Why?"

"Because I think he has something to do with that armoire."

Chris knew things were coming to a head. He would have to explain the kidnapping case to Luna so she wouldn't go off like a gun half-cocked. "Can we please talk about this later?"

"Yes, Marshal," she said smugly.

Within minutes they were back at the hotel. Ordinarily, they would stop for a nightcap, but it had been a long evening and they all had had their fair share of alcoholic beverages. When they reached their floor, Chris took out his key and hesitated. He was waiting for Chi-Chi and Cullen to say good night. But that would mean he wouldn't be able to have a private conversation with Luna. Then he thought about Elle. He wondered if she knew anything about the kidnapping. He thought she must, considering how close she was to Camille. He turned to Chi-Chi and Cullen and said, "I have to go over a few things with Elle and Luna." He looked at Elle, who had a very confused expression on her face. "Elle? Would you mind if we came into your room?"

"Not at all. Please." She gave Luna a questioning look.

Luna frowned slightly in response as Elle opened her hotel room door. They all said good night to Chi-Chi and Cullen before going inside.

Elle looked at Chris. "Is everything all right?"

Luna stood with her hands folded across her chest.

"Please. Sit down," Chris said and gestured. Elle took a seat on the divan, Luna in a side chair. "When you mentioned Camille's name, it rang a bell, but I couldn't remember why." He turned to Luna. "And you, Miss Smarty-Pants, kept bothering me about something bothering me. Well, here it is. Elle, do you remember when J.R. was abducted?"

Elle gasped. "What? When? What are you talking about?"

Chris closed his eyes. He'd honestly thought she would know. *Wrong approach. Hit the reset button.* "Obviously, I have inadvertently divulged some very personal and confidential information. I should never have assumed you knew about it, but you and Camille are such old and very close friends, I just thought . . ."

Elle was dumbfounded. "I don't know anything about any abduction." She looked for a tissue. "When did this happen?" Tears began to flow down her face.

"He's okay now," Chris reassured her. "It happened twenty years ago."

Luna was chomping at the bit. "I *knew* it. I *knew* it."

Elle dabbed her eyes as she moved toward the side bar. "Shall I make it three?" She held up a decanter.

"Yes, please," Luna answered.

"Yes. Thanks." Chris thought he could probably drink the whole bottle at this point.

Elle's hands were shaking, so Luna got up to help her. She took the bottle and poured each of them a drink. When they had settled back into their seats, Chris continued.

"It was my first year at John Jay. We were studying case files of kidnappings. Some had good resolutions, some horrific and some had none whatsoever. In J.R.'s case, there wasn't much in the file except a notation that the family paid a one-million-dollar ransom and J.R. was found walking on the side of a road in Colts Neck, New Jersey."

Elle was still in shock. "You say this happened twenty years ago?"

"Yes."

Elle thought back to when J.R. had spent time in Europe. "Was it here in the States?"

Luna couldn't hold back any longer. "Yes. In Briarcliff." Chris was almost glaring at her. She shrank down and looked up. "Sorry."

He brushed it off. "Yes, it was Briarcliff."

"And the armoire," Luna added.

"We don't know that for sure, Luna. Please do not add information that has not been corroborated."

"Then corroborate it, Marshal." Luna was impatient at this point.

"And how do you suggest I do that?" Chris asked.

Luna quickly pulled the business card out of her purse. "Dust it for prints. Then you can dust the armoire for prints."

Chris had to admit she had a good idea. "But what is that going to prove?"

"Well, for one thing, it will prove the armoire was involved in a crime. You are a law enforcement officer."

"Listen. According to the official report, J.R. had little information to offer. Two men in ski masks came into his room. The next thing he remembered was waking up in a van with something covering his head. They kept him in a bathroom at a motel for three days. Chad got the money and dropped it in a shed in Colts Neck. He was instructed to wait one hour and then go to the intersection of Newman Springs Road and Route 34. The perpetrators let J.R. out on the side of the road about a half mile west, and he walked to the gas station, where Chad picked him up."

Luna squinted. "And that's it?"

"That's it," Chris said.

"I don't think so," Luna disputed, while Elle sat in horror.

"I wonder why Camille never told me," Elle said sadly. "Why wouldn't she?"

"According to the file, they did not contact the authorities until after J.R. was released. The kidnappers were clear about that, but they usually are. No police. Therefore, no publicity. Perhaps the family felt it was something they should keep to themselves. That kind of trauma is very personal, and it stays with you forever. Even though things turned out all right for J.R., the pain stays deep within the cells of your body."

Luna smiled. He really understood the mind-body connection. Even though he might not readily admit it.

Elle winced. "What about Harrison? Was he involved?"

"I have no idea. The file didn't go into detail about any other family members involved, only that Chad withdrew the money and dropped it off."

"What should I do?" Elle asked.

"Nothing," Chris replied. "If Camille wanted you to know, she would have told you."

"But now I *do* know, and I don't know what to do with this information." She was tearing up again.

Luna put her arm around Elle. "Don't fret about it now. Everyone is safe. And it's probably a part of their history they'd prefer to forget."

Elle sighed. "I don't know what I am going to say to her tomorrow."

"Talk about anything else," Chris pleaded. "Please."

"Right." Elle sighed again. "I am certain we will have plenty to talk about tomorrow. Besides, I wouldn't want to rain on Camille's parade, and all her wonderful hospitality."

Chris walked over and put his arm around her, and it turned into a group hug. "That's our Elle."

They sat in silence for a while. Elle finally spoke. "Isn't life full of surprises?"

Luna looked at Chris. "Isn't it?"

"I think I'm going to turn in," Chris said. He was exhausted. Physically, mentally and probably spiritually, but he wasn't about to admit it. "Brunch tomorrow?" He looked at Luna.

It had momentarily skipped her mind. "Oh! Yes! Where are we going?"

"It's a surprise." Chris raised his eyebrows, kissed her on the forehead and said good night.

Luna decided to stay with Elle a little longer. She knew Elle still had to digest this very shocking information. Luna, in contrast, was not the least bit surprised by the revelation.

The two chatted about the gala and what fascinating works the women had on display. Luna was drawn to several pieces of modern sculpture with fluid lines. One piece in particular fascinated her. It was three feet high and looked like a large teardrop. The bottom half was a shade of teal that swirled upward into the white area on the top half. Luna sensed the transition the artist had made from being blue to coming into the light. She'd giggled when she read the artist's statement describing the exact sensation Luna had felt when she was near the sculpture. *Empathy.* "You know, Elle, I really like that sculptor, Marina Delgado. I think she might fit in well at Stillwell. What do you think?" she suggested.

"There were a couple I would consider, but that's a very involved conversation I would have to have with Camille."

"Well, maybe that's one way you can distract yourself from this horror story tomorrow," Luna urged. She could feel how upset Elle was, both with the news and the idea her friend hadn't trusted her with the information. She knew Camille had her reasons, but feelings were feelings, and Elle was feeling a bit sad in the moment.

Luna gave her another hug. "It's late, and I need to get my beauty sleep for my big date tomorrow." She pursed her lips.

"I wish I knew where we were going so I could figure out what to wear."

"Oh, love, you will look lovely no matter what you wear."

"Sunday brunch in New York. Do I try to look boho or chic?" Luna asked. Boho was her normal attire.

"I think you always manage to pull off both at once, my dear." Elle smiled for the first time in the past hour.

"I'll wear the black-and-white-polka-dot maxidress with a wide matching headband, black espadrilles and my black woven shoulder bag."

"See? Sounds lovely, chic and ooh-la-la." Elle walked Luna to the door. "Sweet dreams, my dear."

"You too, Elle. Thanks for being such a good friend and always sharing with us." With that, Luna gave Elle a bear hug.

Chapter Nine

Alone At Last

Sunday

Chris told Luna to be ready by ten thirty. Naturally, she could hardly wait and was ready by nine. "I think I'll give Alex a call and talk to Wylie," she said.

If it were anyone else, Chi-Chi would have thought this woman was out of her mind. Instead, she said, "I think that is a very good idea. You need a distraction." Chi-Chi reached over to the nightstand between their beds and tossed Luna's phone in her direction. "Say hello to the boys for me."

"How can you be so calm?" Luna knew Chi-Chi was in the same state of mind. Excited. Anxious.

"I am not calm. You only think I am calm." Chi-Chi gave Luna a big smile. "I think it is because I am taller and my head is held higher."

Luna furrowed her brow. "Interesting explanation." She turned around. "Do you have time to braid my hair?"

"Of course." Chi-Chi whipped Luna's hair into shape within three minutes. Luna looked absolutely charming and ready for Sunday brunch in New York.

Chi-Chi picked out a yellow kaftan, woven sandals and a straw bag. She, too, wore a large headband, with her braids wrapped through it. "Your brother did not tell me where we were going either."

"Must be a conspiracy." Luna checked her face in the mirror and applied a neutral shade of lipstick.

"He did tell me that we were not going to the same place as you."

"Yep. Conspiracy."

"Well, I think it is very sweet. Both men are trying to please us," Chi-Chi said.

Luna looked at Chi-Chi's reflection in the mirror. "We are lucky. We have two really decent guys."

"I agree." Chi-Chi nodded. "I think it is also because we refuse to settle." Chi-Chi took a seat. "Think about it. We are in our thirties. We are not married. But we could be. And we are not because we did not marry someone for the sake of being married."

"I used to think it was me. Something I was doing wrong," Luna said and then, in a whiny tone, "Why doesn't he like me? What's wrong with me?" She slipped the lipstick into her purse. "Then I realized I am me. I am loving. I am smart. I am kind. Loyal. Generous. And responsible. So if that's not enough, it's not my problem." She tossed her head from side to side.

"You and I are very different in many ways, yet at our core we are very much the same." Chi-Chi smiled.

"When I was in my twenties, I would fall in love in seconds. I thought that was what I was supposed to do. Then it was one failed relationship after another. I really should say one situation after another. Relationships are complicated. They require commitment. I think that's where the rubber met the road. When I wanted a commitment, they were not interested. Therefore no relationship." She squinted at Chi-Chi. "Know what I mean?"

"Maybe not exactly, but I think I know what you are trying to say."

"I must admit, I am so happy none of them worked out. I cannot imagine being with Lew now." She hooted. "They say things work out for the best, but I think things just work out and we move on. And moving on is the best thing we can do."

"You are very philosophical today, my friend," Chi-Chi noted.

"There's been a lot of sensory stimuli these past couple of days." She laughed. Not to mention the bombshell from Chris last night, about which she was sworn to secrecy. Luna jumped at the knock on the door and then took three long, deep breaths, centering herself. She calmly walked to the door.

"Good morning, Marshal Gaines. You look quite dapper today." He was wearing chino slacks, a white collared shirt and a navy cotton blazer with dark burgundy loafers.

"And you look fetching." He peered inside the room. "As do you, Chi-Chi."

"I don't suppose you are going to tell me where Cullen will be taking me today?" Chi-Chi asked.

"You suppose correctly." Chris winked. He turned to Luna and asked, "Shall we?"

"We shall." They strode arm in arm down the hallway toward the elevator. "This feels like a real date." She gave him a little nudge.

"It *is* a real date." He nudged her back.

When they got into the cab, he handed the driver a piece of paper with the address. The driver nodded in the rearview mirror. "Right, sir!" He drove east and got on the FDR Drive, heading uptown. A few miles later, he exited on East 61st, made the turn onto Grand Army Plaza and stopped in front of The Plaza Hotel.

"Oh my goodness," Luna said in a hushed voice. "Are we really going for tea at The Palm Court?"

Chris tapped her on the nose and chuckled. "I can't put anything past you, can I?"

"This is the pinnacle of refinement." Luna spoke with reverence. Not that the super-rich should be held in reverence, but the building itself had been a witness to so much history and culture. The Plaza Hotel was a story unto itself. The Palm Court had hosted more dignitaries, celebrities, socialites and criminals than all of its rivals over the hundred-plus years since it opened. It was the epitome of opulence. Every part of the space was a work of art, from the stained-glass ceiling light to the petits fours. "Let's not forget *Eloise* either." Luna was referring to the children's book about a young girl who lived at The Plaza. "Did you know the book was not initially intended for children? It was for pretentious grown-ups." Luna laughed. "At least that's according to the illustrator. I think that note may also be somewhere in the book."

"Luna, you never cease to amaze me."

"Nor you me." Luna's eyes lit up. She knew she had fallen for this guy. Big-time. He held out his hand to assist her in exiting the taxi. *Chivalrous too.*

They climbed the steps to the double-gilded doors that two uniformed men opened with a flourish. "Welcome to The Plaza Hotel," one of them said as a salutation.

"Thank you. Lovely to be here." Luna had been to many fancy hotels before, but this one was special. It, too, had its own fragrance, a blend of bergamot, grapefruit, leather and amber. It exuded an ambience of grace and style. She took in a long, smooth inhale of the sumptuous atmosphere. It was a symphony for the senses. Chris made a crook in his elbow, pulled Luna's arm through and guided her to the famous restaurant.

Luna relaxed into the comfortable chair, her gaze floating across the room. She could sense many faces, many stories. It struck her that it was important to get out of your routine and have a change of scenery. It was easy to lose your perspective on the rest of the world if you weren't exposed to something more than your own little bubble. Two glasses of champagne were brought to the table. "Oh, lovely!" Luna cooed. She also felt some kind of vibe going on. Now that her earlier feeling had been resolved, she had to unravel this one. Or maybe just let it go. She almost started laughing, thinking about when she had burst into song in front of Chi-Chi. She held back a giggle.

Chris looked at her. "What?"

"Oh, nothing. Really."

"It had to be something. Spill it, Luna Bodman." Chris used his stern, marshal voice.

"Just how I can be at times."

"Such as?" He leaned in.

"Like a dog with a sock in his mouth." She slowly twirled her glass. "I get hold of something and I can't let it go." She laughed again. "Chi-Chi and I were talking about that very thing, and I started to sing." She lowered her voice and croaked out the first two lines of the song.

Chris's eyes darted left and right, and he decided the only thing to do to shut her up was to kiss her. So he did. Lightly. On the lips, but not enough to draw attention to them.

Luna did a double blink. "Was that a compliment to my vocal forte?"

Chris wasn't sure how to answer that question without insulting her. "I am invoking my Fifth Amendment rights."

"Oh, you!" She gave him a playful slap on the arm.

He moved in closer. "I know there is no way on earth you can keep your nose out of this, Ms. Dog with Sock. Or should I say, set the sock free?"

"Ha. Ha."

"Tomorrow, I am going to Colts Neck. I want to check out the drop point of the kidnapping."

Luna almost sprang out of her chair. "Really?" Her eyes were bugging out. "Can I come? Please? Pretty please?"

"Listen. I have a plan. I am going to meet up with one of the deputy commissioners who oversees land development and has site plans. He is going to meet me, and we are going to the location. I am sure it's not at all the same as it was then, but I want to get an idea of proximity."

"Well, I'll be darned." She rested her elbow on the table, and then her chin on her hand. "You are really taking me seriously this time, eh? I am flattered."

"Oh, come on, Luna. I've taken you seriously many times. I just don't say it enough. But blame it on my gender. We're dumbasses, for the most part."

Luna began to giggle. "You won't get an argument out of me."

"From what Ross told me, it was an old farm that lay fallow for about thirty years. I don't know if any of the buildings are still there, but it's worth the drive. I have a feeling about this, too."

Luna looked at him thoughtfully. "You know how I often say the universe puts us in situations that we would not normally have considered or thought of?"

"As in a coincidence?" He had a twinkle in his eye.

"That could be the very definition, but we just don't know. And it's nice to still be able to speculate. Wonder. Let our imagination run free. Aside from the natural wonders of the earth, everything has been born from someone's imagination." She swayed a little in her seat. "Well, I think you were 'sent' here to solve that case. You studied it your first year in college?" She tilted her head. "What are the odds?"

"Ah, the famous Lunatic query." He took her hand. "Now, this is what I need you and Cullen to do."

Luna leaned in closer and used her Natasha voice. "Zo, vot ve do with moose and squirrel?"

"Geez!" Chris burst out laughing, turning a few heads. He nodded at the gawkers and mouthed *sorry* before continuing. "Tomorrow, you and Cullen take Amtrak to Westwood, Route 128. It's over three hours there and back, but I really need you to do this. If you jump on the eight a.m. train, you'll be there around nine thirty. Spend two hours, tops, at the school. What I need is for Cullen to authenticate the piece of furniture. Not that I'm saying it will matter one way or another, but the more information we can gather, the closer we could be to solving this case."

Luna could do nothing but bat her eyes at him. "We're really doing this together."

"Yes, and it's off duty until I have some facts. Evidence. Something."

"Wow." She sat up straight. "If everything runs smoothly, we should be back in time to meet up for dinner and compare notes."

He placed his hand on top of hers. "Are you sure you don't want to join the US Marshals Office?"

"Ha. As if." Luna laughed. "Oh, but maybe you and I could start our own detective agency."

"Hang on there, cowgirl. Let's get through this mission first. Deal?" He held up his glass of champagne.

"Deal!" They clinked glasses.

Around two hours later, they decided to take a walk in Central Park. Depending on who you talked to, Central Park was a terrible or a wonderful place. For a long time, there were muggings, rapes and a couple of murders. But the city buckled down with a greater police presence and added cameras everywhere. Now, if you were to commit a crime, chances were it would be caught on camera.

Luna and Chris crossed Central Park South and decided to walk up Fifth Avenue, where artists sat with easels, hoping someone would sit for their portrait. Only twenty dollars!

There were women selling handmade jewelry, straw hats and a cart of "gently used" books. The avenue resembled an orderly ministreet fair, with plenty of room for passersby. All of the vendors had licenses, which made them legit. Luna and Chris walked arm in arm, commenting on the vast array of wares, hopes and dreams. A young man with an electric cello played soft classical music. It was a civilized slice of the Big Apple. Albeit a very small slice.

They moved on to the park entrance at 66th Street near the zoo. It took no cajoling for Luna to agree to visit the animals. They were just in time to watch the sea lions get fed. When it came to animals, Luna was almost childlike. She would say she could dial into their frequency, and there was some scientific data that supported an innate connection between children and animals. But as people aged, they became less tuned in to their intuition, the many frequencies like a radio receiver. They got distracted, and too easily. Chris gazed at his extraordinary friend as she squatted down to look into the animals' eyes. "Dr. Doolittle?" he said and smiled.

"At your service." She began to stand and saluted. "Aren't they beautiful?" she said with deep respect and awe as Chris helped her up. Not that she needed any aid.

Chris wondered if that was what kept them from moving their relationship further along. Did she *need* him in her life? He tightened his lips. It was something to seriously think about.

Luna looked up at him. "Everything okay?"

"Yes. Of course. Couldn't be better." He put his arm around her shoulders and gave her a friendly hug.

"And we're on a caper together." Luna lowered her voice, pretending it was top secret. In some ways it could be. She didn't know if their efforts to solve this kidnapping would have any ramifications in terms of Chris's job. Was it okay for him to work on a case on his own?

"Please do not invoke Boris and Natasha again. I beg you."

"Party pooper."

"I think you called me that yesterday." He grimaced.

"If not yesterday, certainly once—or many—times before," she teased.

They spent a good part of the next hour visiting the rest of the zoo before walking back toward the Grand Army Plaza exit. It was almost three.

"This has been such a lovely day." Luna looked up at the few light, puffy clouds hanging in the bright, blue sky.

"Shall we head back to the hotel or do you want to do more sightseeing?"

"We're not far from St. Patrick's Cathedral. I'd like to stop in and say hello to a few of my favorite saints."

"Ah, would one be St. Francis?" Chris knew the patron saint of animals was at the top of her list.

"Yes, and St. Jude. I think we can all use a little help."

They walked arm in arm the ten blocks down Fifth Avenue to the famous church. Chris stayed close behind as Luna made her way to the far north wall, where the sanctuary for St. Jude was located. Rows and rows of candles on brass racks flanked the haven of the saint of lost causes. Luna preferred to think of him as a spiritual vitamin.

She reached into the box of fresh candles and pulled out five of the votives. Chris watched as she placed each in a red glass holder, took a stick from the container and lit the candles. She said a silent prayer and moved away to allow others seeking solace to make their offerings. She motioned for Chris to sit with her in one of the empty pews. "Just for a couple of minutes."

Chris gave her a smile and a nod. Luna slid in first and Chris followed. They sat in silence for a while. It was peaceful. Solace in the busiest city in the country. Probably the world. But these days, it was hard to tell. There was just too much going on everywhere. Plain and simple. This bit of calm was the icing on the cake of a delicious experience. No pun intended. Afternoon tea had been scrumptious. Eventually, Luna motioned that it was time to leave. They moved silently through the crowd and back onto the sidewalk. They were right across the street from Rockefeller Center and moved in that direction.

"One more iconic site?" Chris suggested.

"Absolutely." Luna realized she had slowed her pace after her moments of spiritual engagement. New York was a fast city. No doubt about it; it even outpaced her fiery energy.

They walked down the beautifully landscaped Promenade toward the famous rink, which was currently being used for roller staking. No matter how many times you saw it, the statue of Prometheus overlooking the plaza was impressive. They stopped at Del Frisco's Grille for an afternoon beverage, sitting outside under a large market umbrella.

"I think I have had the definitive New York experience." Luna sipped a glass of champagne. "It was very special." She leaned over and pecked Chris on the cheek.

"Luna, there is something I wanted to talk to you about."

Her facial expression changed. *Uh-oh. Here it comes. He's breaking up with me. Just like the time Michael made a fabulous dinner, opened a great bottle of wine, only to tell me he was moving in with someone named Micelle. They think it softens the blow.*

"You okay?" Chris was perplexed.

"Yes, sorry. What did you want to talk to me about?" She tried not to wince. *Why, oh why, was she so insecure?*

He took her hand. "We've been seeing each other for a while. I know it hasn't been ideal."

She didn't respond.

"I have a grueling schedule, and it's important for me to spend time with Carter. He's a teenager now and he could go in any direction. I want to make sure he gets some stability from me."

Luna placed her hand on his. "I know. I totally get it."

"It's really not fair to you for me to be almost three hours away, with a wacky schedule."

She lifted her glass with her other hand and began to take a sip to soften the blow she anticipated was coming.

"And it's not really fair for me to ask, but do you think we could go steady?" he said sheepishly.

The champagne hit the back of Luna's throat and went up and out of her nose. She pulled her hand away from Chris and covered her mouth as champagne dripped from her nose and on to her lips. From that point, she went into a fit of laughter. Laughter from her silly thoughts, and then from making a total dingbat of herself by spewing Moët & Chandon Rosé on herself and the table.

Chris was totally amused. *That's my Luna. I hope.*

She leaned against the back of her chair, checking the reaction of the other patrons. That would be two for two for her. In one day. Two spectacles. She regained her composure. "Steady?" She cocked her head. "Interesting. How does one define that in today's culture?"

Avoiding the word "commitment," Chris explained his position. "I'm on the edge of forty. I still have a few good decades ahead of me. I have a good job, and a great kid. What I don't have is time to date. Until I met you, having any kind of relationship with a woman wasn't even on my radar. But then you showed up in my search party." Chris took a deep breath. "What I'm trying to say is I really like you. You're smart, funny and easy to be with. Most of the time." He stopped to smile. "I like what we have, and I don't want to lose it. I realize what I'm asking is really at the high end of the selfish bar, but I don't want to think about you dating someone else."

Luna thought she would pee in her pants. Her entire body was vibrating. She didn't want to ruin the moment, but she had to dash to the ladies' room unless she wanted to embarrass herself . . . again. She pecked him on the cheek. "Hold that thought. I will be right back." She caught the eye of the hostess, who knew exactly what Luna was looking for and tilted her head toward the back, inside the restaurant.

Chris was dumbfounded. *What kind of response was that?* He would just have to wait. The couple at the next table couldn't help but overhear what they were discussing. You could barely get past anyone's table without brushing against them. They gave him a sympathetic look. *Yeah, the girl who hurled her champagne and then left the table. Sorry, mate.* Chris blinked and then gave a somewhat confident smirk. He certainly wasn't going to let them know he was crestfallen. He was a US Marshal, for heaven's sake.

Luna returned and slipped back into her seat. She took his hand. "So. If we're going to go steady, I need to wear your class ring on a chain." She bit the inside of her lip, trying not to laugh.

"Now, that's funny."

"*You* are funny. And you made some very good points." She took a deep breath. "The thing is, I don't have the time nor do I have the inclination to date either. And I like you very much. I mean I *really, really* like you." She mimicked a high school girl. "I think this could be a very nice situation . . ." *There was that word she'd used the day before with Chi-Chi.* "Let me rephrase that. We've come this far in our elephant-in-the-room conversation. I would like to call it a relationship. I mean, we already have one, but this will expand it." She tilted her head.

"I have to admit, I didn't know how else to approach this except by being a bit old school. *Really* old school," he replied. "My high school ring. I don't think I know where it is anymore."

"I have an idea. Let's walk down Fifth Avenue to one of the souvenir stores. We'll get a ring there." Luna was excited, then quickly asked, "But do you think it's weird?"

Chris laughed. "I wouldn't expect anything else of you."

He paid the bill and they began their stroll. Soon they arrived at a very large shop with every imaginable object stamped, embossed, printed, stitched, bronzed, chained, mugged and snow-globed with some iconic New York logo. They found a signet ring with the New York Yankees logo emblazoned on it.

"That's the one," Luna said. She knew Chris's son Carter was a big fan of the team, giving the ring more meaning. She asked Chris to unfasten her pearl necklace. The ring was large enough to slip over the beads and he clipped it back around her neck. She looked in a mirror sitting on the counter. "Perfect." At that moment, she felt like a schoolgirl. But she often did when she was around Chris. She didn't care if she was being juvenile.

Chris was standing behind her. He placed his hands on her shoulders and kissed her on the temple. "Stunning," he said wryly.

"Thank you." Both of them knew the necklace looked ridiculous. It was the thought that counted.

At the next corner, they hailed a cab and started back to the hotel.

"So, what was Cullen up to today?" Luna snuggled close to Chris. "You know I am eventually going to find out, so you should just give it up now."

"A Manhattan Architectural Yacht Cruise."

"No! Get out!" Luna was surprised it wasn't something more romantic.

"He thought Chi-Chi would appreciate the historic interest."

"The Palm Court is historic," Luna said smugly.

"Well, The River Café may not be historic, but it's grand for dining."

"The River Café?" Luna was impressed. The restaurant boasted a Michelin-starred rating for exclusive fine dining, an impeccable wine list and an incredible view of downtown Manhattan.

"Yes, after their tour they'll go to Brooklyn. They'll take a water taxi from Chelsea Piers to Pier 11 and then hop across the river to the restaurant."

Luna was even more impressed. "I had no idea Cullen could be so romantic."

"Elle helped him," Chris confessed.

"That does not surprise me. Well, I am glad he had the sense to seek her counsel."

The taxi ride took about fifteen minutes and then they arrived at the hotel. It was near five. Luna gave Chris a mischievous look. "So, what shall we do now, Marshal?"

He wasn't sure how he should answer that question.

Earlier that day Chi-Chi and Cullen agreed to meet in the lobby at one. They hopped in a taxi that took them to the West Side of Manhattan. "Are you still not telling me where we are going?" Chi-Chi looked at Cullen closely.

"You'll see. Just a few more minutes."

When the cab pulled up in front of Chelsea Piers, Chi-Chi's face fell. "You are taking me to play golf?"

Cullen laughed out loud. "No. Chelsea Piers has a number of activities. Besides, we aren't going inside." He paid the cab driver and assisted Chi-Chi from the SUV. "Follow me." He took her hand and led her to the actual pier, where several cruise liners were docked. He looked around until he saw the correct sign. "Come on."

As they approached the boat, Chi-Chi gasped at the 1920s-style teak yacht with a glass-enclosed, climate-controlled cabin. With a capacity of fewer than one hundred people, it was a very comfortable setting. Cullen was particularly happy with the style of the boat. The two found a comfortable spot, relaxed and listened to the guide as she pointed out the many interesting sights of Manhattan. Cullen took great pleasure in describing some of the other buildings to Chi-Chi as she listened with great interest. After the two-and-a-half-hour ride, they went from the yacht over to the ferry terminal and took the Water Taxi to the East Side of lower Manhattan.

"Where are we going?" Chi-Chi noticed they weren't taking a taxi back to the hotel.

"The day is not over." Cullen was quite pleased with himself. He ushered her from one dock to another, where they boarded another Water Taxi to Brooklyn.

"This has been rather an aquatic afternoon," Chi-Chi said as she felt the breeze against her cheeks. In less than seven minutes, they arrived at a dock. Cullen held Chi-Chi's hand as he escorted her to the marvelous restaurant. Even though it was still daylight, the sun was glinting through the massive canyon of buildings in lower Manhattan.

"Oh, Cullen. This is wonderful." Her hand touched her throat. "You have given me such an extraordinary day. And now this." Chi-Chi thought she might finally lose her infamous state of composure.

"You have been an extraordinary friend." Cullen didn't know what other word to use. They weren't lovers. But there was love. How much, and what kind? That remained to be seen.

"As have you," she replied and nodded with respect.

The maître d' showed them to a table by the window. The interior walls of the restaurant were covered with mirrors so no matter where you sat, you would not miss the spectacular view from under the Brooklyn Bridge.

They shared the famous River Café oysters, and each ordered their own entrée. One salmon, the other lamb, both promising to share. Dessert was a chocolate soufflé with two spoons. After the meal, Chi-Chi leaned into the back of her chair. "I do not think I have eaten so much in months as I have the past two days." She rested her hand on her stomach. "I am going to get fat."

"Please. You are not. You barely eat during the day. You'll wither away."

Chi-Chi let out a guffaw. "I seriously doubt that."

Cullen smiled.

"What? Did I say something funny?" she asked.

"No. I just like to hear you speak. Your accent. It's enchanting."

"And so is yours," she responded.

Cullen laughed out loud. "Touché!" Then he thought about it. "Do I really have one?"

"Just a little bit of a drawl. Nothing that would make you sound like a hillbilly." She laughed. "Or is it a redneck? I get them confused."

"Oh, you don't ever want to do that." Cullen chuckled. "Hillbillies are very sensitive. It's about where they come from. They come from the hills. Hence the word 'hillbilly.' Rednecks can come from anywhere. The term generally refers to men who work outside, so their necks get red from working in the sun."

Chi-Chi propped her arm on the table and rested her chin on her hand. "You don't say?"

"For real," Cullen said. "If you call a hillbilly a redneck, you could get yourself shot!"

"Well, I will certainly employ discrimination should I encounter such a situation," Chi-Chi commented.

"Good. I wouldn't want to think about you running around Buncombe County yelling the word 'redneck' to any guy you meet."

Chi-Chi laughed out loud. "I can promise you I will not."

"Whew. That's a relief," Cullen said humorously. Changing the subject, he asked, "What time is your flight back tomorrow?"

"Eleven. I should probably leave around eight thirty.

Rush-hour traffic may be coming while I am going, but it doesn't seem to matter, and I don't want to miss my flight. I do not want to think about Abeo being on his own too long." She giggled. "I appreciate him coming to mind the shop over the weekend, but I do not want to imagine what Jennine may have done with him." She laughed.

Cullen wasn't sure how much he should tell Chi-Chi about his plans. He decided to keep it simple, and as close to the truth as possible. "Luna and I are taking Amtrak to Massachusetts to visit Briarcliff. I want to authenticate the armoire."

Chi-Chi gave him a suspicious glance. "Have you ever done that before?"

"Not really. But you know my sister. When she gets a bee in her bonnet, there is no stopping her."

"I do understand. Completely." She gently placed her palms on the table. "I love your sister. And she can be rather insistent at times."

"Try unrelenting." Cullen chuckled. "But I love her, too."

"What is not to love about her?" Chi-Chi smiled brightly.

"Oh, I could think of a few things." He laughed, but they both knew he was joking.

Elle had been pacing around her hotel room the hour before she was to leave to meet Camille. She was still overwrought with the news Chris had shared. But Luna was right. She should stay focused on the exhibit. She stood, adjusted her white shirt, black slacks and black-and-white saddle shoes. She matched from the top of her head to her toes. A fifteen-minute taxi ride brought her to Penelope, where she was meeting Camille. The two greeted each other with a big hug. The hostess showed them to a table in the corner, where they could sit, eat and chat for as long as they wanted.

Elle decided to start the conversation about the sculptor, and the discussion went on from there. Elle suggested Marina spend the summer as a guest artist at her center. She would get a feel for the business end of her craft. Camille thought it was a marvelous idea, and she would foot the bill for Marina's travel and lodging. Marina was recently widowed, and her grown children lived across the country. She was living on social security in a rent-stabilized building. It would be a wonderful opportunity and change of pace for her. Camille was overjoyed her project was resulting in success for someone.

Several hours later, Elle had completely forgotten about the traumatic family history until Camille brought up J.R. "Did he seem a little distant last night?" Camille asked.

"I really couldn't say," Elle offered. "I haven't seen him in years." That much was true. She really had no idea how J.R. normally acted in a social situation.

"I know there was a lot going on, but he was much more reticent than usual." Camille rolled her eyes, "But his wife? Could someone please stuff a sock in her mouth?"

Elle snorted a laugh.

"And she has absolutely nothing meaningful to say," Camille continued. "I know I sound terrible, but it frustrates me to no end that someone who has the means to do good things for the community, the planet, animals, whatever, does nothing. Not a thing." Camille sighed. "She thinks other people will do the things that need to be done."

Elle patted Camille's hand. "I know. It's a generational thing, I'm afraid."

"Didn't we go through that generation gap thing fifty years ago?"

"We did. And as long as there are different generations moving at the speed of light, it would seem the gap will become even greater."

Camille sighed. "Sad but true."

Elle didn't want to push it, but she was curious. "So, what do you think was on J.R.'s mind?"

"I have no idea, although there was a rather seedy-looking man hanging about. I noticed J.R. had a brief conversation with him."

"You didn't recognize him, I suppose," Elle said.

"No."

"Did you ask J.R.?"

"No. I was too busy, but I couldn't help noticing his pensive mood during dinner."

"Men. They are not very forthcoming with their feelings," Elle added.

"Very true." Camille sighed. "Perhaps it's something at work."

"That's probably it," Elle said, trying to assuage her friend's concerns.

"I should be going. I have scads of thank-you notes to write. Want to grab lunch tomorrow?" Camille asked.

"I'll be flying back in the morning with Chi-Chi. We can't leave our artists alone for too long."

"What about Luna and Cullen? And the marshal? He is quite handsome, I must say."

"Cullen said something about meeting a dealer and that Luna was going with him. I think Christopher has some business to attend to."

"I am so happy you were able to come up." Camille hugged her friend. "Let's not wait too long before we see each other again."

"Next time you come down to the center. You haven't seen it yet," Elle reminded her.

"I know and I apologize for not making the trip. But I promise I will. This fall," Camille assured her.

"Splendid. The mountains are glorious that time of year." Elle gave her another hug. "Thank you so much for your generous hospitality. Love you lots."

"Love you, too." Camille was a little weepy. It had been a

big weekend and everything had gone as well as she'd hoped. "Fantastic" would be a good word to describe her efforts.

They finished saying their goodbyes and departed. Elle asked the cab driver to drop her at the Whitney Museum, where she spent a couple of hours before returning to the hotel. She wondered how everyone else's day was progressing.

Luna and Chris took the opportunity to spend some time alone in Luna's room. Knowing Chi-Chi wouldn't be back until after eight, they indulged themselves in the longing they were feeling toward each other. It was sensuous. Loving. Passionate. After they were spent, Luna sat up against the pillows and giggled. She was still wearing the pearls. "I guess we are really going steady now."

While everyone else was having a most glorious day, J.R. was pensive, irritable and anxious. He was completely rattled. His past had come back like a tsunami. First that slime-ball Johnson showed up, and then this guy from North Carolina somehow had an armoire from Briarcliff. How could this be happening? It had been years. He had almost completely put the kidnapping out of his head, except for the last $10,000 he kept in the safe in his office. Just in case. Just in case of what he wasn't sure, but he was comfortable knowing he had extra cash handy. But Johnson . . . What was he going to do about the extortionist? He knew the guy was never going to go away. He certainly couldn't murder him. He looked over at his wife, sleeping next to him with her sleep mask on. Naturally, she had to go out clubbing with her friends after their dinner the night before. Who did that anymore? At her age? Obviously, she did, along with her friends. Her friends. The hangers-on. Most of her acquaintances her age were married, with at least one child. Lindsay relied on the younger set to party, and they were happy to oblige, especially with her picking up the tab. It was abundantly clear he'd married a spoiled, immature brat. The thought ran through his mind again. *Yep. It seemed like a good idea at the time.* He knew he couldn't discuss any of his problems with her. So much for marital vows. The "richer" part was clear. The "poorer" part? Highly unlikely. He was finally seeing what his mother saw, even though she never expressed it. She didn't have to.

J.R. decided a round of tennis might help him unwind and clear his head, so he called the club and reserved a court. But even after two wildly played matches, he was still in a quandary. He comforted himself with the idea that the armoire couldn't prove anything. But that Johnson fellow . . . Maybe a big payoff and a ticket somewhere far away would do the trick. He would contemplate that later. For now, he needed to take a very long shower.

Chapter Ten

Fact-Checking

Monday

Luna and Chi-Chi were up at the crack of dawn. Considering they'd stayed up past midnight sharing the day's events, they were both rather perky. Luna called Cullen's room. Chris answered.

"Good morning, Marshal. How did you sleep?" She was being a bit sassy.

"Rather well, and yourself?"

"Like a log." She wished they could have spent the night together, but it wasn't possible under the circumstances. "What time are you leaving?" she asked.

"In about an hour. And you?"

"As soon as Cullen is ready. Tell him to shake a leg. We gotta train to catch." She hung up with the biggest grin on her face.

"You are on a mission." Chi-Chi shook her head in acknowledgment.

"I am," Luna replied. She gave herself a once-over and made sure she had a couple of protein bars, bottles of water and her copy of *Letting Go: The Pathway of Surrender* by Dr. David Hawkins. She held it up. "See? I don't even have to sing."

"Ah. There are such things as miracles."

"Oh, you have been spending too much time with my brother." Luna laughed.

"I am thinking maybe not enough."

"Ooooh . . ." Luna chided. "Have a little crush on the old boy?"

"Well, you know I do. And after the day he planned for me yesterday? I can tell you, he is a kind and generous man."

"You knew that already." Luna laughed.

"But as you pointed out, sometimes it is important to look at things from a different perspective."

"Amen to that, sister." Luna patted the book and tossed it into her tote. "Gimme a hug."

The women embraced and wished each other safe travels. "See you in a couple of days," Luna said as she waved and went out the door. Cullen was entering the hallway at the same time.

"Ready?" Luna asked him.

"Just give me a minute." Cullen grabbed the door before it shut behind Luna. He wanted to wish Chi-Chi a proper goodbye. And he did. It was one of the most fervent kisses in his life. It almost made him dizzy. Chi-Chi was glad when Cullen left the room so she could fall backward on the bed in delight.

Penn Station was overflowing with commuters, and Luna and Cullen were going against the tide. They had to hold on to each other to avoid being trampled by the busy, oblivious masses. They jostled their way to the Moynihan Train Hall, where they waited near the track entrance. Several minutes later, a silverlike bullet pulled into the station. It was the famed high-speed Acela, the fastest train in the Western Hemisphere, which boasted 150 mph when at maximum speed. Unfortunately, that speed was only possible between New Haven and Boston, where the infrastructure could handle it. The rest of the route was riddled with one-hundred-year-old tracks, causing the train to average less than half its potential.

"Now what kind of stupid is that?" Luna remarked as they were settling into their seats. "Build a really fast train, but don't have the rails to support it. Ugh. Drives me crazy."

"Hey, it's not even eight. Can you tone down the hyperbole at least until we leave the station?"

"I am not being hyperbolic. I am not exaggerating in any way whatsoever." She plunked herself down next to the window. "Stupid is stupid."

Cullen looked over at the man sitting across the aisle. "Don't mind her. They only let her out once a month."

The man laughed. "She's not wrong, you know."

Luna stuck out her tongue at her brother.

"Siblings?" the man asked.

"Can you tell?" Luna joked; then an announcement came over the loudspeaker announcing the train's departure.

"I'll try to keep her under wraps," Cullen assured the gentleman, who was reading the *Wall Street Journal*—the print edition of the newspaper, not on an electronic device.

Luna made an aren't-you-funny kind of face as the train pulled out of the station. She rolled her pashmina, placed it next to the window and used it as a pillow. She needed to get some shut-eye. As soon as her head hit the makeshift pillow, she was out like a light.

Halfway into the journey, Luna woke with a start. She was slightly disoriented and her mouth felt like the Sahara Desert. "Whoa." She blinked several times. "That was some kind of deep sleep." She stretched her neck back and forth and from side to side.

"I was enjoying the quiet," Cullen said from behind his book. He was reading a thriller by Lee Child.

"You really should take your act on the road." Luna elbowed him.

"I am, but it's on the rail instead."

"My, aren't you chipper today." Luna gave him a sideways look.

"And you are, what? Going steady?" Cullen couldn't contain himself any longer. He hadn't said anything earlier, but he'd noticed the ring.

Luna clasped her necklace. "Oh, this. Well, yeah. Kinda."

"Don't be coy." Cullen put down his book. "The two of you have a thing. It's okay. I'm totally cool with it."

"Well, I should hope so." Luna rearranged herself in her seat. "He's a good guy."

"I know. And I am happy you have someone who actually gets you." Cullen was being sincere. "As much as I love you, I know you're not always easy to be with. You and your 'vibes.'" He used air quotes.

"Oh, and you're perfect," Luna chided.

"I was yesterday." Cullen raised his eyebrows.

"Thanks to Elle." Luna was smug.

"Well, I pulled it off. That's all that matters."

Luna hugged her pashmina against her chest. "It was a magical day."

Cullen was going to comment on the use of the word "magical," but she was right.

Another hour went by, and they were finally at their destination. The well-dressed gent had departed several stations before, while Luna was napping. Cullen gestured to the seat where the man had been sitting. "He couldn't take your snoring any longer."

"I don't snore," Luna protested and gave him a gentle shove down the aisle.

A rental car with a driver was waiting for them at the station. They dropped him back at the rental office and then started toward Briarcliff. "This is kind of exciting," Luna said.

"How do you get me into these things?" Cullen asked, looking ahead at the road.

"You love it," Luna replied.

"Sometimes," he half-agreed.

A half hour later, they arrived at an imposing building with a sign reading BRIARCLIFF ACADEMY. It looked more like an asylum than a school from the front. "Kinda creepy," Luna remarked as she poked her head out the passenger window.

"Well, if there is a guy yelling, 'Here's Johnny,' I am outta there!"

"You and me both, bro," Luna agreed wholeheartedly. "So, who are we meeting?"

"Mr. Purcell. He's the headmaster."

"Does he know why we are here?"

"I told him I want to authenticate the piece I got from Longmire. He seemed fine with it."

The main door to the school was locked. They rang the bell. It took several moments for a haggard-looking man to open the heavy wooden door. "Can I help you?" he squeaked.

"Yes. Hello. Cullen and Luna Bodman to see Mr. Purcell," Cullen said.

"Come in." The man stepped aside to let them in and then bolted the door behind them. Both Cullen and Luna jumped. "Follow me."

Luna tried not to laugh. She was remembering Marty Feldman playing Igor in *Young Frankenstein*. She bit her lip. *Walk* this *way*. Cullen knew exactly what she was thinking. They moved past a round table in the foyer and into a large office with bookshelves covering all three walls. A mahogany desk faced the doorway. An equally ragged man stepped out from behind the desk. "How do you do? I am Professor Cuthbert Purcell."

Luna almost lost it. The entire place was a cliché.

"How do you do," Cullen responded. "I am Cullen Bod-man, and this is my sister, Luna."

"Now, what is it you need of me?" The man seemed to be in a hurry.

"I recently purchased a piece that was salvaged from Longmire. They told us it originated here."

"Yes, we send all of our things to them when they are no longer in a useful condition."

Cullen pulled out his cell phone and scrolled through the photos. He always took before and after pictures. Once he found the photo of the armoire, he showed it to the older man. "Does this look familiar?"

"When did you say you got it?"

"A couple of weeks ago."

"That looks quite old." The man peered at the photo more closely. He moved back to his desk and shuffled some papers in a folder. "Longmire has been working with us for many years. Thirty, at least." He tapped his finger on his lips. "Recently, they phoned and told us there was a storage error and they were in possession of several items that had been sitting in the back of their warehouse for a very long time. Evidently, the three pieces were behind other items and were discovered when they were going to demolish one of the buildings. We told them we had no use for them, and they could dispose of them as they wished. We didn't think they would get any money for them, given how long they had been sitting there."

"Do you have any idea when the items were moved from Briarcliff to Longmire?" Cullen asked. He could tell Luna was getting restless.

"Let me see here." The headmaster shuffled through more papers. "April 2003."

Luna resisted the temptation to yell, *Bingo!*

Cullen made a few notes. "So, we can safely say this piece was once the property of Briarcliff."

"I suppose so." The man ran his fingers through the five hairs that were still growing on his head.

"Thank you. I very much appreciate your time," Cullen said.

"Not at all. Is there anything else I can help you with?"

Luna had one question. "Professor, was this taken from someone's room? Or do you have a place where you keep things you are going to donate or sell?"

"We have a back building where we store things, yes. Why?"

"Just curious. So, this could have been sitting in your building for a while as well?"

"Absolutely. We usually wait until we have enough for a pickup."

"And who organizes those pickups?" Luna had to ask the question.

"Usually a student."

"You wouldn't happen to know who that student was?"

"I wasn't here at the time. Does it matter?"

"Just trying to connect the dots." She paused. "For authentication purposes."

"Of course. Let me check." He looked through the file again. "Yes, here is the authorization."

Luna held her breath.

"Chad Pierce Jr. He called for the truck on April 2."

Luna was about to bust a gut. Cullen knew he had to get her out of there pronto. "Thank you, Professor. You have been most helpful."

"No problem at all. Have a good day." He walked back behind his desk, having no idea he might have just cracked a twenty-year-old case.

Cullen and Luna dashed outside. Luna phoned Chris immediately, but the call went to voice mail. She was disappointed she couldn't tell Chris the news directly, but she left a message. "Chris. On April 2, 2003, Chad Pierce Jr. authorized Longmire to pick up some old furniture from a back building at Briarcliff. Coincidence? Ha!"

Luna and Cullen took a car back to the rental office and then were driven to the train station. She could hardly wait to meet up with the marshal later that day.

On the train ride back, Luna couldn't help but ask Cullen about Chi-Chi. She knew he was falling for her big-time.

"So, tell me, bro, how was your date?" She had already heard Chi-Chi's version; now she wanted to hear his.

"Spectacular." He smiled. "Elle's idea was spot-on."

"And?" Luna was pulling taffy now.

"And what?" Cullen refused to continue.

"You know I am not going to stop until you spill it."

"Okay. So here's the big thing." Cullen took a deep breath. "Chi-Chi is from Nigeria. I am from North Carolina. Some people would not think much of our relationship."

"Why should you care what people think?" Luna was quite serious.

"I suppose I really don't, but society . . ." His voice trailed off.

"Oh, bugger society. People will judge you no matter what if they want to. It makes them feel better about themselves. You cannot live your life fearing what people might think because they are going to think what they will no matter what you do." She took a beat. "Look at me. I'm kooky, spooky. But I don't let it bother me anymore." She nudged Cullen. "Of course, I have my big brother to protect me, but you have your Lunatic sister to protect *you*." She patted his arm. "People will feel what they feel, think what they think and do what they do. You cannot live your life wondering and worrying about other people. It's a waste of time worrying about things you have no control over." She sat back and let him digest her words of wisdom. For now, she needed a nap.

Marshal Gaines rented a car and drove to Colts Neck, New Jersey. He was meeting one of the county commissioners at the local municipal office, where he would be able to look at a plot plan of the area in question.

Commissioner Licitra greeted him with a warm welcome and a handshake. "We don't usually get US Marshals visiting here. At least not in the past century."

Chris gave him an odd look. "What changed?"

"The repeal of Prohibition."

"Really?" Chris was intrigued. "I thought that was the realm of the FBI and the IRS."

"Some kind of task force. This was the wilderness during the 1920s." He motioned for Chris to follow him into a small conference room with too much fluorescent lighting. A large map of the area was pinned on the wall. "What were you particularly interested in?"

Chris gave him the rough location. Licitra pointed to an area that looked as if it had been subdivided.

"What is all this?" Chris asked.

"The property you are asking about used to be an old farm. Hadn't been in use for maybe twenty-five years. But the buildings date back to the early part of the twentieth century. They recently demolished the original farmhouse and are about to begin excavating the rest of the property. If you want, we can take a ride over there."

"That would be great. I appreciate it."

The two men got into the commissioner's SUV and rode out to the construction site. There were bulldozers on one side of the property. A group of men were standing together having a heated conversation. Licitra and Gaines approached the men. "What's going on?" Licitra asked.

"When we tore down the old concrete shed, we found a tunnel," one of the men said. "It looks like it leads to where the old barn used to be."

Another chimed in, "So now we have to get a different permit to dig up the pieces of the tunnel."

Licitra grinned. "You guys dug up a bootleg operation."

"Say what?" one of them asked in disbelief.

"Back in the days of Prohibition, the moonshiners would build stills in sheds in the middle of nowhere. The bootleggers would build tunnels and underground passageways that ran from one part of the property to the shed. It was often under the barn or the house itself. It depended on how much money and property they had," Licitra continued. "There were interconnected passageways with trapdoors that enabled them to check on their still without being seen. If the authorities thought there was something going on, they would try to burn down the sheds, so many of them were built with concrete. In New Jersey alone, there are over a thousand records of court cases about gin stills"

Chris's mind was racing. "Is it possible to get the name of the people who owned this land prior to 2003?"

"Sure. Let's go back to the office. Meanwhile, guys, stop working. We need to pull more permits."

The foreman did not look happy. "I'm going to have to call the bank and the developer to let them know there is going to be a delay. We don't want to run out of time before our financing expires."

Chris stopped in his tracks. "What bank is it?"

"Metropolitan Savings and Loan."

J.R. almost had a stroke when he got the call. "What do you mean, they have to halt demolition?"

The foreman explained. "The commissioner was here with someone looking at the property, and the commissioner said we had to get another permit on account of the tunnels. Something about the EPA. They gotta test the soil again."

"But we already had a soil analysis!" J.R. was livid and panicked.

"Yeah, but we didn't have a tunnel at the time." The foreman was used to being yelled at by clients and bankers.

"Cripes. Well, get it done, and fast. Does Davidson Contracting know?"

"I'm calling them now. Thought I'd give you a heads-up since you guys are footing the bill. For now."

J.R. slammed down the phone and dropped his head in his hands. He'd thought he'd successfully buried his past—or was about to. He had been meticulous about rooting out the owners of the farmland and partnering with Davidson. For several years, the farm's owners used it as a tax write-off, selling just enough pumpkins to qualify. But the several million dollars they were being offered represented a far better deal than the few thousand dollars they got to recover on their tax bill.

J.R.'s phone rang again. "What?"

"A Mr. Henry Johnson is on the phone."

"Tell him I'm in a meeting." He slammed the phone down again.

Things were not going well for J.R. The last thing he needed was that nuisance bothering him again. He got up and began to pace. About fifteen minutes later, his phone rang again. "Yeah?"

"Mr. Johnson is here to see you."

J.R. thought his head was going to explode. Before he could say another word, Johnson brazenly walked into his office. J.R.'s assistant was vehemently trying to stop him from behind.

"Hey there, J.R.," said Hank. "I was in the neighborhood and thought I'd stop by to say hello."

"What do you want?" J.R. demanded, shooing his assistant out of the room. The niceties were out the window now.

"Aw, is that any way to talk to an old friend?" Hank was really pressing his luck.

"We are not friends. Never were. You did me a favor once and I repaid you—twice. Now get the hell out of my office before I call security." J.R. was livid as he flung his arm in the direction of the door.

"Okay. Okay. Don't blow a gasket. I'll just come back later when you're in a better mood."

"Don't even think about it." J.R. was at the crossroads of violence. He considered choking the hell out of the guy.

Hank Johnson saw the rage in J.R.'s eyes. He knew he had stepped way over the line and quickly retreated to the outer office. He moved faster than he had in years and dashed to the elevator. When the doors opened, two very large security guards greeted him. "May we escort you to the door?" one of them asked. It wasn't really a question.

Back in his office, J.R. was pacing furiously. Gregory stood in the doorway and asked, "Can I do anything for you?"

J.R. stopped and looked up. "No." He took a deep breath. "Thanks. Just shut the door, please." Gregory slowly and quietly pulled it closed. J.R. moved to the credenza and poured a Scotch. His watch said 11:00 a.m. Too bad. He had to calm his nerves. He had to think of what do to next. Of course he would extend the option. What other choice did he have? The bank stood to make over a million dollars in interest over the next five years. A million dollars. The magic number. Or so he thought.

Chris noticed there was a voice mail waiting for him. He dialed and heard Luna's message. Bingo! He pressed her speed dial number. "You were right again, Luna."

"I am so relieved." Luna truly was. She would hate herself

if she was wrong about J.R. and had all those suspicious thoughts about him. Guilty until proven innocent. She really didn't like approaching things that way. But that was the nature of her gift, such as it was. She continued, "I mean, I'm relieved my intuition was right. It's just kinda bad that it was."

"You were right on the money. No pun intended." Chris chuckled.

"So now what happens?"

"I am going to run those prints, so don't let anyone touch the armoire until I get there. When are you guys heading back to Asheville?"

"Tomorrow."

"Good. So am I. Do you know what flight you're on?"

Luna opened her bag and checked the paper ticket. She always liked a backup. Technology could mess you up if it wasn't working. "Flight leaves Newark at one."

"Good. We're on the same flight. What time do you think you'll be back in the city?"

"We are on the train now, so we should be back at the hotel by five."

"Okay. Good. I'll catch up with you guys there."

"Cool. See you soon." Luna clicked off the phone.

Eventually, the train pulled into the station. Luna and Cullen unfolded themselves from the wide, cushy seats and squeezed their way through the crowded corridor of the Acela, then through another crowd at Penn Station. "I don't know how these people do this every day. I would lose my mind," Cullen noted as the thousands of people scurried to catch their trains to get home.

"I hear ya," Luna concurred. "I wouldn't be able to take all this anxiety. Mine or theirs!" She clung to the back of Cullen's jacket. "This is just crazy. Why do people do this?" She knew it was a rhetorical question, but she couldn't help but ponder, nonetheless. Why? Surely the money couldn't be *that* good. She thought about some of her sociology studies. People tended to do what their parents did. It was called intragenerational mobility. A horizontal move within their social strata. They basically had similar jobs and similar lifestyles. But things like pandemics and war could upend that continuity and force people to make drastic moves. After WWII, many people who were raised in the cities moved to the burgeoning suburbs. The next generation tended to leave the suburbs and move back to more metropolitan areas. Then the pandemic came, and people were moving anywhere to get away from the throngs. So much had happened in the past fifty years, it was quite startling.

Cullen could see his sister's mind ticking. "You okay?"

"Yes. Just pondering the socioeconomics of commuting."

"Deep." Cullen saw an opening in the crowd and moved faster. Again, they were moving against the tide of commuters.

"See? Even when I am trying to be serious, you mock me." She gave him a helpful nudge.

"There are so many reasons to mock you," Cullen teased, ducking his head in anticipation of being clobbered.

They exited the station on 7th Avenue, where a line of taxis were waiting. Most had dropped off passengers entering the station.

Once Luna and Cullen had arrived back at the hotel, they went to their rooms. "I need a shower," Luna said. "I feel gross." She looked at her brother. "Don't you dare say a word."

About an hour later, Chris also returned. He phoned Luna, and they made plans along with Cullen to meet for dinner at seven. Despite all the restaurants at their disposal, Chris wanted them to experience Odeon—the history, the food and its more casual atmosphere.

They met in the lobby at six forty-five and walked the few

blocks to the restaurant. When they were seated, they pulled out their phones, pads and notebooks. Cullen began with the authentication of the armoire. Chris then corroborated that the dates J.R. authorized the armoire for salvage matched with the alleged kidnapping. He went on to tell them about the farm, the tunnels, the shed for the still. "The way I see it, someone, most likely J.R. and perhaps an accomplice, knew about the tunnels."

"But how?" Luna asked.

"I did a little more digging into J.R.'s checkered schooling. Evidently, he was either kicked out or dropped out of several private schools. One was Horace Mann."

"How do you know this?" Luna asked, wide-eyed.

Chris gave her a look. "I know someone who knows someone." Then he smiled. It was a phrase they used with each other frequently.

"Aha." Luna grinned. "Continue, s'il vous plaît."

"Merci." He continued, "During spring break, several of the students went to New Jersey to spend some time in the fresh air. At an old farmhouse. In Colts Neck. It turned out the farmhouse was owned by a bootlegger during Prohibition." He went on to reiterate what he had learned earlier that day. "They built interconnected tunnels from either the main house, a barn or a back building that led to the shack where they had their stills. There were well concealed trapdoors in the floors of the shacks."

"Wow," Luna said in awe.

Chris sat back and took a pull of his beer. "The shack where Pierce dropped the money had an underground tunnel."

"Oh my gosh!" Luna began to put it together.

"Yes. Once the drop was complete, someone, maybe J.R., went through the tunnel and retrieved the money."

"So where did he keep the money?" Luna asked.

"That much we don't know yet. He must have stashed it

somewhere and then gone back to get it at a later date," Chris replied. "We have to trace his steps from the point where his father picked him up."

"But for how long?" Luna asked.

"From what the professor told me, J.R. finished school and then left for Europe for several months. When he came back, he got a job in the loan office of a bank." Chris had a devilish grin on his face. "The very same bank that is funding the construction project on the very same farmland." He knew the next word was coming, so he beat her to it. "Coincidence? I don't think so."

"So what do we do now?" Cullen asked.

"We have a few options. One, I can confront J.R. and tell him we have a lot of evidence that is pointing in his direction and hope for a confession."

"Do you think that would work?" Cullen asked.

"Hard to tell. However, he comes from a powerful family who could quash our attempts to reopen the case."

"Yes, but Camille and Chad seem like very upstanding people," Luna said.

"Yes, and he is their son. They did everything they could to protect him when this happened. They might do the same now," Chris pointed out.

"What's the second option?" Cullen asked.

"I could meet you in Asheville and dust the cabinet for prints."

Luna was overjoyed. "See! I told you!"

"Easy, girl. I could tell him that is my intention, which may also spur a confession." Chris knew they were on to something.

Luna pursed her lips. "True. Kind of a threat."

"More like coaxing him." Chris appreciated Luna's enthusiasm. "Since we are already here, in New York, I think I am going to go for the first idea. He already seemed rattled when

Cullen mentioned the armoire. And then there was that strange dude who got under J.R.'s skin. J.R. just might be ready to spill his guts. Get it over with." Chris motioned for the waiter to take their order. "I've seen people on the brink before, and I think he just might be." Chris made a few recommendations from the menu to the others and ordered a bottle of wine.

"Very good, sir," the waiter concurred. A few minutes later, he returned with a bottle of Whispering Angel, a light, dry rosé. After the server had poured their wine, Chris raised his glass. "To the best amateur detectives I know!" He knew the word "amateur" would gall Luna, and it did.

"Amateur! I beg your pardon." But she knew he was teasing and gave him a big smile in return. "But seriously, think about it." Then she used one of her favorite expressions: "What are the odds?" She held up her thumb. "Cullen gets an armoire." Then came her index finger. "We get invited to New York." Up went the next finger. "To be with people who were involved in a kidnapping." She continued to tick off the incidents on her hand. "You! You just happened to meet with a professor who remembered the case." She stopped. "Okay. That's four things. On their own they would not be of any consequence. But a convergence of related incidents? Again, I ask—what are the odds?"

No one answered. "Well, do you want to know what I think?" she asked.

"I am sure you will tell us." Cullen dabbed his mouth with the linen napkin.

"I think it was karma." She sat back and let that sink in. After a few brief moments, she went on. "It was time J.R. had a reckoning. Look at his parents. They are kind. Generous beyond belief. The angst he put them through. The money he stole from them. No, it was time karma caught up with him."

Chris eyed Cullen. How could they disagree?

"So what do you think, oh, great, wise woman?" Chris asked.

"I think you're right about confronting him. J.R. is about to snap, crackle and pop. I feel that he wants to purge his guilt."

"Cullen? Any thoughts?" Chris looked at him.

"Me? I'm just another bozo on this bus. You're the driver. I mean, the two of you take turns. I'm for whatever you guys decide."

"Then it's settled." Luna stopped. She didn't want to take over the entire evening. "Just one more thing." The men rolled their eyes. "It was also *your* karma." She pointed her fork in Chris's direction. "You were meant to solve this. The end." She'd said what she had to say.

"I'm going to call J.R. tomorrow morning to set up an appointment to meet in his office. I'll lay it all out for him. He might be outraged at the insinuation, but he won't have much choice if I tell him we plan to dust the armoire for his prints. He could claim it was in his room, but I don't think he's willing to go the distance on this. It would involve his family. His job. It could turn into a horribly embarrassing circus. And I think J.R. is the type who would rather avoid such controversy."

"Tell me something," Cullen asked. "In legal terms. How did he break the law if it wasn't a real kidnapping?"

"Extortion, for one."

"And how would you prove it if his family doesn't cooperate?" Cullen asked.

"It can either be very complicated or very simple. If he protests, it gets complicated. We—law enforcement, that is— would have to try to prove an illegal act was committed. We can't do that unless his parents file a complaint. Remember, he was only eighteen at the time, so the court could be sympathetic."

"And the simple way?" Luna queried.

"He tells his parents and lets them decide. If they don't press charges and he offers restitution, there is nothing I can do. Legally, that is." Chris motioned for the waiter to pour everyone another glass of wine. "Morally? That is the thing I am going to do tomorrow. Challenge his ethics and his integrity."

Luna raised her glass. "Here's to integrity." They clinked glasses and finished their entrées, then polished off the meal with Odeon's famous ice cream sandwiches. They casually strolled back to the hotel, Luna's arms linked through both Cullen's and Chris's. She sighed. "My two favorite men."

As they approached their floor, an awkward moment occurred between Luna and Chris. Chi-Chi and Elle had departed earlier that day, leaving Luna with the room to herself. She decided to let Chris make the move. But he was a gentleman and wanted *her* to suggest what they were both thinking. But she didn't, and so they parted outside each other's doors and had to be satisfied with a brief kiss good night. When Luna shut the door behind her, she wanted to kick herself. She would have to be satisfied with that kiss and knowing they would meet up for breakfast in the morning. She fingered the ring by her neck, wondering where the relationship might go. For the first time, she didn't feel anything but love and admiration to and from a man. Not fear, not the need to be needed or wanted, possessed or trapped. Just love. The love that comes from a deep friendship. From your best friend.

Once she settled in, she phoned Chi-Chi and told her they wouldn't be back until Wednesday, and promised to fill her in once they got home. She then phoned Elle and let her know about her travel plans. Elle assured Luna everything at the center would be covered and that she would phone Alex to ask him to bring Wylie over to her house so he would have some company with Ziggy and Marley.

Everything was falling into place.

Chapter Eleven

The Reckoning

Luna, Cullen and Chris met in the lobby at eight and walked two blocks to the local café where they were planning to have breakfast. After the waitress took their order, Chris pulled out his cell and called the number on the business card J.R. had given Luna. At this point, the fingerprints were irrelevant. He could get them at any time moving forward if necessary.

A polite young gentleman's voice answered Chris's call. "Good morning, Chad Pierce Jr.'s office. This is Gregory. How may I help you?"

"Good morning. This is Marshal Christopher Gaines. I met J.R., Mr. Pierce, the other night at his mother's gallery opening. I was wondering if he had a few minutes to meet with me today."

Gregory hesitated. "What is this regarding, may I ask?"

"A follow-up to our conversation at dinner." He paused briefly. "At the Tribeca Grill." Chris figured the more personal the association he could prove to the assistant, the more accommodating he would be.

"Oh, yes, of course. Let me check his schedule." Gregory

normally asked J.R. before he put anything on his calendar, but J.R. was behind closed doors, having an argument with someone. Better to just put this man in the book. "It looks like he has an opening at eleven thirty. Would that work for you?"

Chris took a beat. "Yes. That will be fine. Thank you very much, Gregory." He looked over at Luna, who was sopping up her eggs with toasted rye bread. "Eleven thirty. Zero hour."

Dribbles of yoke just missed her mouth. "Really?" she said with glee. Chris resisted the temptation to wipe her mouth and gestured for her to pick up her napkin. *Gosh, she can be so cute sometimes.* She got the signal and wiped her mouth.

"Yes. And no, you cannot come with me."

"Party pooper," Luna said.

"Is that your favorite term now?" Cullen asked.

"Only when it fits." She mugged. "Let's not forget 'what are the odds.' "

"Ha. Ha." Cullen smirked.

"I need to prep for my meeting," Chris said. "I want to have everything lined up. I'm going to head back to the hotel and pull my presentation together."

"I'm going to head over to the Oculus," Luna added. "The building that resembles a dove's tail. I've been curious to go inside. There's supposed to be some interesting shops and art there. Cullen, want to join me?"

"I have one more meeting with a dealer on the Lower East Side."

"Looks like we are all on our own. Let's meet up for lunch and I'll recap my meeting with J.R.," Chris said.

"Sounds like a plan. Any place in particular?" Cullen asked.

"How about Bryant Park Grill, behind the New York Public Library? Say twelve thirty? I'm not sure how long my meeting with J.R. is going to last. If I start running late, I'll let you know."

"I'll make the rez," Luna offered. "Do I dare try to take the subway?"

"Uh, maybe that's not such a good idea. You. Underground. Alone," Chris said.

"I was simply trying to complete my New York experience."

"That's something you can try another time. It's not something of the finest of what New York has to offer." Chris grinned.

"Got it. Taxi," Luna acquiesced.

Cullen picked up the check for breakfast, and they went in different directions. Cullen headed east, Luna walked west and Chris went back to the hotel to put his notes together.

After an hour perusing them, along with the information Cullen and Luna had gathered, Chris was satisfied he had a timeline. The motive? Obviously, money. But why? That was something he wondered if J.R. would be willing to share. It wasn't as if he was poor. His family could surely have given him whatever he wanted. And it was rather apparent they did. He decided on a more casual, less imposing look, so opted for slacks, a button-down shirt and a blazer. He didn't think a tie would be necessary for the chat he was going to have. By eleven he was ready to take on this challenge. For one thing, he was not officially on the case. He wasn't sure if there would be any ramifications should this go to a higher level.

He arrived at the main building of the Metropolitan Savings and Loan. He checked in with security, using his US Marshal identification. The security guard stood at attention when he saw Chris's credentials. "To your left. Eighth floor, sir."

Chris was often amused at the reaction he got from people who *thought* they were in law enforcement. Not that there was anything wrong with being a security guard. It was a respectable living. But when push came to shove—or worse—you wanted an experienced law enforcement officer backing you. He was also aware that many security guards were former NYPD. If you started in the police force at twenty-three, you could retire by age forty-five and start another career. That was if you wanted to keep working and stay in the metropolitan area.

The receptionist greeted Chris as he entered through the glass doors. "Good morning. How may I help you?"

"Good morning. I have an appointment with J.R. Pierce."

She looked at his ID and sat up straighter. He smiled to himself. What was with people and the US Marshals Service? Was he that intimidating? Or maybe it was because most people didn't interact with marshals on a regular basis. Face it: Most people never did. She dialed a number. "Gregory? Marshal Gaines is here to see J.R. Okay. Will do." She pointed her pen over her right shoulder. "Around the corner and down the hall."

"Thanks." He gave her his friendliest smile and made his way to the outer office. "Gregory?" Chris asked the impeccably dressed young man seated at the desk.

"Yes!" He stood. "Marshal Gaines?"

"Correct."

"I was able to speak to J.R. and let him know you were coming. He is rather busy today. Some big to-do in Jersey, but he can spare a few minutes. I'll let him know you're here."

J.R. had almost soiled his pants when Gregory told him a US marshal was stopping by. The walls were closing in. He could feel it. He felt trapped. He had reached for a glass of Scotch a few minutes before Gaines was due to arrive. He jumped when the intercom buzzed.

"Marshal Gaines is here."

"Send him in." J.R. was dreading every minute of what was to come. He straightened his tie and rose from his desk. Gregory opened the door and Gaines strode in.

"Thanks for taking the time to see me, J.R." Chris shook his hand. "That was quite an event on Saturday."

J.R. knew in his gut this man was not there to recap the gallery opening or discuss the merits of the grilled octopus at the Tribeca Grill. "Yes, it was. But I don't think that's why you are here. Is it?" He went back to the credenza and poured an inch of Scotch into his glass. He turned to the marshal. "Care to join me?"

"It's a little early for me."

"Official business?" J.R. asked suspiciously.

"Perhaps. That's up to you." Chris waited for J.R. to offer him a seat.

"Fine. So, why don't you tell me why you are really here." He finally gestured for Chris to sit. J.R. took the chair facing him.

Chris began. "In 2003, while you were attending Briarcliff Academy, an incident occurred in which you were allegedly abducted." He let the word "allegedly" sink in for a moment. "According to the official report, you were taken from your room by two men in masks. You had little recollection from the time they took you until you realized you were in a delivery van. They then took you to a motel, where they held you captive in a bathroom. You never saw their faces. Two days later, they brought you to the side of the road near the intersection of Newman Springs Road and Route 34." Chris paused. "Do I have it right so far? As far as the report goes?" he clarified. "In the interim, the kidnappers asked your parents for one million dollars to be delivered to a shack in Colts Neck. Shortly thereafter you were released."

"That's what the report says," J.R. said curtly.

"It does. But we are working on another theory." He failed to mention the "we" was Luna, Cullen and himself and not the US Marshals Service.

J.R. pretended to be surprised. "Oh?"

Chris flipped open his notebook. "We also have information indicating you called Longmire Salvage and arranged for them to pick up some furniture that had been sitting in a back building for some time."

"Yes. So?"

"So, that happened to be around the same time as your abduction."

"What are you getting at, Marshal?" J.R. was becoming unglued but was trying to hold it together.

"What I am getting at is that you staged the entire thing. You locked yourself in an armoire knowing it was going to be removed. You made your way to New Jersey to a farm you visited when you attended Horace Mann. When you were at the farm during a spring break trip, you and your friends discovered a series of tunnels that led to a shack in the middle of a field." Chris paused. "How am I doing so far?"

J.R. saw exactly where this was going. "Continue."

"Either you were in it alone or you had some help. In any case, you essentially extorted money from your family."

J.R. couldn't hold it in any longer. "I was up to my neck in debt."

"But how? You were only eighteen." Chris tried to keep the surprise from his voice.

"Yes, and I had a fake ID and there was a casino within an hour of the school. One of the kids had a car and we would sneak out to gamble."

"But where did you get the money to gamble with?" Chris was taking notes now.

"I borrowed it."

"That was probably your second mistake," Chris said plainly.

"My second?" J.R. wasn't sure what the first one was.

"You went to the casino in the first place. Ergo, your second mistake was to borrow money." Chris continued, "But why did you carve 'HELP!' into a panel of the armoire?"

"Just in case my plan went sideways. I could pretend I got locked in as a prank. I got bored waiting for them to drop it off. I was a teenager. Teenagers do stupid things. Obviously."

That was probably his biggest mistake of all, Chris thought to himself. *It's what got Luna on the case.*

J.R. was starting to feel a strange sensation wash over him. He was cleansing himself of years of shame and guilt. "Yes, and the third mistake was to borrow the money from a loan shark."

"The things we do when we think we know it all, eh?" Chris acted more sympathetic now. The guy was spilling his guts and he wanted to be sure he collected every bit of info.

J.R. looked up at Chris. "I owed him two hundred fifty thousand dollars."

Chris whistled. "How did you manage to rack up a bill like that without getting your legs broken?"

"I made promises. Used my family name. Blah. Blah. Blah. He took a pull from his glass. "I told him I'd have all of it within a certain time frame, which was when I cooked up the kidnapping scheme."

"Why didn't you just go straight to your parents?"

"Are you kidding? After all I put them through and all the money I blew?"

"So you decided to extort money from them instead?" Chris was incredulous at J.R.'s reasoning.

"Like I said, I was a teenager. I figured they would hate me if I told them I gambled away two hundred fifty thousand dollars, and this way they would feel bad for me after it was over."

Chris was almost speechless. Almost. "Then you went to Europe."

"Yep. And gambled away another two hundred fifty thousand dollars."

Chris thought for a moment. "Let's back it up. When your father dropped the money in the shack, where were you?"

"I was hiding in the barn on the property. I crawled to the shack and dragged the bags to the barn, then stashed them there until I could get back."

"Which was when?" Chris continued to write. He hadn't thought the confession would come this easily, but occasionally, when people started to talk, they couldn't stop. They had to unburden themselves. He was grateful this was proving to be the case—in more ways than one—with J.R.

"It was the next day. I told my parents I needed to go for a drive. Clear my head. I went back to the barn and lugged the bags to a storage unit in Jersey City. Then I drove to the casino in Massachusetts and paid off the loan shark."

"What about the rest of the money?" Chris asked casually.

"As you said, I went to Europe. Blew the other quarter mil in Monaco."

Chris was stunned at how cavalier J.R. had been at the time. "And then what happened?"

"I dropped a lot of coin in Nice and then came home." J.R. was finally getting the color back in his face. "My father got me a job. By the way, I am very proud of the work I've done. Not that it makes up for my sins." He paused. "Then I bought a car, clothes and put a down payment on a co-op. I met Lindsay and wined and dined her."

"Anything left of your indiscretion?"

"About ten grand." He gestured toward the credenza. "It's in the safe."

"You kept that money all these years?" Chris asked calmly.

"I really didn't need it. I've been doing very well, and my wife has her own money."

"I see." Chris closed his notebook. "One last question. How did you get from Longmire to New Jersey?"

"I stupidly asked one of my former classmates to pick me up and drive me there. He was down and out and I knew he could use the money. Another mistake in the grand scheme of things." He sighed. "Now what?" J.R. looked at him pleadingly.

"Now we go and tell your parents."

"It will kill my mother," J.R. said, his eyes welling up.

"The other option is I turn this report over to the district attorney." Chris knew the DA couldn't really do anything with the information, but he thought the bluff might move the needle with J.R. "What do you think would hurt your mother more? Learning the truth from you or the police and the press? You know as soon as this becomes public record, the media will be all over it." Chris paused. "This can be handled with the utmost diplomacy. It would stay within your family. No one else has to know."

J.R. straightened up. "You mean if I confess to my parents and promise restitution, this might go away?"

"Quite possibly." Chris was relieved he didn't have to resort to Plan B. Whatever that would be.

J.R. nodded. "I owe them that much."

Chris was satisfied. In truth, he had been almost sure J.R. would cave and repent. His parents were good, decent people. He had to have at least some of their DNA inside him. "I agree. Why don't you call them now?"

J.R. got up and went to his phone, dialed and hit the Speaker button. "Dad? I need to see you and Mom." He held back a sob. "Today. As in now."

"Everything all right, son?" Chad's voice sounded very concerned.

"Yeah, Pop." He hiccupped another sob. "Call Mom and call me back." He disengaged the call and then completely broke down into tears.

Chris almost felt sorry for him. Almost.

J.R. snapped out of it when his phone rang. He cleared his throat before answering. "Yes, Gregory."

"A Mr. Johnson is on the line."

For the first time, J.R. was happy Hank had called. "Hello, Hank. What is it you want today? Before you say anything, you should know I am sitting with a US Marshal." He listened on the phone for a moment before saying, "Yes, a US Marshal. Well, you tell me why you think he's here." J.R. nodded. "Correct. Let's be abundantly clear. You will never call me or come anywhere near me or my family ever again." He waited for an answer. "Goodbye." It was also the first time J.R. felt such a sense of relief. From the guilt, and from the looming pressure of a very greedy, despicable man.

Chris looked at J.R. "I take it he was your ride?"

"Yep.," J.R. answered.

An hour later, Marshal Gaines and J.R. walked into Sniffen Court. Camille met them at the door. "J.R.! What is going on?" She threw her arms around him. "Christopher. What are you doing here?"

J.R. took both her hands. "Let's go inside."

Camille was visibly shaken. The call from Chad had been alarming. J.R. had to meet with them immediately. What could possibly be wrong? Was it his health? Lindsay?

"Where's Dad?"

"In his study." Camille looped her arm through J.R.'s and escorted him to the paneled room where Chad waited.

Chad gestured toward the carafes of liquor. "Should I pour us all something?"

"Perhaps you should," J.R. encouraged him.

Once everyone but Chris, who declined, had a glass of a calming beverage and took a seat, J.R. began his story. "What I am about to tell you will appall you. Probably disgust you. But before I begin, I want you to know I will make every effort to make it up to you."

"For heaven's sake, son. Get to the point." Chad had also been on tenterhooks since J.R. phoned.

J.R. began with an apology. "First, let me say how very sorry I am for what I am about to tell you."

Camille couldn't stand the suspense. "Are you okay?"

"Yes, I am fine," J.R. continued. "But I wasn't fine when I was eighteen."

Camille tried to interrupt. "Of course—"

"Mom, please let me get through this." J.R. took in a gulp of air. "When I was eighteen, I got into some trouble. Much more than you ever knew about." He spoke slowly, detailing each step of his undoing from the gambling in the casino, to the bogus kidnapping and his ride from Longmire. He added the details about his fake trip the day after he returned and where he kept the money. Camille and Chad stared into space as J.R. finished his saga, including blowing almost all the rest of the money in Europe and on Lindsay. He further explained the convergence of Cullen's acquisition and Chris's recollection of the case from when he was in college.

The first thing to come out of Camille's mouth was, "It was that dreadful man at the gallery, wasn't it? He was blackmailing you."

"I suppose you could call it that." J.R. looked at both his parents, expecting a barrage of insults. There were none. The silence was heavy. Then he said, "I promise I will pay the ransom money back. Every penny of it. I cannot tell you how sorry I am." For the second time that day he broke down in sobs. Camille followed with tears. Chad took a big swig of Scotch.

Chris stood. "My work here is done."

Chad met his gaze. "You mean . . . that's it?"

"What's it?" Chris said.

"His confession. Doesn't that mean you have to arrest him?"

"Not unless you want to press charges," Chris replied. He turned and let himself out. He knew J.R.'s parents wouldn't press charges. But he also knew that they now had to deal with the emotional fallout of their son's confession. For the family, the real work was just BEGINNING.

Epilogue

Shortly after the big reveal, J.R. began to reset the course of his life. He filed for divorce. Lindsay was ambivalent. She'd find someone else's arm to cling to. Once J.R. moved to his own place, he scaled back his lifestyle. It was easier than he thought. Keeping up with Lindsay had been costing him a lot more than he realized. He did whatever he could to support his mother's charitable efforts and spent more time with his father. Golf wasn't as bad as he thought. At least the experience wasn't. It was his game that needed help.

During one of their conversations, Camille finally told Elle the whole horrible story. It felt good to know she had a friend she could confide in.Before Chris returned from New York, he made a quick call to Balfour. They had exactly what he was looking for. He couldn't wait to see Luna and the rest of the gang and planned to go to Asheville the following weekend. Chi-Chi invited everyone to her house for an authentic Nigerian dinner to celebrate the resolution of their investigation.

Chris wanted a few minutes alone with Luna before dinner and stopped at her house to pick her up. He handed her a small box. She gave him a sideways glance.

"Open it," he urged her.

Luna gasped, then laughed when she pulled out a chain with a ring on it. Into the ring was carved the words JOHN JAY COLLEGE OF CRIMINAL JUSTICE.

"I couldn't find the original, so I had this made instead," Chris explained

Luna looped the chain over her head and gave him a big hug. "Now we really are going steady!"